RAVAGED FOR YOU

(RAVAGED ROCKSTARS I)

REBECCA CASTLE

Copyright © 2022 by Rebecca Castle

All rights reserved.

No part of this book may be reproduced in any form or by any electronic or mechanical means, including information storage and retrieval systems, without written permission from the author, except for the use of brief quotations in a book review.

ISBN: 9780645395990

This series is for all my past loves
We may not talk anymore, but a small part of my heart will forever be inscribed with your name
Thank you for the verse of my life you wrote for me

PLAYLIST

Let Me Down Easy - Gang of Youths
Anything Could Happen - The Academic
Wildest Dreams - Taylor Swift
About A Girl - Nirvana
Late Night Talking - Harry Styles
Shut Off The Lights - Bastille
Mr. Brightside - The Killers
Little Lion Man - Mumford and Sons
Are You Gonna Be My Girl - Jet
She Is Love - Oasis

You say we're only friends
You say this is not love
But I'm not blind, girl
I know it when two people fall
And falling is what we're doing

Are you sure you want to do this?
Because, girl, I can hurt
I know what's happening to you
You're opening your heart to me
You're inviting my pain in

PROLOGUE

AXEL

WHAT IS the point of being a rockstar if you can't sleep around, and what is the point of being a rockstar if you can't perform live in front of thousands of adoring fans screaming your name? Those two things are the *only* two things that matter for a world-famous rockstar like me.

The music. And the women.

And I am currently doing one of them. I'll let you guess which. Here's a clue: this one doesn't involve someone else in your bed.

I'm standing on stage at London's biggest arena - right next to the river Thames - with my beloved bass guitar in my talented hands; my fingers expertly sliding up and down the strings as chart-topping rock music blares out at ear-deafening levels. I gaze out into the crowd arrayed before me.

All those faces staring right back.

Hell yeah.

All those thousands of people out there in the crowd

admiring my skill as I play. Admiring my innate ability. My charisma.

My pure sexual energy.

Fuck yes.

All those fucking girls out there ready to get down and dirty with one of the most famous musicians on the fucking planet.

I see it all reflected in their eyes. *I* am who they've come for tonight. *I* am who they've paid to see.

I am a fucking rockstar.

I'm here with my band. Ravaged. One of the top rock bands on the entire planet. Sexy-as-hell musicians in their mid-twenties with an entire list of number-one hits comfortably under our belts. Known throughout the world from Timbuctoo to the top of Canada. Say one of our names and I bet you can even get a Mongolian villager to start singing one of our songs.

The lights are bright…

The crowd is in the palm of our hands…

Yep. I'm on top of the fucking world, baby.

I turn my gaze from the audience to my fellow bandmates.

Next to me on stage stands Bishop Hayes. He's the tallest of us four boys, and that's saying something because we all clear six feet easily. Bishop's the guitarist of the group and, boy, does he *know* it. The way he holds his instrument… it's like he's making sweet passionate love to it. Scrap that. Raw, *rough* love. The beautiful sounds he can wring from that thing with his hands can make girls instantly swoon. He's the hardworking musical genius of the group, always able to use his melodic flair to flip an average song-in-progress into a bestselling crowd-pleaser. His dark brown hair, the same color as his eyes, is slicked back stylishly. Bishop is outgoing, optimistic, and *super* competitive;

Bishop and I are infamously known to get into messy and sometimes violent scraps over anything remotely like a contest, all the way from a simple darts game to the decision of the name of the next Ravaged single.

I smile at him, and he smiles back absentmindedly. He's lost in the music like a true craftsman. This is Bishop's art, and, boy, he's a maestro.

Like the rest of us in Ravaged, he's wearing a black leather jacket; our signature look on stage. The jacket thing was my idea. I reckon I pull it off the best in the group. That's another piece of contention between Bishop and me.

Behind us, on the drums, is Caspian Ford. He's the burly muscle of the band. Stoic and silent, he is a real BFFG. *Big Friendly Fucking Giant*. But don't get him wrong; he can easily rip your arms off if you dare cross him. Caspian is the brawler of the group. Sure, we all think we could fight anyone if we could - we're young men with pure testosterone pumping through our veins - but we all know, without a doubt, Caspian can knock any one of us out stone cold.

You can never tell what Caspian's thinking behind that infamous brooding stare of his, but I've seen the aggression that he can unleash and it ain't pretty. The gallery of tattoos over his ripped torso tells the story of a dark past, mysterious even to his bandmates. But the man's loyal to a tee, ready to give his own physical safety for his closest friends. And, hell, he can belt out a fucking drum solo like the best of them.

His black hair, long like a Viking's, trails down his back. His dark brown eyes spell danger.

Many girls have tried and failed to reach the drummer's guarded heart. The man's a wall of brute physical force, and that certainly applies to the defenses around his innermost emotions. No girl's getting through that. Maybe Caspian's worried about what his power can do to someone else. How he can hurt other people. A man with a dark history and a dark soul, that's for sure.

We make eye contact and I start nodding along to his beat. Caspian nods back.

And up front on the stage, *of course*, is the lead singer of Ravaged. Drake Sharpe. As much as I hate to admit it, Drake's the one that *all* the girls love. He's the classic playboy rockstar, carrying on the tradition of rock bands from the past. Effeminate, and yet fiercely driven by a pure male sexual energy that tempts the female species like a moth to a flame; Drake's like a Mick Jagger or David Bowie reincarnate. Charismatic without even trying, and that pisses me off. The man knows how to move his slender, toned body around the stage with ease, wooing the audience with his flashy dancing. And, back in the hotel, there is always at least a girl in his bed. Well, most likely several. Despite the women, though, Drake's got one rule he lives by, and that's to never get into a relationship. He's pretty public about that decree, leaving a trail of broken hearts in his wake in every city we visit. Drake and a relationship lasting more than a single night are two things that don't exist in the same universe. He's all about the music. That's his number one priority. Girls are just collateral for him.

And he doesn't give a fuck.

Drake flicks his thick, wavy hair back theatrically, making the London crowd go wild. He sees me staring at him and he winks playfully. I wink back.

And as for me? Like Drake, I also abide by that one rule in this rockstar game. *No relationships*. I left my small town to experience and soak in what the world has to offer me, not to settle down and live a normal, boring life. As I've said... *I'm a fucking rockstar*. I am simply built differently from other men.

Sure, some people may call me cocky. Some people may call me an arrogant ass or impulsive to the point of annoyance. I prefer the term *free-spirited.*

Truth be told, I've become a wee bit notorious for my playboy ways. I mean, even the press has started to dub me the nickname *Active Axel* due to the fact I have a new girl around my arm every night of the week. In my long and checkered past I have had the delight of spending long nights with musicians, supermodels, actresses, influencers… but the main thing is that I have been with a *fuck load* of women.

Snobby-ass critics may moan and bitch about my womanizing antics, but, hey, I'm just taking full advantage of my rockstar life. I'm a young man with testosterone pumping through my veins and a never-satiated sex drive spurring me on, who else could I be? Find one girl and settle down?

Hah.

Nope.

Not me. I'm Axel Stoll, and I'm here on this planet to fuck women and play music. Because otherwise what's the *fucking point*?

I run a hand through my short jet-black hair and cause chaos on my bass.

Following Drake's lead, we launch into our most famous song, *Lightning and Thunder*. He raises the microphone to his full lips and begins to sing.

Come with me to the edge of the world
Don't let me fall when we stand
on those cliffs as I tell you you're mine
You and me, girl, we can go anywhere
Anywhere our hearts desire

I know you're scared
And so am I
But when you're with me
I feel I can do anything
Come with me to the edge of the world
where we'll know we're meant
to be together
like lightning and thunder
So follow me up there
and let's storm into our destiny

THE ROAR of a thousand fans blows over us like a wave of ecstatic sound and that's when I think...

This – being on stage with my four best friends playing music – *is the whole fucking point of being a rockstar.*

1

MADDIE

I HAVE ABSOLUTELY no need to be concerned about if I'm at the right place; with the sheer amount of squealing and excitable girls currently surrounding me, I think I can deduce I am at *exactly* the correct location for the show tonight.

The LA Forum.

Ravaged's one-night-only performance in this city.

And things are getting quite crowded.

There are so many people around me waiting to get inside that I'm beginning to feel claustrophobic, and I worry that I won't find my friend...

But then I see her.

"Marie!"

I worm my way through the mass of fans to the girl I recognize. She's pretty easy to spot, wearing a black t-shirt that's emblazoned with the word *RAVAGED* written in white painted font over the front. Official merchandise, I suspect. I wonder how much the band must make from selling cheap products like that.

Nope, Maddie. Less criticizing. You're here to experience something new and unfamiliar, remember?

I'm happy to find her in the crowd; I'm a pretty short girl, but Marie is even shorter. She turns her head in my direction and gestures me over. I'm practically breathless by the time I reach her.

I flick my light brown wavy hair back.

"So. Many. People. To. Get. Through."

Marie envelops me in a hug. I hang onto my ticket with dear life. Don't want to lose that.

"Hey, girl. I'm so glad you could make it! I honestly didn't think you would come in the end," Marie says. "I didn't think this was your cup of tea at all."

I shake my head. "It was a nightmare trying to get through security. I was practically manhandled like I was in prison or something."

"Ravaged are the biggest band on the planet," Marie replies. "Gotta vet everyone coming in to see them."

I look around at all the people streaming into the arena. "They sure are the biggest thing I've ever seen."

"Well, we're here now," Marie says. "How about we get inside?"

"Yep. Let's get ready to fight our way in."

Marie is a colleague from work. We're not exactly the best of friends or anything, and we don't have much in common, but my New Year's resolution has been to make more friends and just be more... friendly. It all comes back to my mother. "You're so alone in that condo of yours in the middle of LA," she told me the last time I saw her.

And those words stung. Because they're the truth. I've isolated myself.

So, yeah. I made a New Year's resolution to say yes to

more opportunities and to be less, well, *isolated*. I've had a life cowering away from life, and now I want things to change. Accept life more. With my mother's words ringing in my ears, I woke up sober and regretful on New Year's Day a few months ago and the first thing I did that morning was to write out *say yes more* on a post-it note. I stuck it on the wall next to my bed to remind myself every morning.

And I also wrote something else under it.

Stand up for yourself, Maddie.

The two things I'm going to live by this year. Hopefully.

So when Marie approached me in the office out of the blue and invited me to see Ravaged and said she had a spare ticket, I instantly put my hand up instead of naturally declining.

Say yes more. Stand up for yourself.

Got it.

Hey, it's either see this band or spend my Sunday night doing something geeky and alone and isolating in my condo. Something that *definitely* goes against my New Year's resolution.

As we slowly make it up the stairs to Door A – where we're meant to go as marked on our tickets – Marie leans in close to me.

"You watched those YouTube clips I sent you, right? Ravaged's music videos?"

"Um. Maybe not, sorry. I know I should've before I came here, but I didn't have time between work and getting ready and..."

"So you're saying that you don't know who Ravaged is?" she asks me, completely bewildered. Like I said, we have very little in common.

"Of course I know who Ravaged are," I reply. "I've heard their songs before. Everyone has. You've got to be living under a rock to not know these guys."

"But you haven't seen one of their music videos?" Marie asks.

Long pause.

"I don't think so."

Marie throws her hands in the air dramatically. "Maddie, are you crazy?"

"I mean, sure I know their songs," I reply. "I've heard them… around in shopping malls and stuff. But I wouldn't be able to pick any of the members of this band in a police line-up. I don't think I could pick out any famous musician, come to think of it. Actually, no. I'll be able to pick out Michael Jackson, for sure."

"You're such a geek, Maddie."

"And you're such a teenage girl for liking this band, Marie, even though you're in your twenties."

She twirls a lock of her brown hair cheekily.

"I can appreciate high art."

I cock an eyebrow. "High art?"

"Okay," Marie replies. "So I *appreciate* how gorgeous they are, is that what you want me to say? I might be an adult, but I'm still allowed to salivate over a cool rock band."

"Look," I say. "It's not like I'm proud of not knowing who Ravaged are. I just don't really pay much attention to things like this."

"Yeah, you are *totally* a geek," Marie remarks. She points up to four giant posters dangling above us just inside the arena. Each one has a different boy on it, staring sternly into the camera like they're trying to be brooding. I can see teenage girls all around us looking up at said boys in open-mouthed wonder, practically drooling over the members of Ravaged. "See, that's them."

"I guessed."

"At least now that you can actually see their faces I can

give you a proper education on the best band in the world," Marie says.

"Well, thank you again for the ticket."

"My pleasure."

"I'm looking forward to this education. It's what I'm here for."

Marie gets giddy at the prospect of telling me. Her face lights up.

"Okay, let me go through them all with you. Individually."

"Shoot."

"So, they were formed in some small town called Crystal River a few years ago. The boys all met at the same high school in that town; that's where they made the band. None of their parents are famous or whatever, so you just know that they got to this position purely on talent."

"Is that why you like them?" I ask.

"One of the reasons I do. That and how nice their faces are."

"Ah, I see."

"They've sold millions of copies and go on world tours all the time. I can't believe their energy. I think they're one of the top-selling bands of all time. Their closest rival is some other band called Tainted Lives."

"Surely that's a PR move? Rival bands like to make beef to sell tickets and all that jazz..."

"Nope. The two bands really don't like each other. You should see how the fans react online. It's crazy stuff."

"Right, okay. You've basically just narrated their Wikipedia page. So, tell me. Who's your favorite? Everyone always has a favorite."

Marie takes a moment to think about the question like it's some deep philosophical one. "Well, of course I would get with Drake if I could. I mean, who wouldn't? But I also think Axel is super cool, although he is well-known for being such a playboy and such a mischievous free spirit. Caspian's got those muscles and that deep mysterious look about him. So brooding and quiet. I like how you don't know what he's thinking. Bishop has that devil-may-care introverted bad boy attitude, and he's the musical genius of the band, so he's super smart. That's so attractive. Apparently, he's such a worker, and there's something sexy about a man with a passion. And Drake is the loud show-off charmer, which is just irresistible to me. So, I guess they're all cute. In their own way."

"That's not a single answer, Marie."

"Jeez, Maddie. I like them all, alright? A girl can dream, can't she? Every girl's had that fantasy of hooking up with a famous rockstar, hasn't she? Get them noticing you in the crowd. Taking you back to their hotel suite. Having them write songs about you..."

I laugh. "I'll just hope they'd buy me a drink first."

"You're such a spoil-sport. You're telling me you've never had a fantasy like that?"

I shrug. "Sure." I take another look at the giant posters. "Once or twice. And, hey, they're not bad-looking dudes. I wouldn't mind them... getting to know me better. But that kind of stuff only exists in fiction. It never happens to a girl like me. I should just dream on."

Marie smiles. "Simply close your eyes and listen to one of their songs. It makes you feel like they're only performing *to* you. That's what I do."

"I'll give it a go."

We make our way towards the bar, where there's another line for drinks. There are just so many people trying to cram into this place that it makes moving faster than a snail impossible.

"I'm just glad to spend a night out for once," I say to

Marie as we wait. "Winston at work has me working overtime."

"Has he?"

Winston's our boss. A real horse-whipper. He's been breathing down my neck for the last few weeks in his trademark fashion. I'm so worried that I might get fired soon, thanks to his attitude towards me. Marie and I work at a big marketing company, pretentiously called Focus. One word, I know. We work with big-name companies and big-name products; our last contact has been with a sunglasses brand. We have had some pretty famous actors feature in ads for the brand. I was lucky enough to spend a day on the film set, watching these people I'd seen in my favorite movies in the flesh promoting sunglasses. It sounds all very Hollywood and glamorous but, trust me, it ain't. I'm merely an assistant there, slowly rising up through the ranks and praying for my ass not to get fired. I just spend most of my time reading and copying numbers in a spreadsheet.

Winston's recently been trusting me with projects of my own. Little side things, nothing too important. But it's hard to tell with him. One minute he's actively promoting me, and then the next he's tearing me back down. One day he's telling me I could really make it far in this industry, then next he's telling me that my work is a failure. Despite me spending time on set, I barely ever meet the actual celebrities we have in, and even then, why would they care to talk to some geeky marketing assistant who's too shy to even make eye contact? I'm about as removed from the celebrity world as Ravaged is to a bad-selling album.

"Yeah, Winston's really got it out for me at the moment," I continue. "He thinks I'm failing at my job. Well, that's what he told me in our last meeting."

"But you're really good at what you do," Marie replies.

"Tell that to him. It's like I'm his target. I'm scared of

bumping into him at the office. Every day I go to work worried if I might be leaving at the end of the day with a brown box of my things."

We finally reach the bar. Marie tries to pay for the drinks, but I don't let her.

"I'm getting these. You've brought me along tonight, Marie, and I want to thank you properly."

"You're sweet, Maddie," my work colleague replies. "When I first met you, I thought you were so shy. But underneath that, you're a smart, nice person."

I blush. I'm not used to compliments.

As we move inside the actual auditorium of the concert arena, we chink our glasses together and take a sip.

"Thanks again for inviting me," I say to Marie. Inside, the pre-show music is blaring out invitingly.

"Stop doing that," she replies. "I'm glad you decided to come and that I get to tell you all about the best freaking band on the planet."

I am happy I'm here. I'm happy I decided against my cautious impulse and followed my New Year's resolution.

"Let's find our seats quickly," Marie says. "I think the show's about to start."

2

MADDIE

Marie guides me through the crowd, taking us further and further inside the arena's vast auditorium.

"Where the heck are our seats?" I ask her above the noise of the audience. Marie shoots me back a devilish look.

"Wait and see."

She leads me all the way to the front, just two rows from the very front of the stage. We're so close that I feel like I can just reach up and grab the microphone from off its stand.

Holy moly.

I did not expect this at all.

"Wow," I say to my co-worker as we sit. "We're *really* quite close to the action here."

Marie taps me on the shoulder to make me look behind at the giant arena surrounding us. There must be thousands of people here. So many seats, and we're practically at the very front.

"I know someone who works high-up in the ticketing

office at this place," she explains. "I was able to sweet-talk them into these seats, plus I'm willing to fork out a bit extra to be close to the closest guys our modern world has to Greek gods."

I roll my eyes.

"It's a great atmosphere alright," I reply. "We're in the thick of it."

I decide not to thank her again. She'll just get snappy at me for being such a damp towel.

The closest thing I've come close to something like this was a few years ago when I went to Comic Con in San Diego. Back then, I'd dressed up as a superhero and spent the day wandering around the conference floor, looking at the different stalls and seeing interviews with actors from big blockbuster films. That was a fun day. I'd saved up a lot of money to attend, which is unusual for me. I'm not a big spender, and certainly not for things like this or Comic Con. The truth is that my bank account is a bit dry and has been for some time.

It's fair to say I don't usually do things like see a band live, and certainly not on my own. I know who I am. Shy and introverted. Happier to spend the night at home than on the dancefloor. But I *have* made a commitment to change this year.

We make ourselves comfy in our seats and gossip about work as the pre-show ends.

Then, soon enough, it's time for the main event.

The lights go down in LA Forum.

The music roars up.

The crowd goes crazy as everything gears up for Ravaged's appearance.

Marie, next to me, is practically trembling in excitement, and it's starting to rub off on me. The expectation is killing me now…

What will these boys be like, especially when we're so close?

A thousand girls scream as the band sprints onto the stage. I feel myself let out an involuntary gasp as the boys take their positions just in front of me.

We really are so freaking close.

I could reach out and touch them.

The lead singer – I'm presuming that's Drake – raises his hand in a welcoming salute. He bites his lip and smiles at the crowd. He's wearing a silver chain around his neck and there's a really cute solitary curl of hair dropped over his brow. Blue eyes that shine forth.

He. Is. Gorgeous.

Now I understand Marie's dramatic comment about them being Greek gods. They are all perfect specimens of the male species.

Drake brings the microphone to his full lips and speaks.

"Los Angeles, ready to make some noise?"

The arena roars again. I find myself cheering along with Marie.

This is certainly not my usual style, but you just can't resist the atmosphere. Even an introvert like me. I'm whipped up in it with all these other women ecstatic for these rockstars.

Drake points to the man holding a guitar next to him. "Give it up for Bishop."

The guitarist nonchalantly waves to the crowd as if it's perfectly normal there's a thousand people are calling your name. There's more deafening wooing and squealing from behind me. It's clear as day that Bishop is a bad boy. He's tall and cool. I'm guessing he's a real heartbreaker. He doesn't look like he gives a single damn in the whole wide world.

Bishop's sharp straight hair is an elegant dark brown. I

can tell a deep intelligence hides behind those eyes of his. He's got the confidence of a man who knows *exactly* what he's doing.

Drake spins behind him. "You all know Caspian on the drums."

Caspian's already seated at his drum kit. Unlike Bishop, he doesn't even wave. He just broodingly stares into the crowd. But the arena isn't disappointed; this behavior seems to be exactly what they want from this hulking mass of muscles and strength. From where I sit, I can see that Caspian is covered in tattoos from the neck down. He's so dark. Dangerous. His hands are the size of my face. He's got a kind of bro-flow long hair that reaches down past his shoulders. An old-fashioned rocker look. With those muscles of his, he looks like a barbarian from Roman times. And he's got that menacing air of violence to match.

Drake turns to the bassist. "And, of course, here's Axel. *Active* Axel, as he's come to be known. He's such a *naughty* boy."

The bassist gives Drake the finger and the lead singer lifts his fists in a mock boxing pose. Axel pretends to kick him back. The two guys laugh giddily like two schoolboys.

It's fair to say their audience *loves* it.

Axel clearly lives up to his reputation as a playboy. I can so picture him right now seducing girls back to his bedroom like a modern-day Pied Piper. His hair is perfectly tousled, and his dimples are irresistible. With chains around his neck and rings on his fingers, he's wearing an open black leather jacket. No shirt underneath, just his toned muscles. Man, I can't stop staring at his defined abs as he stands there with his bass guitar hanging loosely by his side. I notice he's wearing just a touch of black eyeliner, making his green eyes pop under the arena's lights. He probably doesn't even need to open his mouth to seduce women. I bet his mere look alone will send them crazy.

I mean, it's kinda sending me a bit crazy now.

Look at you, Maddie, letting your hair down for once...

In each of their own way, those boys on the stage are perfect.

The lead singer turns back to his loving audience.

"And I am, of course, Drake Sharpe. And. We. Are. Ravaged."

He blares out those final words. The music starts.

The whole arena throbs with rock and roll.

I find myself not actually minding the songs. They're good. *Great*, even. Alongside Marie, I'm bobbing along to the beat. She smiles at me, clearly satisfied that I'm enjoying the show.

I certainly am.

I follow her advice from earlier and close my eyes. I simply listen to the words and let the music take me like a wave. Like Marie said, it does feel like Drake's honeyed voice is speaking directly to me as I stand there. With the entire world shut out of my head, it makes me feel like those words are written *just* for me.

Are you sure you want to do this?
Because, girl, I can hurt
I know what's happening to you
You're opening your heart to me
You're inviting my pain in

MAN, the shiver that goes down my body as those lyrics wash over me.

I wish someone would say those words to me one day.

I lose myself to the fantasy until, seemingly as soon as it began, the show is over.

The boys do one last song and then exit the stage. Gone forever. They came and went like supernatural beings.

Wow, I'm really being dramatic, aren't I? I'm turning into Marie.

I let out a sigh. It feels like I've been holding my breath in this entire time.

"What did you think?" Marie asks me, a big grin spread across her face.

I shake my head. "I think I need a minute to recover."

"That good, huh?"

"Yeah, really good. I'm impressed, actually. Super impressed. I think I understand your passion for those boys now."

She's elated by my response.

"Oh, look at you, Maddie. I've converted you into being a signed-up Ravaged fangirl," she says, dangerously close to a fit of giggles.

"How about we go back to mine for a drink and a cool down?" I suggest. "I don't know about you, but I certainly need it."

She leans in conspiratorially. "I've got a better idea," she says in a whisper. "Let's go backstage and meet the band."

3

MADDIE

I BLUSH at my friend's suggestion.

"No, I can't," I say.

Backstage? Now? Here?

I am terrified of the suggestion.

Marie looks at me with pleading puppy dog eyes. "Please. Pretty please. I want to meet them, and I'm sure you do too."

I sigh. "What do you mean *backstage*?" I ask her. "I'm sure we need special VIP passes or something to do that, and we definitely don't otherwise you'd have almost certainly told me by now."

"We don't need passes," she says.

"What do you mean?"

Marie smiles cheekily. "I've done this before, trust me. All you've got to do is follow my lead."

"How many times have you seen this band again?"

"Look, I think we'll manage getting through to the back of here. Catch them as they leave. Maybe one of them will spot me in the crowd and instantly fall in love with me and then I'll be his cool girlfriend who everyone is jealous of, and we'll have amazing sex and I'll have all his babies..."

"And then live happily ever after?"

"*Exactly.*"

"I think you and I have very different fantasies, Marie."

"Come on, Maddie. It'll be fun. Let's do something fun and dangerous before we're old and regretful. You never know, one of those rockstars might instantly fall in love with you too."

"*Ha.* I doubt it."

"What do you say? Worth a try?"

I take a last look around us at all the fans slowly making their way to the exits. I don't want to sneak past security. I don't want to ruin the rest of my night. I am certainly not a rule-breaker. I don't creep around the back of arenas.

But I gotta remember my New Year's resolution. Gotta say *yes* to more things.

And this is exactly one of those things.

"Okay. Just because it'll keep you happy," I reply to Marie's excited giggles with a quiver of trepidation in my voice. "Let's try and see one of these famous rockstars, then."

* * *

WELL, as it turns out, we are not the *only* ones to have the idea of meeting the members of Ravaged and hopefully have them instantly fall in love with us. Judging from who's waiting outside at the back of the arena, half the audience tonight seems to have the exact same plan in their heads.

We have to fight through the crowds of screaming teenage girls and their bored fathers to even get close to reaching the front of the imposing metal barriers that separate the horde from the arena exit.

I'm in my mid-twenties and super introverted. I shouldn't be doing this.

"Great," I say sarcastically when we manage to squeeze to the front. "What now?"

Marie nods in the direction of a giant black bus, undeterred by the increase in her estimated competition for the hearts of the rockstars. "That's their tour bus," she says like a wise old sage.

The bus windows are tinted. You can't see anything inside.

What are we doing here?

Surrounding the parked bus are half a dozen black vehicles with big men in dark suits standing guard. Very imposing.

"Wow, they have enough security to form a small army," I remark.

"Guess that's the condition of being the biggest band in the world," Marie replies.

We continue to watch as a line of very attractive women of my age stroll out from backstage. They all look very... aroused and talkative.

Damn. They're all so very *hot*.

Marie and I instantly know what they're doing and who they are.

One word. *Groupies.*

"Maybe one of the boys won't instantly fall in love with me tonight, after all," Marie remarks as we watch the girls board the tour bus one by one with their long slender legs and very full chests; much more slender and much more full than either Marie or mine.

"Typical boy band behavior," I say. "They're rockstars. This is what they do. Of course, they're going to have a whole selection of groupies to choose from every night. This is the life they lead."

Marie sighs, dejected. "Yeah."

"They merely have to glimpse in a direction and there will be a hundred squealing women throwing their panties at them."

Although I'm mocking them, I'm also a tiny bit jealous. It's been some time since I've been intimate with someone. I'm not the best at dating or making myself available for guys. I'm just so damn awkward and clumsy and shy that I don't think any guy I'm vaguely interested in will look at me that way. If they notice me at all.

And then, from around us, there's a torrent of screaming. It can mean only one thing. I glance over to the door to the arena and, sure enough, the members of Ravaged suddenly appear.

Even though they're no longer on stage under the lights, they still look otherworldly. Like, they shouldn't *be* real. They all grin and wave at their adoring, screaming audience. Lapping up the attention.

They swagger with all the confidence in the world. Axel is, by far, the worse. Two gorgeous girls are on either side of him, his arms wrapped around their waists. He gives a cheeky wink to the waiting crowd as he struts by. He's so cocky and yet so handsome that it's irritating. No one should be gifted all that. I know I was fawning over him a minute ago by the stage, but he's just so conceited that it's hard not to find him so frustrating when he comes out with multiple girls dangling from his hands like the world owes him something.

These boys walk through life so easily with a smirk on their faces. It makes me wonder if they've ever heard *no* or experienced any kind of pushback. They live like kings with all the riches of the world.

Oh, well. They're talented rockstars. What should I expect? It's wrong of me to sit back and judge. A waste of my time.

We've seen what we came to see.

"Come on, let's go home," I say to Marie. "This is too much for me. Especially *him*."

I'm pointing at Axel Stoll.

4

MADDIE

As I give Marie the glass of wine, she places her hand over her chest. "My heart is still beating," she says dreamily.

I sit down beside her on my couch. "So is mine," I reply.

"I can't believe we got to see them so close up," Marie continues. "I could swear that some of Drake's sweat landed on me from the stage."

"Ew. Gross."

"No, it was actually *amazing*."

I giggle and take a sip of wine before I reach for her shoulder. "You know what, Marie? It was pretty damn amazing for me as well. Exhilarating. Well, everything *was* great up until I saw all those groupies get into the bus with them."

"What can you expect from rockstars?" Marie shrugs. "And, hey, I would love to be invited onto that bus."

My mouth drops. "No way."

"Yep," she replies. "Just for one night. I wouldn't mind being a groupie."

I giggle. "Have some respect for yourself, Marie."

"Yeah, but it would be so much fun."

"I know what goes on in those buses, Marie."

"Oh, do you now?"

I drink my wine. "Yeah, orgies and... *stuff*."

She laughs. "Stuff? Very informative. You really are such a geek, Maddie."

I check my heartbeat. "Yeah, I'm still beating super fast, though. That was a great night, no matter how it ended."

"All thanks to me."

"Yep. All thanks to you."

Marie's eyes dart to my kitchen counter. "Are those choc chip cookies?" she asks, sleuthing the results of my baking.

There's a mountain of giant choc chip cookies placed on a plate in the middle of the counter. "Yep," I reply. "I baked them today but I didn't get the chance to put them away properly."

"Can I try one?"

"Go ahead."

Marie reaches for one and takes a bite and then her eyes roll back into her head like she's experiencing a rush of endorphins. "Holy shit, this cookie is to die for. I *should* be counting my calories, but this is perfection. I didn't know you were so good at baking, Maddie. You're so shy to ever show off at the office. If you brought these in, then everyone will love you. Guaranteed."

It's so nice to have someone other than my mom to test the cookies on. Seeing Marie's reaction makes me glow. Mom doesn't like my cookies. She doesn't like sugar. In fact, she basically doesn't like anything that might dare bring you pleasure.

"You think people at the office will like them?" I ask my work colleague. "They're actually my own recipe that I've developed through a lot of trial and error. I don't know if I've struck the right balance yet."

"They're so good," she says as she takes another giant bite. "You should definitely start some kind of online business selling these. I would buy them for sure."

I blush. "I don't know about that."

"Come, let's sit and talk," Marie instructs, bringing me back over the couch, choc chip cookie crumbs dropping from her full mouth. "I feel like I barely know you, Maddie. We work together but we haven't had the chance to have an honest deep and meaningful conversation."

"Sure."

"And don't you dare get all shy and introverted like you usually do at the office whenever someone wants to chat. It's just us here now."

"Okay..."

I plow through another glass of wine for some Dutch courage as Marie wrings out my past from me. Things I've not told anyone since I moved to Los Angeles.

I tell her about how I grew up. I tell her about my mother and the close bond we shared as I grew up. I recount how I moved to LA and found the assistant job at Focus.

Marie, in turn, tells me all about her life and how she ended up working in marketing and publicity. Hint: it's to do with her love for celebrities. It seems like she got into this game for meeting famous people, and I got into it because I just wanted to get out of my hometown and get any job I could in LA. Focus was the first, and only place, to hire my sorry ass.

Marie's side of the story is all something I've heard before. Where I'm the introvert of the office, Marie is the extrovert. She's retold her life's story enough times and at a loud enough volume around the watercooler that even I could probably write her autobiography.

But then the conversation moves on, and we get to the inevitable question that any introvert dreads...

"So, how's your dating life?" Marie asks me. My cheeks immediately flush with red and I lower my half-empty glass of wine.

"Um... well..."

"Okay, I'll rephrase that," Marie continues. "How's your *sex* life?"

"Hey, that's a worse question."

"That bad, huh?"

"Look..."

"Come on, you can tell me how things are going? I swear I won't tell anyone else in the office."

It's only because I've drunk my way through a near entire bottle of wine that I even attempt to answer, and when I do, I almost instantly regret opening my mouth.

"It's been, like, a year and a half since I've gotten any..."

Now it's Marie's turn to drop her jaw. "Your pussy must be full of cobwebs," she remarks, and I shoot her a dirty look for her language. "You know what I mean. Come on, admit it."

"It kinda is."

"So what's wrong, Maddie? I mean, look at you. You're *pretty*. You've got lovely blue eyes and light brown hair to die for."

"My skin's paler than a zombie..."

"You are pretty, Maddie. Can't you see that?"

I don't usually receive compliments, even from other women. I'm very good at sort of fading away into the background. Not get noticed.

"I'm just not a confident person," I explain. "I can't get boys interested in me."

"Well, you should be confident with a face like yours. You are a bit geeky, but you're stunning."

"Thank you, Marie."

"So are you looking for a guy, or?"

I shake my head. "I just find it hard to trust men. My parents went through a messy divorce and it kinda scarred me ever since."

"So," Marie says. "What you're really telling me is that the men of Ravaged wouldn't have a chance of getting into your panties?"

"*Definitely.*"

We both laugh and chink our wine glasses together.

"Here's to not having sex or to trusting rockstars," Marie cheers.

"I can drink to that."

We continue drinking far later into the night than we ever planned to, especially because work is in the morning. We drink until Marie finally stands up from the couch, swaying on her tipsy feet.

"Goodnight, Maddie. You know, I didn't think you were as much fun as you turned out to be. You're generally so... mousey. But you're so smart and funny. We should definitely do this again sometime."

Even drunk, my cautious side looms. "Hey, you can't be planning to drive home like this, surely?"

She blinks at me. "Yeah."

"But... you've had a few."

"Oh, you really are such a strait-laced geek, Maddie."

"You keep saying."

She tries to unlock her phone, but the thing slips from her unsteady hands and falls to the floor. "I could order a taxi," she says as she bends over to pick it up.

I wave her suggestion away. "How about you stay the night, and we'll go to work together in the morning?"

"You sure?" Marie asks.

"Yeah."

"I don't want to put you to any trouble."

"You got me that awesome nearly front row ticket," I reply. "It's the least I can do."

"Well, okay then."

I nod towards my bedroom. "You can take my bed if you like."

"Where will you sleep?"

"Here on the couch."

Despite more protestation from Marie, I eventually manage to force her into my bedroom. Gratefully, she falls asleep immediately upon lying on my bed. I make myself at home on the couch and close my eyes as the world dizzyingly spins around me. I groggily come to the realization I've not drunk this much alcohol for a very long time.

Probably not since my last date.

Yeah, that was a really long time ago.

Maybe I should message that guy I last slept with. Well, he's probably forgotten all about me. I can't blame him.

My thoughts drift away from the past and to the show I witnessed tonight. Those rockstars lead a very different life to me...

I start to fall asleep, and I begin to dream of being one of those hot girls invited onto the Ravaged tour bus. Just for a night, like Marie said she imagines.

I have to admit there's a secret part of me that quite likes that impossible fantasy.

5

AXEL

Lucas Mac wakes me up, and he does so in the most egregious of fashions.

"Fuck off," I say when he violently throws open the hotel suite's curtains, revealing the late morning sun in all its blinding glory. The sunlight rays shine directly into my face as I lie in my massive bed. It takes me a moment to blink my eyes open and have them adjust to all the fucking brightness pouring in like lava.

"Up. Up," Lucas commands, clapping his hand obnoxiously as he does so. "Time to get up, Axel."

"Fuck off." I groan again and try to turn away from the garish sunshine.

Lucas is the manager for Ravaged. He's been with us since we signed our first record deal years ago. Lucas can sometimes be a complete asshole with his trademark honesty and all his *responsible-ness*, but he's essentially the glue that keeps the band together and running like a world-class record-selling machine. Without Lucas and his ability to untie any tricky knot that flings our way, we wouldn't be a band at this point, despite how much I want to kill him sometimes. He works us boys like a racehorse, and it seems like today it is *my* turn to face the end of Lucas' famous fiery rod of discipline.

Lying naked under the sheets next to me, a girl sleepily moans. I forget which one she is from last night, let alone her name. I *think* I remember her legs around mine at some point in the early morning. There are currently three girls in my bed right now, and I don't have a clue who any of them are, even though I was fucking all three simultaneously mere hours ago.

"Alright, girls, you've had your fun," Lucas says in his loud, no-nonsense managerial voice. "You all have to leave now. Axel has got to get up. The rockstar has to do what he's paid obscene amounts of money for and *work*. For a change."

I feel warm female bodies around me lazily shift. It appears to me that they aren't leaving any time soon.

"Give us another minute, Lucas," I protest. "I still need my morning blowjob."

Lucas completely ignores me.

"Get out, girls, or I'm suing your asses into the next century."

Now, that gets them moving. Regrettably, I feel their comforting warmth slide out of my bed. I groan again.

Man, I really wanted that morning blowjob.

"Don't go, girls," I implore, but it's too fucking late. Lucas has frightened them straight out of the hotel suite like a flock of panicked seagulls. They're gone, and so are my chances of getting my dick wet this morning. "Fuck."

"Fuck, indeed," Lucas says, turning his attention back to me. "It's time for you, young man, to get up."

I shield my face from the morning glare and stare at

the man defiantly standing at the end of my bed. He's got short blonde hair that's slowly graying, and tired rings under his eyes despite being in his mid-thirties. Being Ravaged's manager is a stressful job, and it shows on Lucas. Drake's told me the man hasn't been on a date for years. I can't even remember Lucas' last boyfriend; he's been single for that long. Married to the job and all that. Despite all the shit that he deals out to me on a daily basis, I can't help but love the old bastard and his devotion to Ravaged's success.

"Stop pretending to be so old and wise," I say with a just-awake crack in my voice. I really went hard on the drink last night. God, it was fun. Right until Lucas set foot in this room. "You're not even ten years older than me, Lucas."

He mockingly snorts. "That still makes me your elder, so you should listen to me."

"Well, I have about a hundred million more dollars than you sitting in my bank account right now. How about that?"

"I think you'll find that, in Ravaged, my title is *manager,* and that technically means I'm higher on the pecking order," Lucas retorts with a sly smile. "Unlike those ladies in your bed, your ass is mine."

"Fuck off, Lucas. You couldn't take me on even if you tried."

"I may be a flaming homosexual, Axel, but I can still whoop your ass. Now it's time to get out of bed."

I leisurely take my time to crawl out from under the bedsheets. I *am* going to do what he says, but that doesn't mean I can't make a petty show of reluctance while I'm at it.

Lucas stands there just watching me. He's a loud man. Very flamboyant. We all love him. Lucas and I have an easy-going banter that I don't have with anyone outside of Ravaged. Unlike everyone else that we meet, Lucas truly doesn't give a shit about our fame or money, only that we stick to his perfectly timed schedule. That earns my respect.

He's the only man in the world I allow to lecture me without repercussions. Mainly because he's right about everything all the time, though he will *never* hear me admit that.

"You're all about the asses today, Lucas, aren't you?"

"I hope you can forgive me. Because of your band's silly little tour, I've ended up being too busy kicking girls out of your bed every night to not get any."

I grimace at him, and he stares impassibly back.

I rip the sheet away from my body and then realize I'm completely naked.

"Fuck."

"Don't blush," Lucas says, not taking his eyes off mine. "I might be gay, but I've seen your cock a million times to even give a shit. There's nothing you can do to impress me. With you boys, I'm less of a manager and more of a dignified childcare minder."

"You should be proud of me," I say as I collect a spare clean pair of Calvin Klein's from the other side of the hotel suite bedroom. "Kicking girls out of my bed and all that. This is the rockstar lifestyle I signed up for."

Lucas raises a concerned eyebrow. "Being a bad boy might sell a lot of albums and have girls frothing to get under your... Calvin Kleins, but people nowadays expect boybands selling music to teenage girls to have at least a teeny tiny ounce of moral fiber in their bones."

"You mean settle down?" I ask, incredulous. "Find one woman? Live a boring life? Not fall out of nightclubs at two in the morning?"

"Exactly."

"Where's the rockstar spirit, Lucas? Where's the adventure? I'm carrying on a tradition here that dates back to the sexual revolution of the fifties and sixties, man. The Rolling Stones. All of them."

My manager simply rolls his eyes at my passion. "Just get ready, Mick Jagger." He checks the time on his phone. "It's midday already and we have an important meeting in an hour."

"Great. A meeting. How very rockstar."

"You really do live in the moment, don't you? No thought of the future, huh?"

I stand before him proudly in only my underwear. I know I look fucking good; I can see my toned muscular body in the mirror. Before I respond, I take a long, hard look at myself.

I am fucking sexy.

"Yep."

"Put some damn clothes on, Elvis."

"Yes, sir," I reply snarkily. "Is the whole band coming to this meeting, or is it just a special treat for me?"

"Yes, the whole band will be there."

"It better be fucking important, then."

6

MADDIE

Making myself a cup of tea in work's kitchen takes me a lot longer than usual on account of my severe hangover from last night. Yeah, I haven't drunk that much in years, and it's pretty evident in the way I look, feel, and walk. I haven't been able to even think about eating anything this morning, which is very unlike me. A very weak cup of tea is the only thing I can digest that isn't going to make me spew all over my desk.

I just hope Winston - my boss - doesn't see me like this. I'm already on such thin ice with him. I don't think I can even bear to talk to him today.

I stagger back into the office, careful not to spill any of my hot beverage as I make my way, staggering, toward my desk.

I pass Marie. She's slumped over her own desk, clearly feeling the same effects as me. She turns to me and makes a dramatic puking expression, which makes me laugh loudly.

"We're so hungover," I mouth to her. She nods.

I manage to make it to my chair before my weak legs make me fall over myself. I sit down and take a cautious sip of my tea. It's not going to make me spew, thank God.

Knowing I need to actually start my work sometime today, I open my computer and check my emails. Any thought that this might be a simple task is undone the moment I see the first message that pops up on my screen. It's my landlord saying my rent is long overdue.

"Damn," I mutter as I dare read the threatening email.

I am broke, that's true. I haven't been able to pay the rent for some time. But that's because I send money home to Mom. I feel so guilty about her living on her own back home in Wisconsin. I left her to come here, and I'm torn up about it. She doesn't help the situation at all; always reminding me about my *abandonment* of her every time we talk on the phone. I swear it wasn't like that at all, but I can't help but feel like I did a bad thing to her. That's what she calls it. A *selfish* act. But I needed to get away from my town and start my life. I didn't want to hurt her.

My parents got divorced when I was young, and it wasn't an amicable good one either. It was very messy. In the years after, Mom slowly shifted towards religion to the point where now she's practically a fundamentalist. Nothing wrong with that, but it now seems like every conversation I have with her is about sin and death and hell and how everything is somehow my fault. There's no trace of the mom I remember from my childhood left. Even though I send my money back – even to the point of falling behind rent payments to do so – Mom is absolutely convinced I must live a life of sin in Los Angeles.

Ha. I could only wish to live a life of sin. That'll be something different from my dull routine at least.

I came here to escape that negative stranglehold back home, but it seems like every month Mom asks for yet even more money and I can't deny her that. I do feel... dutybound to make sure she's okay.

How can I tell her *no*? How do I tell my mom that I'm about to lose both my condo and my job? That would just confirm the state of sin I'm living in, wouldn't it? My irresponsibleness.

A notification pops up on my computer screen. A new email. From my boss.

With a gulp full of trepidation, I read it.

He's requesting an urgent meeting. Right now.

Oh shit, what can it be?

I stand up and start walking towards the office meeting room, gripping my cup of tea as something to keep my hands from nervously shaking.

Marie takes my arm. "What is it?" she asks, sensing that something's up.

"Winston wants me to see him."

Her eyes widen. "Crap."

"Yeah. *Crap.*"

"Do you think you're going to get fired?" she asks. "Like you were telling me last night..."

"Wow, so blunt."

"What do you think?"

Truth be told, I honestly don't know. I can't give her any answer but a shrug.

I just know that this meeting can't be good.

7

MADDIE

"So, Maddie, why do you think I've pulled you in here today?"

I look down at my steaming mug of tea, trying to avoid the strong eye contact of Winston sitting opposite me. I better drink this thing before it gets cold.

"Um... I don't exactly know why," I reply, hesitant.

Winston shuffles some papers in a resigned way and sighs. It's all so very theatrical. My boss is a man who's known around the office for being a tricky character. I've found him to be stern and grouchy, but also very knowledgeable when it comes to marketing. He's not the *easiest* person to get along with, let's leave it at that. Winston's in his mid-fifties, but he's got a sort of silver fox thing about him.

But I'm not thinking about that now.

"Things don't look so good," he says, rubbing his short gray hair. "For you."

Shit.

"Yeah?"

"Look, the last two projects you spearheaded basically died on their feet, didn't they?"

I try to reply.

"Yes, I know but..."

"They really were not good," Winston interrupts. "Lackluster performances. No sales. The clients weren't happy. Total disasters, don't you think? You got anything to say in response?"

Stand up for yourself, Maddie. Remember?

"I've been working to improve," I hastily say. "I know what mistakes I made, and I will not repeat them in the future."

"Right."

He's not buying it.

I've got to stay positive. I smile at my boss, trying not to show how I'm practically freaking out inside. "They were good learning exercises," I continue. "I've been through all the reports and the analysis. I know what I have to do in the future now to avoid those mistakes. I can go into the future knowing what works best and what doesn't."

"You sure about that?"

"Yes. I learn quickly. I may have made some novice errors, but I'm dedicated. I really like this job, Winston. I *really* like it. I really want to show you what I can do. I *can* do better."

My boss shuffles his papers again. "I like *you*, Maddie," he starts. "I really do. You've got grit and you work hard. You're smart and a perfectionist. Always on time. You don't gossip. You put your head down and just get on with the task."

"I'm glad you can see that. I really do try and make myself an asset to the team. I can show you what I'm capable of, I'm sure of it."

There, standing up for myself.

My boss purses his lips together and pauses, leaving me in dreadful suspense.

My stomach churns, both on account of the lingering thudding hangover from last night and my fluttering nerves.

I really don't want to get fired. I really *can't* get fired, especially not after that threatening email from my landlord.

How the hell am I going to live with no job and no condo?

I did not plan for any of this when I ventured to this city dreaming of a better life.

Eventually, my boss speaks again.

"You want to show me what you can do? Well, we have some potential new clients coming in today, and I'll like you to accompany me to the meeting with them. There'll be no need for you to say or do anything, just be in the room. Observe. Take notes."

"Oh, okay."

I can't believe this. Is this Winston giving me a second chance? I can't let this slip out of my grasp.

"They would be incredibly big and lucrative clients if we manage to snare them," Winston continues. "Enough for you and me to rest easy in our jobs for the foreseeable future."

"That would be great."

"The higher-ups are pressuring me to make some cuts."

Oh, crap.

"Yeah?"

"I don't want to cut you, Maddie. I *haven't* cut you. Like I said, you're a good worker."

"Thank you, Winston. For this opportunity as well. I promise I won't let you down."

"It's just a meeting today, but hopefully it'll lead to good things."

"So, who are these clients, then?" I ask, but before Winston can answer, his phone beeps with an incoming message. He checks it, frowning.

"Speaking of the clients," he says. "They're actually here now. That was the receptionist pinging me to say they're making their way up."

"Really?"

"To be honest, I was expecting them, with their reputation, to be late," Winston says. "I spent all night watching their material. Of course, I've heard of them before, but I'm not a fourteen year old girl, so I'm not exactly their target demographic. I once had a career in music. Did you know that?"

I blink.

Where's he going with this?

"I didn't know."

"Yeah, I was a roadie," he says with a faraway glaze. "I used to do everything for a band. Moved their gear. Cleaned their vans. Good times they were. Met the most amazing woman..."

And then he's back in the room.

"Sorry, Maddie. Got lost there."

I wave him off.

I don't get why he's talking about being a roadie, but it sounds like the clients *are* the product we'll be advertising. That's unusual for a marketing agency like Focus. We deal with brands, not personalities.

Who are these clients and why are they so special?

Glancing at the window behind me that looks into the office, Winston suddenly stands up.

I spin in my seat to see what he's looking at.

It seems like the new clients have made it to our floor.

And it's not just any regular old clients you might expect as a marketing agency. A bunch of lawyers in suits or corporate guys.

These ones are definitely special.

Instead of the usual old men in suits, the very same Greek gods I saw on stage last night are strolling through the office. They are walking through the shocked room like they own the ground they step on.

Ravaged the band is the client Winston has been talking about.

8

MADDIE

I want to pinch myself.

Is this real? Is this actually freaking happening?

I spot Marie standing at her desk, eyes widening as she takes in Ravaged not even ten yards away from her. What remains, after the hangover, of any color in her face is quickly draining away. It appears that she's dangerously close to fainting.

I also can't take my eyes off our new visitors. Oh, it's definitely them, for sure. That unmistakable swagger and cocky confidence and *everything*. Caspian's at the back; a wide burly frame who strolls in with a cool silent alertness. He doesn't look real. I mean, Jesus, he's built like Dwayne Johnson. In front of him is Drake, flicking his curly hair back in a very sexy way and very much enjoying the attention like the show-off he is. Next is Bishop, taking in the office surroundings with his dark, intelligent gaze.

And up front is Axel, sauntering ahead of the pack with a rockstar's flourish. He's wearing a leather jacket over a tight t-shirt that reveals an outline of his hard pecs, a black pair of skinny jeans, and boots. The band all appear so out of place in a corporate office like this, but everyone is staring at them with awe and respect. Even the old men of the office, who I have long suspected wouldn't know what pop culture is even when slapping them in the face, are unblinkingly gawping at Ravaged.

It seems the only person in the entire building who doesn't care that four of the biggest names in the world have just walked into the office is Winston. He gets up from the desk calmly opposite me and points to the meeting room's door.

"Okay, Maddie, you want to follow me and meet the new clients?" he asks.

What did he just say?

I gulp. "Meet them?" My voice breaks.

Winston nods like what he's just said is such a normal run-of-the-mill thing to say and not the craziest thing I've heard all year. "Yes, Maddie, they're our potential clients. And, unfortunately, your last hope of remaining here."

"Um. Okay..."

So. I simply follow Winston out of the meeting room to just *casually* meet the most famous band on the planet. In my shock, I quickly take my mug of tea with me. I don't know why. I don't even want to drink it anymore. I don't think I can stomach it. Anyway, it's gone cold now.

Winston is already shaking their hands when I reach him from the meeting room. They all stand in a semi-circle in the middle of the office, watched silently by everyone I work with like it's some kind of theater show. Some guy who looks deadly serious accompanies the band. I assume he's their manager. Winston speaks to him for a moment and then turns to the rest of the band. Names are exchanged. It's all such a blur.

But then it's my turn.

"This is Maddie," Winston introduces, waving his hand at me. "She's one of the publicists who will take care of you."

Winston's not mentioning the fact that I am *technically* an assistant, not a publicist. He's really laying all the responsibility of this at my feet, isn't he?

"*Potentially* take care of us," Drake replies with his perfectly smooth voice. I can't get it out of my head that the last time I heard that voice was through the sound system of an arena filled with thousands of fans. "We still need to decide on who our band will go with now that we've left our old PR agency."

"Right," Winston says. "Of course. Hopefully, we can convince you to go with us."

During the whole interaction, Axel does nothing else but stare at me, his green eyes indecipherable under his sexy dark fringe. He offers out his hand in order to shake mine. Somehow, by the unserious vibe he gives off when doing it, I feel like him offering his hand to me is some kind of joke for him. A dare.

He wants to see if I'll do it. Some awestruck commoner.

I bet he can see the nerves in my eyes; the same nerves I imagine Ravaged see on a daily basis from other people when they meet them. Is there anything more infuriating than a man who thinks he's above you just because he has a pretty face and a hot smolder that can burn through metal?

Well, I'll shake your hand, mister. I can stand up for myself.

I go for it, but I also completely forget I'm holding a full mug of tea in my other hand. The mug tips forward, and all its contents go flying over the front of Axel.

"Holy moly."

Those exact words fly out of my mouth as I watch the tea drip down the rockstar's shirt and jacket.

So much tea.

At least it's cooled down by now and isn't burning.

Axel continues staring at me, seemingly unfazed by the liquid currently trickling down his front.

Oh, he's going to be so angry...

Everyone in the office seems to hold their breath, afraid of what's about to happen next. The rest of Ravaged look on with amusing smirks.

And I'm freaking the freak out.

"So sorry," I stutter to the bassist. "That was totally my fault."

His jacket is probably so expensive. I certainly can't afford to pay him back for what I've done. A piece of clothing like that is definitely worth a few months of payday. I would have to work day and night to even think about paying for it.

Ha. If I even last that long in this job. I've screwed everything up.

I sense Winston glaring at me. I don't want to even acknowledge him or his condescending expression. I know I have definitely fucked up.

Well, this is the end...

Axel then laughs. It's so easygoing.

"I've never heard anyone say *holy moly* outside of an old English children's book before," he remarks, breaking the tension and making me feel like a total idiot.

"I am so sorry. I can clean this up," I say, reaching into my pocket for a spare tissue. I go to dry the stain, but Axel immediately backs off.

"Don't touch me, sweetheart."

It's a deep growl. A warning that hits me in the gut.

"Sorry," I deferentially reply, but Axel laughs again.

"I'm just joking," he sniggers. And then, without a single fuck given, Axel takes off his jacket. He drops it in a nearby trash can, followed by his shirt. "It's no matter. I'll just get a new one."

He's now completely topless. His toned body displayed gloriously right in front of me. My eyes – and those of the rest of the office - instinctively follow down his V shape straight to the rim of his skinny jeans. He's wearing a metal chain around his neck. His chest is adorned with tattoos. Only inches from my face, I can identify them all so clearly. Sparrows, a deck of playing cards, a guitar, a vinyl record. A quote on the underside of his collarbone. *Don't let anybody get in your way*. I wonder where that's from. From what I know about the rockstar, it sounds very Axel. There's a striped tiger on his left upper arm. A crystal and a winding river on his other shoulder. A cross down the top of his chest between his pecs. I think it's fair to say he loves tattoos. I want to just reach out and trace my fingers over his hard muscles. Find out where those ink markings have come from and what they all mean. There must be a story behind each one, I guess. I notice, on his lefthand side covering his heart proudly, - the most prominent one - is a lightning bolt R tattoo.

Consumed with the irresistible naked torso in front of me, I've completely forgotten about the spilled tea, or even about the fact that everyone present in the office has been watching this strange little interaction.

"Ah, sorry," I say in a mousey way to the gaggle of onlookers.

"All good," Axel replies. "I didn't like that shirt anyway. I'm more comfortable like this. Is that what you wanted when you went to spill tea down me, girl?"

Somehow, I have the suspicion that he's mocking me.

"It was an accident..."

Axel smiles. His dimples flare. "Sure, it was. I bet you *wanted* a look under my shirt, you bad little girl."

"I didn't..."

"How about we head into the meeting room now," Winston suggests from behind me, clearly wanting to move on as fast as possible. I'm guessing he's shooting daggers into my back with his eyes.

"Sounds like a plan," says Axel.

As the band follows my boss into the room, Axel doesn't take his eyes off me. He follows me close behind. I can feel his penetrating gaze on my back the entire way.

Oh, Lord, what have I done?

9

AXEL

People tend to act... *different* around rockstars. That's one of the biggest realizations you get when you become one. Everyone treats you differently. Looks at you differently.

Forget about all the other bullshit; that's what fame is.

When the whole marketing office stopped dead in their tracks as we walked in, none of us band members barely noticed. That's what tends to happen to Ravaged now wherever we go. It's become such a part of normal life for us that an entire building fainting at our feet barely registers.

Yeah, I noted that mousey little publicist girl freak out when I offered her my hand to shake. Sure, I was toying with her – having fun with that fear in her eyes - but even I didn't expect her to be so nervous as to spill that tea all over me.

But I honestly don't give a solitary shit about a ruined jacket. I've taken much more expensive shirts and jackets off in the past and flung them into adoring crowds during shows to even care about something I hastily chucked on I found lying on my hotel suite this afternoon. I've hurled enough shit into crowds that Drake has helpfully suggested maybe I should start charging fans for it.

And so we follow the mousey girl and her boss, taking our seats in some crappy little meeting room. Not very rockstar, I must say.

I don't know why the fuck I'm here, nor do I give a fuck.

"I'll rather be practicing bass or getting my dick sucked than be sitting in this shithole," I tell Bishop.

He can't help but chortle at my joke. "You're so immature, Axel," he says. "Grow the fuck up."

"That's bold coming from you."

"Shut up and focus for once in your life."

"I'm not the one who needs time to practice," I retort snarkily. "I certainly heard that wrong note you played last night, and so did ten thousand of our fans..."

Bishop turns to face me. "Oh really? You're making that accusation?"

"Yeah, I am. What are you gonna do about it, coward?"

"I'm gonna whoop your ass, that's what. And then I'm going to whoop it again for calling me a coward."

"What? You can't bear the competition?"

He takes a swing at me, and I easily dodge it. I ram into his chest like a football player, pushing him back in his chair.

"Gotcha," I grunt as I wrap my arms around his waist, pinning his hands.

"Asshole," he snaps back as he knees my stomach.

It's play fighting, something we members of Ravaged like to do. It's what happens when you get four testosterone-fueled young men in the same band together. We gotta let off our aggression somehow.

Caspian quickly breaks us up, as he usually does. I feel

his firm hand pull me away from Bishop. There's no real damage done.

"Everyone's watching," Caspian growls to us, keeping his voice down. That's a lot of words coming from him, basically a full disciplinary lecture. I raise my hands in mock surrender and sit back in my cheap-ass office chair.

Everyone *is* watching. Well, except for Lucas who has his head in his hands in despair. Drake tuts at Bishop and me. We smirk back.

I spot the tea-spilling girl across the room. She's staring at me and awkwardly drops eye contact when I match hers. I shoot her a cheeky grin, just to make her heart beat even more. She's absolutely petrified, the poor girl.

She's kinda cute in a way, though clearly some kind of nerd. I can read her like a book. She's just a strait-laced geek who's never seen such a sexy guy like me before.

Oh, I love playing games with girls like these.

The head honcho of the marketing agency coughs loudly to start the meeting. I think he said his name was Winston.

Like I said, I don't really care.

"The purpose of getting you all here today is to show you what our agency has to offer..."

He doesn't get very far into his little spiel before Drake interrupts him.

"We – and I'm going to be frank, Winston – don't care about any of that corporate bullshit. We're *artists*. Emotional beings who don't have time for money or numbers. All we care about is one thing at the moment. One single target. That's to beat Tainted Lives."

"Tainted Lives? What's that?" Winston asks, clueless.

I roll my eyes and stifle a yawn. The man wants us as his clients but hasn't read up about our closest rival? That's already a point deducted from our analysis of him. There are plenty of other marketing firms we can go and meet. Anyone in this sorry-ass town would be over the moon to represent us.

"They are another rockband," the tea girl squeaks up to her boss. "Ravaged are in direct competition with them."

Winston stares at her for a fleeting moment, then turns back to us. He's clearly annoyed she knows more about us than him.

"For a year, we've worked on our latest album, Staying At Her Place," Drake continues. "We announce it's going to release on a certain day, and then Tainted Lives announce their own album is releasing on the same day. Just to spite us. Basically, they're assholes, Winston, and we'll very much like to beat them at their own game. You're the marketing company; what can we do to make sure our album crushes theirs on release day?"

Winston strokes his chin, thinking. "We'll look into it," he says. "Actually, I'm going to suggest Maddie to take a closer analysis, seeing as she seems to know everything about Ravaged..."

The tea girl perks up. She blinks, an even more shocked expression on her face now.

"Sorry?"

She likes to apologize, doesn't she? The pretty thing.

"You can make a report, to be delivered to Ravaged, about what we can do to help them beat Tainted Lives."

"Oh. Okay."

"What do you think?" Winston asks us.

Lucas nods. "We'll like to see what you can do and your plan. We'll be speaking to other firms and seeing their proposals too. How about we put a time limit on this, seeing as we want to move fast?"

What am I even doing here? This is such a fucking

waste of time. Lucas can handle all this paperwork and admin. I should be out there with my bass...

Although playing with tea girl has been a hell of a lot of fun...

"What are you proposing?"

"Tomorrow?" Lucas suggests.

Winston glances at the tea girl. She obviously tries to express to him, with the sheer panicked look on her face, that maybe tomorrow is *too* short of a time limit for her to compile a comprehensive marketing report, but her boss turns back to Lucas and says one word that seals her fate.

"Done."

Oh, this is fun to watch. Tea-spiller's gonna have to work hard.

I shoot her another grin. Just to rub it in.

Our band manager shrugs, clearly happy and impressed to get a report so quickly. "You think you'll have a plan by tomorrow?" he asks.

"Maddie won't let you down," Winston replies. "She's reliable."

"I hope she doesn't," Drake adds. I can visibly see tea girl's heart sinking.

She definitely won't be able to do this, the poor girl.

"Hopefully you won't spill tea down any report you do," I interject from across the room.

"What?" this Maddie girl asks, not believing what I just said. Yeah, she heard me. As a rockstar, you can get away with saying anything. That's why I like little games like this. I have no inhibitions at all, and I like to scare people with my open mouth.

I raise my feet and comfortably rest them on the table as I smugly study the girl standing by the wall. Winston beholds me and my disrespectful act in disgust, but he should guess by now that I don't give a shit about manners. I do whatever the fuck I want. I'm Axel *fucking* Stoll.

"I don't think you'll be able to handle a band like ours," I continue to tell Maddie. "We make music for people who like to have fun, and I doubt you've partied or held a proper strong drink down in your entire life, though I would love to see you at a party losing your shit. Oh, I imagine that would be fun to witness. What do you think?"

I grin once more at her, expecting her to avert her eyes again, but she doesn't. She seems pissed at me. She stares me back down. Not flinching.

Oh. Now *there's* a little spark of a challenge. A little fire in her. She wants to tell me she doesn't want to put up with my bullshit.

Yes.

I like a girl with a bit of pushback in her.

My opinion of her instantly changes with that little stare of hers.

I like her.

Today hasn't been such a waste of time after all.

10

MADDIE

Winston pulls me aside once Ravaged leaves the meeting room.

"You have a lot of responsibility now," he tells me. Truth is, I can barely hear what he's saying; I am still in shock and processing that those boys just walked in here today. During the whole meeting I had to resist the urge to pinch myself over and over to check if it was some kind of dream that Ravaged was actually in my workplace. Rockstars like that, flaunting *those* bodies, shouldn't be allowed in mundane everyday places like an office, with all the crappy computers and fluorescent lighting and gossip about the latest reality TV show. They should stay forever on stages or private jets or expensive hotels where they belong.

"Responsibility. I got it."

"You need to really work on getting this report for the band exactly right. There can't be no mistakes, you got it?"

I nod, trying to take a breath to quiet my beating heart. "Yep."

"You're a perfectionist, Maddie. That's a trait I admire about you. Get this done right."

"And I definitely have to do it by tomorrow, right?"

"Yes."

"Ah."

"You can't screw this up, Maddie," Winston continues in a near whisper so that no one else in the office can hear. "Remember what I told you earlier? The bosses upstairs want me to make some cuts…"

Like I didn't know that. Like I haven't been both a mixture of extremely terrified and fluttering nervous since he told me that this was my last chance at keeping my job.

"I'm going to start on it straight away."

"Good," Winston replies.

I make my way to my desk and let out a very long and needed exhale of my entire lungs.

How am I ever going to make this report when it seems like the band was mocking me the entire time, especially Axel? Oh, boy, he was out to get me in that meeting room. I feel kinda proud that I finally stood up to him at the end there and stared him back down after his shitty remarks about me not being cool or whatever. He certainly didn't say anything from that point on. Just stared back at me with those pretty green eyes of his until it was time for him to leave.

He was so infuriating, slouching back in the chair like that and shooting insults in my direction. So cocky. He thought he was so clever, ripping into me like that. And, yeah, he can be *like that*. He's a multi-millionaire celebrity and I really am some geek low on the corporate ladder who works with numbers all day. Technically, I'm not worth the heel on the bottom of his very expensive boot.

But how am I even going to do this crazy report? It

seems completely hopeless even attempting to design a marketing plan for the biggest band on the planet.

You know what? I might as well pack up everything, including my job and my condo, and just move back to Wisconsin to live with my mother. There's no way I can do this. Look at me, I've failed...

Hang on. You can do this, Maddie. You are good at your job.

"Excuse me, can you tell me what the fuck just happened?"

Marie appears at the side of my desk, her eyes wild. Does she not know that I can't explain what just happened either?

"Um. Easy. Just the most famous band in the world popped by to say hello and to make sure my job is on the line if I don't do the impossible and come up with a marketing solution for them by tomorrow afternoon. That's what has just happened."

"But you actually got to meet Ravaged." Marie can barely contain her giddiness. She claps her hands together. I'm very much not in the same mood as her.

"Well, more like spill my tea all over them..."

"I saw that," she says. "But then he took his shirt off and, well, *yum*."

"I would say Axel Stoll is a lot ruder in person than *yum*," I reply flatly. "He's just an entitled brat who feels like he can do whatever he wants to people."

"A very gorgeous brat, you've got to admit."

"Sure, he's got it in the looks department, but it doesn't matter though."

"You are so lucky to have met them and actually chatted with them. It's *so* Sagittarius of you. See, I knew star signs are real. You're living up to yours right now."

"This wasn't luck," I say.

"I saw those sparks flying between the two of you..."

My jaw drops. "*Sparks?*"

"Come on, you didn't see it? There was something between you two."

"Not in a million years, Marie."

"You really don't like each other."

"It doesn't matter, none of it does. There are no sparks between Axel Stoll and me. I'm going to lose my job. Simple as that."

"Unless you write up an excellent report to show them, right?"

"Yep. The most impossible task. Due in just twenty-four hours." I sigh. "Thank you, Winston. That isn't very lucky, so I'm not exactly living up to my star sign."

"You know what? I'm so envious that you got to meet them, Maddie."

"You want to do the report instead?" I ask her. "I'll happily give it over to you."

She snorts. "No way. I don't want that kind of pressure, not in a million years."

I sigh. "Great."

"Think of it this way," Marie says, pointing at me. "At least you got to talk to Ravaged, and now they know your name. How many girls get that opportunity?"

I roll my eyes. "What an opportunity of a lifetime."

Not content with just sending an angry email about the rent, my landlord also posts a very threatening letter under my door. I read it when I get home. It's the same set of points he was getting at in the email.

"Lovely."

I put it away on a desk, just wishing it would magically

disappear, and I go and make myself a cup of tea in my tiny little kitchen.

"Hopefully, I won't spill this one over any bad boy celebrities," I mutter to myself like a madwoman.

My phone vibrates in my pocket. I check the message that's just come through. My mother. Of course it is.

Honey, I'm going to need another hundred.

That's it. That's all she sends me.

I really don't have the spare hundred to gift her at the moment. My bank account has been wrung dry.

Stand up for myself? Yeah, not against my mother. I can't do that.

I put away my phone, just like the landlord's letter, in a vain hope that if I ignore it, then it'll go away. Feeling overwhelmed and with nothing else to do this evening, I sit down next to my laptop with my tea and fire it up.

I've decided I'm going to deep dive into Ravaged tonight. Find out everything I need to know to write this damn report. I guess that means I have to know as much about them as a super fan would, so that's who I have to become. I go straight onto the fan sites and social media to start my research. It isn't hard to piece together Ravaged's history from all the stuff about them online.

Like Marie told me at the arena, the boys are all from the same small town. Crystal River. They met at high school when Drake held auditions for a band. They sort of just launched into the stratosphere from there, really. Gigs around the country and then their first album, No Foundation, which went global. They just grew and grew until they're at the chart-topping stage they're at now. I scroll through various articles and interviews, skim-reading. They literally are the biggest thing in music at the moment. They outsell everyone except for Tainted Lives, their closest competitor.

No wonder they want to defeat their rival band. They both really hate each other, even beyond a commercial beef in the press. I can tell this is a real rivalry between two bands. Between two groups of men who hate each other with a passion.

I watch all the videos Marie sent me the other day before the performance. Music videos. Talk show appearances. I watch the boys talk and sing and play.

God, they really are gorgeous, aren't they?

Axel is a total dick, sure, but there's something in the way he plays that bass. So freaking talented. No wonder he gets away with all his crap when he's got skill like that.

I go deep into the night really trying to paint a picture as to what this band is truly about. I should just sign up at their fan club right now.

But this isn't about enjoyment. If I'm to pay my rent and have enough cash to send to Mom, then I gotta do this research. I gotta do this damn report.

I start typing. Piecing together what I've learned and what I think. I doubt myself with every word. Winston was right when he called me a perfectionist.

It's well past midnight when I start to drift off, dreaming about Axel and the way he stared at me in that meeting room. He was trying to test me. Play with me. And I pushed back. That made him go quiet.

I wonder what went through his head then.

Maybe, just maybe, I passed his little test.

11

AXEL

Sweat pours off my brow as the song comes to an end. The last drum beat from Caspian echoes behind me, and I close my eyes as the crowd applauds ecstatically in approval. I soak in the sound. The applause is as sweet as it was the first time I heard it, at Ravaged's first ever gig all those years ago back in Crystal River.

God, this is always my favorite moment.

We all salute the audience before we head off the stage. I raise my fingers to my lips and blow a kiss into the crowd. I think I see a few girls in the front row visibly swoon. That makes my dick hard.

I follow the rest of the band as we jump backstage. Immediately, Drake turns around and his eyes scan up and down my topless torso.

"Lost another shirt, have we?" he asks me sarcastically. I grin in response. Some crewmember for the arena guides us down some hallway back to our dressing room.

"I can't help it if I throw them in the crowd, can I? The girls love it."

"It's the only way Axel can get laid," Bishop juts in as we enter the dressing room. I give him a dirty look.

"You should've seen the girl who caught it," I say. "A real emo girl. Black hair. Black eyeliner. Full of sass."

"Your type, then?" Bishop asks as he slings his guitar off from around his shoulder. With a relaxed grunt, Caspian collapses onto the sofa. He's exhausted.

We all look a sight. Sweat pours off us, but we still smell amazing. My hands are tired from playing my bass all night, but in that good, *worked-hard* kind of way. I grab a hanging sweat towel and use it to dry my wet hair.

My body feels tight. I've worked hard tonight. My muscles ache and I relish the rush of accomplishment that surges through me. I made the crowd reach musical nirvana tonight with just the use of my talented fingers.

This is the greatest fucking job in the world.

"That girl licked her lips when she caught my shirt," I exclaim. "I would love a piece of that ass."

Caspian cracks open a cold bottle of beer.

"You are such a fantasist," Bishop responds. I ignore his taunts and head for the bathroom. I wet my face with water and check myself out in the mirror.

Staring at the reflection of my chiseled jaw and piercing green eyes, I get that feeling again. That strange shudder through my body I sometimes get. The thought that, once upon a time, I was just an ordinary teenage boy living in small town America, and now I'm actually *this*. Internationally renowned rockstar. I'm an entirely different person from that boy practicing his guitar in his bedroom.

I fish for my phone in my pocket and bring up an old photo of me and my sister, taken years ago. Long before albums and records and girls dominated everything. Before Ravaged. She and I are standing in our family's living room, our crappy little TV behind us. We're both super young. I'm ten, and Chloe's eight. We're posing for the camera, pretending to be little Elton Johns with the flashy sunglasses and big microphones pressed against our faces. I gotta admit we look adorable. Back then, Chloe and I were inseparable. It's my favorite photo of us; that's why I keep it stored on my phone and why I check it at moments like these. The memories flood back, and I'm grounded again. I'm back to being that little boy with a dream.

I chuckle to myself. Who knew a few years later everything would change? Chloe and I grew up. Became teenagers. I devoted myself to music, and she developed a fling with one of my best friends. Bishop and I had a major falling out over the fact he and Chloe got together behind my back in high school. Bishop and Chloe then had some kind of major fight and still won't even speak to each other. Even now.

But then Drake formed Ravaged, and the rest is history. People grow up. People change. Lovers come and go.

And now I'm not just Axel Stoll from Crystal River who does Elton John karaoke with my sister, I'm now *Axel Stoll the rockstar*.

I don't know how long this rockstar life will last for, but I know we have to stay on top for as long as possible. I have to soak in every experience.

I lock my phone and dry my face before stepping back into the dressing room. The boys are seated around each other, beers in their hands. Laughing.

"What are you guys chatting about?" I ask, taking a bottle from Bishop and settling down.

Man, I'm spent after that show.

"What else do you think we're talking about?" Drake asks. "*Girls.*"

"Ah."

"Drake thinks we should pay more attention to our upcoming album and its release rather than on getting laid every night," Bishop adds. "Caspian agrees."

I laugh. "You think so?" I ask the mountain of a man.

Caspian just growls.

I raise my hands defensively. "Settle down, big guy. I'm not planning on a fight."

"Your playboy ways are getting a bit out of control," Drake tells me. "And I know that's rich coming from me."

"Hang on," I reply. "I may not be prepared to fight Caspian, but I'm sure as hell ready to take on you, Drake."

"I'm just saying. *Active Axel*," Drake explains. "You're starting to develop a name for yourself. Even Lucas has been talking about it. It won't help us sell albums if you get that kind of reputation. That shit sticks. What parents of teenage girls will want to buy our albums with a guy like you with your status on the cover?"

"What's this? An ambush by my own brothers?"

Before any of them can answer, there's a knock on our dressing room door. We've told security that we don't want to be interrupted by anyone unless it's the fucking President or a hot babe.

This turns out to be the latter.

The door opens, and it's the emo girl from the audience tonight. The one who snagged my sweaty shirt. She's even more sexy up close. Her black lipstick makes me instantly hard again. She takes us all in with her eyes, but her focus drops on me.

"Is this your shirt?" she asks me with a raised eyebrow, holding up the clothing I was just wearing not twenty minutes ago.

"How did you sneak past security?" I ask her.

"I have my ways..."

I turn to my fellow bandmates and smile. Oh, they know this particular smile of mine. They know *precisely* where this night is heading for me.

Active Axel. I gotta live up to my nickname somehow.

* * *

I'm speaking before I even open my eyes the next morning. "That was a good night," I say.

And it most certainly was. That emo chick knows her shit. This isn't her first rodeo, that's for sure. She had a real hunger for me. A lust that seemingly consumed her. I love being wanted like that. I love the noises I made her make.

Fuck, that must be my problem. I'm addicted to the applause.

Both on stage and in the bedroom.

I turn over in my hotel bed, expecting to feel her body, but she's gone.

What.

I open my eyes and search around the room. Girls don't usually leave until I tell them to. Girls like to cuddle, even if it is for a one-night stand. I have to push them out of my bed.

But, yeah, she's nowhere to be seen.

My hotel suite door barges open, and in walks Lucas. As usual, he's completely undeterred by my shabby appearance, or the fact I've clearly just woken up.

"You know there's such a thing as *knocking*?" I ask him, incredulous.

Lucas just grimaces at me and turns on the TV. He's looking a lot more dour than usual.

"Shut up and watch this," he barks.

"What is it?"

It takes a moment for my bleary eyes to adjust to the screen, but when I do, I actually fucking gasp.

It's footage of me. Footage clearly taken in this very room. Just last night.

Footage of me fucking the emo girl, taken from behind and clearly on a phone. Her face is obscured, but mine definitely isn't.

"Wait, was she filming us?" I ask, incredulous yet again.

"*She* was not just some fawning fangirl," Lucas says in an authoritative tone. "*She* was a plant from a tabloid website. Presumably, she was paid a handsome sum for that footage."

"Fuck, fuck, fuck."

What will the band think? What will my fans think? What will my mom say? Chloe?

Sure, it's the modern era and people aren't so squeamish about sex, but I just know people will hate to see something like this on their screens. I'm not that much of an idiot to comprehend the consequences of this. I'm really living up to my stupid nickname, that's for sure.

"Fuck, indeed," Lucas remarks, turning off the TV to spare me some dignity. "I'm sure I don't have to tell you that this isn't going to play well. At all."

I shake my head and swear a few more times. "Yep. Fuck."

"I've gone into damage control mode. I'm trying to limit it. Call in favors from the press. But even I can't work miracles, Axel. This is bad."

"What do the boys think?"

Lucas sighs and rubs his forehead. I've rarely seen him so rattled.

"You'll have to talk to them yourself. I'm not going to be some messenger."

"Fuck."

"You're going to have to sort this," my manager says. "Somehow."

"Fuck."

"Come on," my manager says. "Less swearing and more action. Time to get up and dressed. We've still got that meeting at the publicity office today. Let's see what they make of this."

12

MADDIE

OF COURSE I see the news. I may be a geek and sometimes completely clueless about modern pop culture trends, but even the footage of Axel Stoll fucking some emo girl with a very high-pitched annoying voice is hard for me to avoid. Especially so when every single person at work badly wants to thrust that same footage in my face everywhere I go because they know I'm supposed to have a meeting with said guy in a matter of hours.

Let's just say that the footage has thrown a real spanner in the works when it comes to the report I'm supposed to present to the band today. I've been working on a marketing strategy for Ravaged's latest album all night, sleeping on and off, trying so desperately to save my ass at work, that when I eventually see the footage in the morning, my heart immediately drops.

"Oh, *crap.*"

That was my initial reaction to seeing Axel's bare ass as he fucks the girl. The footage is pretty damn raw, but at least the tabloid has the decency to blur his cock. But not his ass.

And what a damn fine ass it is.

No, don't think about Axel's perfectly tight ass, instead let's think about the fact you're about to lose your job, Maddie.

I try to avoid watching the video till the very end, which is hard when people constantly try to show me it all day. I get the gist. There's no need to watch five minutes of two people grunting to-and-fro to understand that this whole thing really ruins the report I had ready.

It's perfect timing. Just as they're about to start the promotional tour for Staying At Her Place.

To be honest, I didn't expect Ravaged to even turn up to the meeting today. I would've thought they view the whole thing as a lost cause.

But they do.

They come to the office. Again. Still looking like they really don't belong in such a banal and humdrum setting as this.

I rise from my desk as they enter the office. Everyone's head turns, and I know they're looking at Axel especially. So do I.

He's actually got a pretty ashen-faced expression. That's a surprise. Knowing his usual arrogant attitude, I would've guessed he wouldn't give a fuck about the whole situation. I guess he only cares about things once they affect his band. It seems like the most vain and pompous guy on the planet actually gives a damn about something, even if it is about his ass in the thralls of sex plastered all over the internet.

Well, serves the cocky asshole right, I guess.

The band's manager, Lucas, spots me and heads straight on over.

Oh, shit. They really want me to present this half-assed report to them, don't they?

I hastily step away from my desk to greet the band. They all look very grim, and I know that the next hour is going to be difficult.

"Hello, Maddie," Lucas says.

"Hello. Bad day, isn't it?"

The manager sighs. "Bad day."

I face each member of Ravaged in turn, eventually settling on Axel himself. His green eyes shine back at mine.

And then I speak, mustering up all my courage to address these incredibly famous men.

"Let's do this meeting then, shall we?"

13

AXEL

THE TEA GIRL – *what was her name again* – throws me shade from the minute I step into the office. Oh, I know that look of disgust on her face. She's not very good at being subtle. But despite her scornful shots aimed in my direction, I have to admit she's pretty cute. In a nerdy sort of fashion.

I sense her eyes trawling my body up and down in resigned revulsion.

Yeah, yeah, yeah. I have sex. Whoop-de-do.

She's probably too highly strung to have even *touched* a member of the opposite sex, let alone have the level of fun I had last night.

I sigh at the girl and turn to my bandmates for support. I want them to see how obvious the girl is being before we've even started this stupid meeting. They ignore me.

Okay, so the rest of Ravaged didn't take too kindly to the sex tape this morning. Things got quite... *heated* between me and my bandmates. But despite their condemnations, there's no doubt that they won't stick by me. We're brothers, not by blood but by equally deep bonds, and we weather whatever storms get thrown our way. Together.

Lucas, meanwhile, is taking this all as some sort of managerial crisis. He doesn't give a shit about the contents of the footage – no judgment at all – he's simply purely focused on what we can do to recover from this scandal.

A scandal of my own making.

Why was I so stupid as to trust that emo girl?

Now my bare ass is on every fucking screen on the fucking planet. It's a good ass, sure, but I still don't want every fucker in the world to admire it.

I knew my playboy antics would turn around and bite me on the ass one day. Turns out it did, in quite a literal way.

The paparazzi were waiting ravenously for us outside my hotel. I didn't breathe a word to them as I strolled to be chauffeured limousine. They followed us here to the stupid marketing agency, trying to catch me out with their stupid *gotcha* questions.

Facing my fellow bandmates outside this building was one of the worst things this morning. The looks on their faces... I know I fucked up.

And Drake gave me hell for it. He pulled me aside from the rest of Ravaged outside the office and gave me a real talk-down.

"The band is the most important thing, Axel," he told me. Deadly seriously. "The band is *everything*."

"I know."

Fuck. He's right. Ravaged is our heart and soul. Our fucking baby.

I'd do anything for my boys. I'd do anything to save our band.

But I'm not going to admit publicly that any of this was

my fault. Especially not with this fucking tea girl and her boss.

Maddie takes us all into the meeting room and promptly begins her presentation. She's clearly worked hard at this thing. But I want her to know I don't give a shit if she's spent all night on it or not.

Halfway through her slides and her little speech, I raise my hand and stop her dead in her tracks.

"I'm tired of all this talk," I say loudly.

"Oh, really?" Maddie asks. She blinks. Once. Twice. She's clearly never come across anyone like me before. I really don't give a shit about manners.

"I was up all night," I continue with a smirk on my face. I'm loving her reaction. "So I'd rather be sleeping than listening to some boring-ass lecture..."

Maddie just stares at me. She takes her time to respond.

"We all know *why* you weren't sleeping last night," she says coldly and calmly. "And it's my job to solve that problem, so why don't you sit still like a good boy and listen for once in your life?"

There's a moment of silence.

And then my bandmates are whooping and clapping. Cheering the mousey little publicist standing in front of us,

"Yes, Maddie!" Bishop yells.

I remain motionless. Seething.

She's blushing. She didn't want to go that far.

Well, it's too late now, girl.

"She showed you up there," Drake says, giving me an aggressive pat on the shoulder. Even Caspian is clapping, a small hint of a smile at the corners of his lips.

"*Ha ha.*" I try to shake her comments off with a sarcastic laugh, but even I have to admit she's got me. The rest of Ravaged is clearly loving how some lowly publicist has the balls to take me down.

I spot Lucas smirking at my misfortune by the door. The sneaky fucker.

Even the fucking marketing boss, Winston, is carefully repressing a snicker with the palm of his hand.

These motherfuckers...

"You're free to walk back outside to the waiting camera of the paparazzi if you'd like," Maddie says. "But we're trying to make a plan here for your band. Please let me finish."

"You're going to regret saying that bullshit," I snarl back to her.

She looks frightened by that.

Good.

"Just let me do my job," she squeaks in reply.

"Alright then," I say to the girl. "Continue your wonderful plan."

I feel my bandmates' eyes on me. Those fuckers are going to pay for cheering on Maddie when we're back in private. Oh, they certainly are going to pay...

"I've looked at all the focus group data comparing Ravaged with Tainted Lives. Everything Lucas sent over to my company. I have come to one conclusion as to why your band is slipping behind Tainted Lives," Maddie says. "Do you want me to continue?"

That final question from the girl is delivered with a generous helping of snark and passive aggressiveness. Targeted straight at me.

"Please do," Drake says with his charming grin. He knows what Maddie's going to say next, and he's lapping it up. We *all* know what she's going to say next.

She glances at me and takes a deep breath.

"It's you, Axel. Your... *sleeping around*. The most common negative factor coming from all the focus groups is that they want you to act like an adult. People don't mind a rockstar enjoying life, but they think you've gone too far. Too cocky. Too loud about things in the press. People want you to reform your bad boy ways. Parents are viewing your band in a worse light than Tainted Lives because of that very reason."

She stops. And there's another long pause as everyone digests her words.

I'm the fucking problem? Me? For being a goddamn rockstar? For continuing the tradition set for decades?

"What do people want from their musicians?" I ask the room, outraged. "Do they want fucking morality? No. I don't buy it. This all sounds like level-A bullshit to my ears."

I cross my arms and sulk.

Bishop raises his arm. "What about Drake? He doesn't exactly have the *cleanest* record. Is he as bad as Axel?"

Maddie shakes her head. "No. People like Drake. With Axel, they think his arrogance is the problem, not just the girls. They consider him worse than Drake because of that."

"I'm a problem?" I ask, my teeth bared. "Is that all who I am now? A fucking *problem*?"

Maddie doesn't say a word. Her mouth opens and closes.

Drake delivers another aggressive pat on my shoulder, reveling in all this.

"Yep. Seems like you're a problem, Axel."

I flick Drake's hand away from my shoulder and stand up. I take one long look around the room. I'm not putting up with this bullshit.

No. Way.

"Fuck this," I say before I storm straight out of the room and out the office.

14

AXEL

Lucas manages to stop me before I get the chance to duck into the waiting taxi. I turn to him slowly as he calls my name, pissed about everything. Pissed about Maddie. Pissed about my bandmates. Pissed about that emo girl from last night. The leaked footage.

"What is it, Lucas?" I growl like a caged animal.

I can't stay out here on the sidewalk in public for long. A fan might spot me or, even worse, the paparazzi might get tipped off and swoop down like the vultures they are. I just want to get back to my hotel suite. I can't be dealing with the bullshit spewing forth from the pretty little mouth of the short tea-spilling girl in that fucking marketing office room.

"Axel. Just stop."

I sigh and nod at the taxi driver to just continue driving on past. I face back to Lucas with my arms crossed defensively.

Fuck all this.

"You're going to shout at me, I know. I shouldn't have stormed out of there, *blah, blah, blah*. Let's get it over with."

My manager and close friend merely shakes his head sadly. "Look, I'm not going to go crazy at you, Axel. This whole situation doesn't warrant that. Besides, I don't have the energy."

"I'm not going to put up with a girl like that insulting me or with my own bandmates being complete dicks," I say. "We're here to find a solution to the problem, not rub it in my face like shit."

I bet they're still up there now, gloating over how I'm such a wuss who can't handle a few jokes. But I'm not going to sit idly by in some shitty office meeting room when everyone in said room is making *me* the butt of their lame-ass jokes, even if they're my best mates. No, sir.

I'm a rockstar, not a punching bag.

"Well, you have kinda caused this whole mess, Axel."

"Fuck off."

"I'm being serious."

"You're as bad as Drake and Bishop and Caspian, Lucas."

"Last night was a massive mistake, Axel. Even you can see that, surely."

I frown. "I fucked up, okay? I should have made sure she wasn't filming me. I should've vetted her more before I brought her back to my bed. I'll be better next time, alright?"

"It's not about that or her," Lucas replies. "It's not even about *one* woman, can't you see?"

"Then what is it about?" I ask. "Enlighten me, wise man."

"You heard what Maddie had to say up there."

I roll my eyes and groan. "For fuck's sake, all I hear

about is that fucking Maddie. First, she spills tea all over me and now she's daring to lecture me about how to live my fucking multi-millionaire life."

Lucas smiles. "I know you like her, Axel. I know you've got a grudging respect for her standing up to you like that."

"Not many people do that," I add. "Not many people have the balls. It doesn't change how goddamn annoying – how goddamn wrong – she is."

"But you heard what she was going on about, right?" he asks me. "What she was trying to say with all the evidence she had?"

I uncross my arms and take in a deep breath. "Yeah. About the perception of me out there with our audience. *Active Axel* and all that bullshit."

"About the reputation you have as a crazy, unrestrained playboy."

"Yeah, that. Whatever."

"You gotta hand it to her that she's good at her job. She's not wrong."

"What is she, your fucking daughter?"

Lucas chuckles. "So, what do you say? Do you want to beat Tainted Lives? Do you want Ravaged's new album to be number one?"

"More than anything in the fucking world, Lucas. You know that."

"Then what should we do about it?" he asks me.

"I care more about Ravaged being the best band than anything else."

"Then what should *you* do to make that happen, Axel?"

"I ain't giving up the girls, man, if that's what you're trying to say," I snarl. "What do you want me to do? Fake a *happy-as-Larry* relationship until Staying At Her Place's release? Pretend I'm all reformed or some shit?"

Lucas thinks about that comment much longer than he should do. He sighs.

What the fuck is going through his head?

"Yeah," he eventually says quietly. "That's exactly what you might have to do."

15

MADDIE

Lucas and Axel don't return to the office. Which, of course, leaves me stranded in the meeting room with the rest of Ravaged. I just stand in front of them awkwardly, not knowing what to do with my hands or anything.

Things are pretty damn awkward, to say the least.

I am completely clueless on how to proceed until Drake finally speaks up.

"Well, I guess that's the meeting over. Thank you, Maddie."

And then the band walks straight on out of the room, back through the office, and out the front doors.

I let out a sigh of relief once they've gone.

That was not easy, putting it mildly.

It was the scariest meeting I've ever had, and I can't make a guess at what the outcome of it even was. I blindly insulted Axel – *well, because he was being a total dick* – and then he stormed out, closely followed by his manager. Did they even like the report I gave? Were they even listening?

Am I... *fired*?

I don't know what came over me. That snarky attitude I exhibited in front of the band. I'm usually such a reserved person, always so frightened of conflict and causing a storm, and yet Axel somehow makes my inner... *bad girl* come out. He's so infuriating and annoying and rude and... and... so freaking gorgeous. I just couldn't help but stand up to the bassist.

And things weren't helped by the fact that his little randy sojourn in the early hours of this morning completely ruined the presentation I had spent all night carefully crafting. If there's one thing to rile perfectionist me up, it's to ruin my work.

Axel certainly knows how to ruin things.

And now I've done the same.

Maybe this is the end of my career. Gone before it even practically started.

Winston was in the room the entire time, silently observing my presentation. When Ravaged finally leaves, he turns to me.

But he doesn't say a word. I think he might be as equally confused as I am.

"Can I go on lunch early?" I ask him, my voice squeaking from all the tension inside of me.

I need a break. I need to get out of this cramped office. I need to be on my own.

Yep, I've probably lost my job.

"That was a big meeting," Winston says slowly, his tone indecipherable. I can't tell if he's angry or shocked. Probably both. "You deserve a coffee."

"Um. Right. Thanks."

"Good."

"How do you think that... went?" I nervously ask my boss.

He shrugs. "We'll wait until we hear back from the band's team."

"Okay."

That doesn't help me in the slightest.

* * *

Marie stops me in the hallway before I get the chance to escape the office.

"What were they like?" she asks me, gripping my arm. Her voice is barely a whisper.

"Exactly how you'd think."

My curt reply doesn't deter my co-worker.

"Please elaborate. I want to hear all the juicy details."

"Well," I start. There's no need to get deep into what the hell just happened in there, especially not to Marie. "They all seem nice. In their own way. All of them except for that Axel. He's on another level entirely."

Marie nods in agreement. "Oh, I saw the footage of him and that girl. Everyone has. What was it like being in the same room as him? Did he say anything about it? What does he think?"

"He had a lot to say."

"I'm so jealous of you. They're the biggest story on the news today and you're having a private meeting with them..."

I think back on Axel storming out of the room. How it made my heart crumble. I was such an idiot to talk back to him, but he pushed me to the edge with his constant insults about my presentation. That one act of snapping back at him has probably cost me my job. "I don't think you'll want to trade places with me, Marie."

"After today, Ravaged would be difficult clients," she remarks. "That sex tape is not good."

"Yep, certainly not good."

We bid farewell and I carry on walking past reception and out into the LA sunshine.

I'm going to walk a couple of blocks. Clear my head. Maybe get that coffee, sit down, and think about how I'm going to move back home. Think about what I'm going to say to my mother when I walk through the front door of my childhood home having failed at trying to escape.

But I don't even make it more than twenty yards down the sidewalk when a mysterious black car dramatically pulls up alongside me, the engine roaring.

I jump back in surprise as one of the vehicle's tinted windows winds down.

It's Lucas. Alone in the backseat.

I am at a loss for words.

"What are you doing..."

"Get in," he commands me coolly. "We have to talk."

16

MADDIE

"If you're going to kidnap me, then at least buy me a coffee."

Lucas sighs and orders his driver to take us to the nearest Starbucks drive-thru. In the short drive over, we sit uncomfortably together in the back of the car, silent. I fidget with my hands in my lap, nervous.

Why does Lucas want to talk to me?

I just *knew* I shouldn't have messed with Axel back in that meeting room, and now I'm somehow embroiled in Ravaged's problems. What did Mom always tell me as a kid? Don't go into strangers' cars? Stranger danger is the least of my problems now.

I take the coffee from the driver and hold it between my hands, hoping that by gripping onto something it doesn't make me look so on edge.

"Don't worry," I say to Lucas. "I'm not going to spill it all over you."

That makes the man laugh. It's good to see his serious face light up for a brief moment. "I like you, Maddie," he replies. "You've got spirit."

"So, what do you want to talk to me about? Why have you kidnapped me?"

Lucas orders the driver to pull over by the side of the road on a quiet street a few blocks away from work.

"Just here."

"This feels very much like a scene in a Mafia movie," I remark. I'm just trying to fill the awkward dead air. "Am I going to be whacked or something?"

"I wouldn't worry," Lucas replies. "I don't have the stomach for violence. I am here to make you an offer you can't refuse, though."

"Good pun."

"Thanks."

"So?" I ask him with a raised eyebrow. "What's this offer, then?"

"I've got a job for you."

"A job? You're joking."

"I'm being serious."

Why would Ravaged need me?

"Does this job involve something to do with Axel?" I ask him. "I've got a teeny tiny feeling that it does."

Lucas leans toward me. He smells fantastic. He must have some really expensive aftershave. "You're very insightful, Maddie. This job I'm offering pays well. Way better than your current job, I must add."

"What are you getting at?"

"You'll have to quit working at Focus."

"Wait, you want me to leave my publicity job to come work for you and Axel? To do *what*, exactly?"

Lucas blinks. "I thought you might've already guessed," he says.

"I think I'm thinking in the right ballpark, but please enlighten me."

The pieces of the jigsaw are starting to line up in my mind...

"You gave that presentation to the band, and you looked through the figures and the focus groups, so you know more than anyone how important it is that we change the public perception of Axel, right? We both know it boils down to one thing. One immediate thing he can do to salvage this train crash. He needs a relationship. Right now. With someone that the press and his fans don't find too threatening or fake. Axel needs a steady girl."

Oh. Just as I suspected.

This can't be serious, surely?

This is pure freaking insanity, dreamed of by a band that doesn't live in the real world.

"You're not suggesting what I think you're suggesting..."

"I am," Lucas replies. "What do you think?"

"What do I *think*? Did you just call me not threatening?"

Lucas shakes his head. "Are you in or out, Maddie? It would be a shame if you don't commit, because I think you could be the best candidate for this."

I take in a long, deep breath, trying to wrap my mind around all this. "Let me get this straight... So, what you're attempting to ask me is for me to enter some kind of fake relationship with Axel? Purely on the basis of making him appear less of a playboy so that you can sell Ravaged's next album?"

Lucas nods. "Yes. Obviously, being a publicist, you should understand what I'm asking of you."

"I'm *technically* an assistant."

Lucas sighs. "Right. An assistant. Even better to have a low-status job. People can get behind someone working hard for no recognition. They'll connect to you. So, do you understand what I'm saying?"

"Of course I *understand*," I say, trying my best to ignore that he's already finding a way to positively spin my job title. "It's just that I might need a minute here. You're asking me to pretend to date – in a totally fake way - one of the most famous bachelors on the planet?"

"Yes."

"Right. Wow. For how long?"

Lucas waves at the air in front of him. "Only until Staying At Her Place comes out, and then we'll manufacture some kind of... amicable split. Make you all break apart in a way that reflects well for you."

"Okay," I sigh. "That's a lot to take in."

"Look," Lucas says quietly. "I know it's crazy..."

"You got that right."

"And it may sound like the stupidest thing in the world, but – trust me - I've thought it through. *You* would be good for Axel's image. I know people would like you. Maddie Leaver is a real, typical American girl, not some rich supermodel from LA. This job will be the most insane thing you'll ever do, but I promise you it's only for a few months. And, as I've already said, the reimbursement for your trouble will be substantial. *Very* substantial. Enough to make you pause."

"How much are we talking about?" I ask him.

Lucas jots down a number on his phone, then shows it to me. The number makes my jaw drop. And it does make me pause.

Yes. It's very substantial.

My thoughts turn to my condo. With the kind of money Lucas is offering in my bank, I will be able to never worry about my bills again. I'll be able to pay Mom to live in a nicer place back home. I'll never stress about a thing for the next twenty years.

But, then again, it's never been about the money for me. I won't give up my dignity just for extra cash. I'm not about that life. I've never wanted to lose my self-respect just to get money from a man.

And, most of all, I can't imagine being with Axel. The playboy who fucks around. Every time we've met, there's been a tension between us. We're opposites in every way, and it clearly shows. He smirks at me like a cat toying with a mouse. We shouldn't even be in the same room together. How could we last faking a relationship for *months*?

We'd kill each other.

I take in another deep breath and face Lucas. "It's all a good idea," I start. "I understand what you're trying to do with changing Axel's public image. It's a solid, if crazy, plan that I think might actually work, but it isn't for me. I'm not cut out for this. I'm not that kind of girl, even if the money would be very nice to have. So thank you, but no thanks. Sorry."

Lucas purses his lips together and frowns. I've let him down. "I thought you might say that," he replies.

"I'm sorry."

"It's okay. You're very kind, Maddie, you know that? It does throw a spanner in the works. You were perfect for the job. Can I persuade you to at least think about it for a couple of nights?"

This guy's fantastic at being a hard-negotiating manager. No wonder Ravaged are in the position they're in. I actually feel guilty for refusing him the opportunity to ruin my life.

I slowly shake my head. "No, sorry."

"Alright. At least I tried. I'm going to go home and have a headache now."

"Thank you for the coffee, anyway."
"Should I drop you back at work?" he asks me.
"Yes, please."

17

MADDIE

Nothing else eventful happens for the rest of the day at work, certainly nothing that would rival my afternoon meeting and then that weird job offer from Lucas. I just waste away the few hours at my desk until it's time for me to head home, subtly watching for any news from Winston across the room as to my job status. He doesn't say a word to me at all, which is either the worse or the best sign.

As I drive home, I think about what he'd said to me after the meeting. I can't shake the ominous gut instinct that I am going to get fired.

All because some goddamn rockstar can't control his dick.

I pull up alongside my condo building. I spot a gigantic pile of things outside the front door. It takes me a moment to realize exactly what they are.

Those are *my* things, all in one enormous mass. Everything I own from inside the condo. My TV, bedding, even my couch. All my stuff is just heaped up next to the sidewalk like trash.

I quickly park and haste across to my things. There are bags containing all my clothes just dumped on the lawn.

"Oh, crap."

I run up to the front door of the condo building, attempting to use my key to get inside.

But the locks have changed. There's a note pinned to the front door addressed to me. I read it with crushing defeat.

MADDIE,

You are behind in your rent. After many letters to you, I have now decided to kick you out. Please find all your possessions outside the building. Do not contact me again.

IGNORING my Eastern European landlord's scrawled handwriting, I crumble up the letter and throw it as far away from me as possible.

He can't do this. Surely, he can't. It must be illegal somehow.

Yeah, but I don't know how it might be illegal. And I'm not exactly in a position to argue with some crazy landlord when everything I've ever owned is out in public for anyone to simply take. I just gotta stay here and... *I don't know.*

I don't know what the hell I'm supposed to do now.

I slide despondently down the condo wall until I'm sitting down in the dirt with my head in my hands, and I begin to cry.

So much for standing up for myself.

Everything seems pointless. I've probably lost my job today, I have no money at all, and I can't even get into my own freaking condo. Where am I going to sleep tonight? What am I going to do with all my stuff out in the street? They won't all fit into my tiny-ass car.

This has been, without a doubt, the *worst* day of my life. And I just know that things are going to get a hell of a lot more terrible.

Tears fall from my face as I just think about how hopeless everything has turned out to be. I gently sob as my ass cramps up from sitting on the hard ground.

The roar of a motorbike brings me screeching back to reality. A dark figure on a vintage bike zooms up alongside the curb, their face obscured by a black helmet. They're clad all in leather. A real cool biker.

As far as I know, no one around here rides a motorbike that looks as ferocious – and as seemingly *expensive* – as that. He must be a real daredevil, whoever the hell he is.

Probably someone willing to steal my things.

I look up as the biker turns off the ignition and steps off their ride. They remove their helmet.

It's the very last person I ever expected to see again.

Axel Stoll.

He dumps the helmet on his bike's seat and starts walking around my pile of crap towards me.

I try to wipe the tears from my eyes on the back of my sleeve in a futile attempt to show face, but it's clear Axel notices my sorry state.

"What the hell are you doing here?" I ask him, my voice breaking through my sobs.

He doesn't say a word as he approaches. His sharp green eyes are the only thing that I see.

"I don't want you here," I tell him.

He stops then, just a few yards away. Next to my things. He ruffles his helmet hair, letting the dark wavy quiff of his to flop forward.

"I don't want to be here either," he says, pouting with those full lips of his. "But I am here for a reason."

I blink.

"What for?"

"I'm here to persuade you, Maddie."

I chortle. You've just got to laugh at the ridiculousness of all this. First Lucas and now Axel on a motorbike.

"I know exactly what you're saying," I reply curtly. "And I know what you want. The answer is no, just what I told Lucas earlier."

Axel seems unfazed by my retort. He glances down at my things scattered around his feet. "What's all this shit doing outside your condo?" he asks. "Is it yours?"

"Yep. It's all my stuff."

"Why is all your stuff out on the street, Maddie?"

I stare at the rockstar. "You have no idea of what normal life is, don't you?" I ask him. "You have no idea what it's like to have no money, no power, no hope."

"Well, educate me," he smirks.

"I didn't put my stuff out here on purpose," I reply, my voice low. "If you must know, my landlord has locked me out of my place and threw my shit out."

"For what?"

"You wouldn't understand. What do you think, Axel? I'm unable to pay my rent. Of course you would not comprehend a problem like that, would you, being so rich and sexy beyond comprehension?"

"You're calling me sexy?"

I groan. "I would rather you just leave me alone. Can't you see I'm kinda having a problem right now? I would like you to go. Immediately."

Axel, again, doesn't say a word to my request. He simply steps forward and then, in a surprise move, sits down beside me in the dirt.

We're quiet for a long time. Neither of us speaks nor even looks at each other. I gaze upon my things just lying there. I feel a tear drip past my chin and fall to the ground. I wipe my face for a second time.

I hate how vulnerable I am next to this Greek god.

"It's pretty obvious you need cash," Axel eventually says softly.

"What does that mean?"

He waves a hand towards my scattered things. "There. Pretty obvious."

"Get lost," I retort.

"I can help clean this all up," he tells me. "All I have to do is call Lucas and all your things will be off the street and into a storage unit within the hour."

I snort. "I don't need your help."

"What about the money for the job Lucas offered you?"

"I won't do it, Axel."

"I didn't *want* to come here and ask you today," he says. "It's fucking demeaning for me, and I still haven't forgiven you for the crap presentation you gave today."

"Gee, thanks."

"But even I can see how good Lucas' plan might be. It would work. For both of us. I mean, you *do* need the money."

"I'm not doing it."

"Look, it's gonna be easy. A few months pretending to be my girlfriend, that's it. Think about it as spending time with someone you just called sexy beyond comprehension. Your words."

I bow my head. I'm not in the exact right headspace to talk to Axel about this insane job. He seems to understand that. Instead of pressuring me even more, he hands me a card.

"Call me." I glance down at the card he's giving me. It

has his phone number written on it. "I don't know why I'm doing it, but as a favor to you I'll get Lucas to move this stuff for you, free of charge."

"No conditions?"

"None."

"Well, thank you."

"You're one lucky girl," Axel says.

"How am I lucky?" I ask him in disbelief. "I'm sitting outside my condo building that's locked to me with absolutely zero money in my bank account and every chance I'm about to lose my job. How is that lucky?"

"You're a lucky girl because a rockstar like me has just handed you my actual personal phone number. Not a dummy, not a fake one, but the actual one I use for friends and family. There're not many girls who can claim that, so yeah, you are very much a very lucky girl."

"And you're one very lucky guy not to have my fist smack bang in the middle of your face," I reply. "Although that's pretty tempting."

Axel chuckles and stands up.

"Call me," he says before he puts his helmet back on. "Consider the job offer. Things like that don't come along every day, don't they? Even *I'm* not too removed from normal life to know that. Consider the money, Maddie."

And then, with another roar, the rockstar and his vintage motorbike are gone into the evening.

18

MADDIE

Well, I've scrambled up enough of my pitiful savings to book myself a grungy little motel room for the night, and now I don't have a clue what I'm supposed to do with myself.

I flick through the TV channels on the room's crappy little box, my eyes not even focusing on the moving images.

True to Axel's word, Lucas' guys appeared within the hour to take my unorganized pile of things to a storage unit. Thank God for that, otherwise I would be completely screwed. Then, with only my overnight bag, I walked to this cheap motel. I didn't even dare waste any money on gas or a taxi.

To be honest, I don't even want to watch TV. I'm just trying to keep my mind from wandering. I try not to think about my parents getting divorced. How that really hurt me as a little kid, witnessing that. The arguments. My mother telling me that this is what the endpoint of every relationship with a man is like. I usually try to never reflect on those childhood years of pain and turmoil, but with all this talk about Axel and this fake relationship job, I keep turning back to it. Mom told me not to trust men. And do I trust Axel?

Hell no.

What the freak am I even thinking entering this strange not-real pretending-to-be-someone's-girlfriend routine? Why am I even giving it a moment's consideration?

I glance around this crappy little motel room. Well, I *do* need the money.

"Ugh."

I switch off the TV using the remote and roll back onto the bed. The old cheap mattress creaks under me.

I have to call him. There's no other way.

It's either do this crazy-ass job, or head back home to Mom. And that's the last thing I want to do, even worse than spending months playing house with Axel.

And, yeah, I did make that stupid New Year's resolution. Say *yes* more.

Right. *Okay.*

It's midnight, so I don't expect him to pick up when I finally do summon the courage to dial my phone, but he does answer.

"Hello, Maddie."

His voice is calm. Unsurprised.

"Axel."

"Truth be told, I was actually predicting you wouldn't call. I was going to bet Lucas you wouldn't."

"I'll do it."

"What?"

"I'll do you and Lucas' job."

There's a brief pause on the other end.

"I'll have Lucas call you back to arrange the details."

It sounds like he's about to hang up, but I get in there quicker.

"I'm not finished yet."

"Yeah?"

"I am going to do it, but on conditions."

"Just talk it over with Lucas. I ain't got time to comb through some contract. I'm not that kind of guy, sweetheart."

He's already irritating my socks off.

"I want you to hear these conditions. In person. I want to talk things through with my not-real boyfriend. I'm not entering into something without laying down some ground rules."

There's another momentary pause. I can practically hear Axel mulling things over.

"We better meet up," he eventually says.

"Yeah," I reply. "We better meet up."

19

AXEL

Maddie is already at Lucas' condo when I arrive. I mean, I *am* late as per my reputation, so I shouldn't be surprised when I see her in Lucas' living room. She's got a very serious expression on her pretty little face, more so than usual, and she briskly stands up when I enter the condo.

"You're late," she tells me. Like it's some complicated riddle she's figured out all on her own.

"And you're on time like a goody-two-shoes loser," I reply.

She sighs, clearly trying her best to hide her frustration, but then offers to shake my hand, obviously ready to get down immediately to business.

Yeah, as if I'm going to allow her to do that.

"Why are you trying to shake my hand?" I ask her, smirking. "A little bit stiff and formal, don't you think?"

Maddie pulls her hand back, flustered.

"I don't know," she replies.

She's very cute, being so uptight. She is *such* a geek. I wonder what her last boyfriend was like. Probably some socially awkward nerd as well. What a change from someone like that to me, hey.

"You look nervous," I remark, my eyes skimming down from her pale, attractive face with her mid-length brown hair tied in a cute ponytail to her shaking hands.

I can't help but notice what she's wearing. A cute little red dress with dark long boots. I can even glimpse a teasing passing sight of her cleavage. This is not something I'm guessing Maddie usually wears.

Is she trying to impress me?

Or is she trying to make my blood boil? Because it's certainly working. Dressed like this, she's very alluring.

"I've never really negotiated a fake relationship before," she replies. I like her honesty.

"Oh, well I've done it plenty of times," I say, trying not to stare at the hint of her breasts.

"Really?"

I snort. "I'm joking."

In the corner, Lucas rolls his eyes at my little attempt at humor. Maddie just nods.

"Okay. Well, should we sit?"

"Of course," I reply, following her over to Lucas' couch. We're very close together around my manager's table. Her arm rubs up against mine. I can't help realizing it's our first proper physical contact other than the time Maddie shook my hand in the office and then spilled tea all over me. Lucas sits opposite us, watching with his silent judgy attitude.

"Can I ask a question?" Maddie asks. I can see she's still nervous.

"Shoot."

"Why did you suggest we talk this through here? Why not where you live, Axel?"

"I'm currently living from a hotel suite," I explain. "The paparazzi are waiting for me there all the fucking time. If I brought you there, then your face will be all over the tabloids within the hour. Trust me, you don't want that just yet."

Maddie nods, biting her lip and thinking. I like how cautious she is. She wants to make sure everything's accounted for and that she'll be safe doing this job.

She has no idea what's coming to her.

"Okay, shall we start?" she asks Lucas and me. "This is so awkward; I just want to get it over and done with."

"Can I have a drink?" I ask Lucas.

"Help yourself."

"You?" I ask Maddie.

"Oh, no. I'm fine."

She's so rattled by all of this, and I can see why. This is going to be more money than she's seen in her life. I'm about to change her life, for the better and for the worse. Her reaction is sweet; it makes me remember my first taste of fame and how terrified I was when I realized that everything was going to be different from now on. Ravaged's first review. The first time I appeared in the tabloids and on social media. The first time complete strangers knew my name.

Maddie is about to face all of that.

And she doesn't have a clue how bad it's going to get.

At least she'll have me to hold her hand - metaphorically speaking, of course – through all of it.

I pour myself a whisky from Lucas' kitchen and sit back down in the living room, this time in a chair opposite Maddie. Lucas stands and proceeds to walk out.

"I'll leave you two alone while you discuss," he tells us. "Give you a little privacy. Just give me a shout when you need me."

Maddie looks at Lucas like she doesn't want him to go. Like she doesn't want to be left alone in the room with me.

I don't blame her.

"Don't fret," I tell her. "I'm not going to eat you."

"I'm not fretting, Axel."

I sip from my drink as Lucas shuts the door on the way out.

"Obviously, you know what you want, so tell me," I say to her. "I want to hear these *ground rules* of yours."

"Tell me your conditions first," Maddie replies.

There's that spark of defiance I liked so much in the meeting room. The same spark of defiance that probably led her into wearing that gorgeous red dress of hers today.

"Oh, you wanna play hardball?" I ask her with a laugh. "Okay. Here are the rules. You'll enter into a fake relationship with me until the new album's dropped. You'll get paid half your fee now, and then the other half once we're finished and you've upheld your end of the deal. During the relationship, you'll live with me while Ravaged is on tour promoting Staying At Her Place. Is that all fine with you?"

"Considering I'm practically homeless, I don't really have a choice."

"Great. Lucas will talk to your work and organize you to work exclusively as a publicist for the band and, in return, the band will become your work's clients. That'll make your boss happy enough not to fire you, right?"

"It sure will. And I'm technically not a publicist. I'm still just an assistant."

I groan. Fuck.

"Wow. I'm dating an *assistant*? For heaven's sake."

"Hey, I am a real human person."

I think about how fucking embarrassing this all is. "An assistant…"

I curse Lucas under my breath for putting me in this damn position.

Maddie glowers at me. Hm. She doesn't like me treating her as just a lowly assistant. Note taken.

"You won't lose your job, then?" I ask her.

"No, that'll be more than enough."

"Okay, then." I lie back in my chair and drink the rest of the whisky. "That's my cards all out there on the table. Tell me your conditions, Maddie."

"Right."

She reaches into a backpack she's kept by her feet and pulls out a notebook.

"You've prepared notes?" I ask her, gobsmacked and amused in equal measure.

"Yeah, is that a problem?"

"You are hilarious."

"Why?"

"Such a straight-A student," I remark. "All prepared and shit. Little perfectionist."

"What's wrong with having a notebook?" she asks me.

"Nothing. Just that it means you're a nerd."

"Very funny. What are we in, high school?"

"If this were high school, we wouldn't even be talking, Maddie. You'd be stuck in the library and I'll be the popular jock surrounded by the horny cheerleading squad."

"You can drop your bad boy façade, Axel. It's just us two. You don't need to impress me. I saw your show the other night."

That bite returns. Yes. "And what did you think of us?" I ask her.

"Yeah. Good." She's nervous as hell.

"Only just good. Maybe I should try and impress you, then."

"Axel..."

"Okay. Fine. Go ahead and list out your conditions."

I would never tell her, but I find it adorable she's brought notes along to this. She's a good choice for this fake relationship. When Lucas revealed this whole idea to me, I thought I would have to get him sectioned. I did not want this. I did not want to spend months pretending to be all hunky-dory with some chick who insulted me and who very clearly hates my guts. But Maddie does tick all the right boxes for the perfect candidate. Smart, honest, down-to-earth, and – above all - *pretty*. It's better to get a geek than some supermodel.

As if reading my mind, Maddie perks up.

"Why did you choose me for this, Axel?" she asks. "It's what I've been wondering since last night when you turned up at my condo."

I sigh. "You're strait-laced, Maddie. Lucas has looked into you and you're practically faultless. No history of drugs or anything. You're not a groupie, so therefore you're not threatening to my female fans. You've got that virginal quality, even though I'm pretty sure even you have had sex before. You're the ideal candidate."

She brushes a strand of hair away from her face, and I notice her lightly blushing. "You think I'm pretty?"

"I also just basically called you a virgin."

"Yeah, I won't forget that."

"Is that a threat?"

"You may think of me as some *virgin*, Axel, but let me make you understand something," she says, her voice lowering. "I'm not some wide-eyed princess who's been locked away in an ivory tower all my life. I've been through shit myself. You seem to have this perception of me as being some naïve young girl who'll bow at your feet and call you master, but I'm here today to tell you I'm not. I know what I'm getting into. I'm prepared for it."

I'm taken aback by her forthrightness. She's sassy, I'll give her that. That revealing red dress is starting to really fit her.

"Are you sure that you're prepared?" I ask her quietly. "Are you ready to deal with my life?"

"Look, Axel," she closes her notebook and stares me right in the eyes. "I want to get a few things clear. Emotions can't get in the way of this fake relationship. I'm not one of your conquests you can boss around. In fact, that's my first condition."

"Fine."

She straightens her back. She's bolder. Less nervous than when I first entered this room. "I also want no girls at all during the length of the relationship. No groupies coming and going from your bedroom, alright? No busloads of women at every stop, you got that?"

"Well, since I'm not actually physically fucking you, I should be allowed to get my fix," I reply. I can't do *no sex*. Not me, not *Active* Axel.

"That's not how I operate," she retorts bluntly. "No girls. *Period*. The contract is terminated if I even see another girl's panties in your room."

"Well then, I have a condition of my own," I growl back in response.

"Spit it out, then."

"You have to do what I say in public. Be like my doting girlfriend. Can you do that? Act besotted with me. Act like you're in love. All the time, please."

Maddie sighs. "If I must, I must."

"Hey, you don't find me that bad of a looker, do you?"

"Maybe not," Maddie replies. "But no funny business, okay? No groping or anything. I'll walk straight home if you do."

"But if I kiss you in public, then you must kiss back. That's how the game's played."

She raises an eyebrow. I want to see her squirm at that suggestion, and she doesn't disappoint. "You want to kiss in public?"

"That'll be what everyone expects. What the paparazzi expect. You'll be meeting those assholes soon enough."

"Okay, so kisses and hugs in public are fine."

"Good."

Picturing her kissing me does things to my cock. She despises me so much that it would be fun to have her hold that all in and pretend to like me in public. Pretend to be obsessively in love with me. Put aside all her morals to make me look good in front of the cameras. There's something about this girl that makes the pleasure signals in my brain go into overdrive. The thought that we're going to spend the next few weeks basically tied at the hip makes me go crazy.

Yeah, who cares about fucking other women when I've got Maddie Leaver to tease?

"Do you understand how weird this all is for me, Axel?" she asks.

"Ditto."

"Good that you feel the same. I thought I was crazy for thinking this is all crazy."

"Is there anything else?" I ask her.

She pauses, biting her lip again. She doesn't know, but it's very adorable when she does that. "You must remain honorable," she says finally.

I snort. "*Honorable?* What era are we living in, the Age of Chivalry?"

"This is a job for me, nothing more," she replies, deadly serious. "And it should be the same for you. This is about restoring your reputation. This is about this contract and nothing else. Once this is all done, then it's done. We're back to being strangers, okay? This is just a job."

"Gotcha. No need to repeat yourself."

"So, are you fully agreed?" she asks.

"Yep."

Maddie nods. "I'll do it then," she says. "This is utterly insane, but I will be your fake girlfriend, Axel Stoll. Where do I sign?"

"One last thing," I growl. "One last condition of mine. I do not beg. I do not grovel. I do not get on my knees for anyone. You got that?"

Maddie looks at me. "I got it. Now let me sign the damn thing."

20

AXEL

I stop Maddie by the door before she leaves Lucas' condo. After we agreed to everything in the fake relationship and signed the appropriate papers, she immediately got up and announced she was going to head back to the motel and pack.

But I'm not done with her yet.

No girl walks out on me until I'm finished with her.

I take her by the hand as she reaches the front door, forcing her to stop and turn back at me. She's got a glint in her eye. A hardness that makes me momentarily pause.

"What do you want now?" she asks me in a sharp whisper.

"I better get to know the girl I'm dating," I reply back.

"You really want to do this now? In here, of all places?"

"Yes."

She shrugs and lets go of my hand. "What do you want to know?"

Time to play.

"Well, we better understand things about each other only a couple would know in order to avoid suspicion. Trust me, those tabloid journalists are like vultures. They will descend on you the minute you show weakness. The whole fake relationship façade has got to work for any of this to be believable, and that means we've got to be able to pretend we've been on enough dates that we intimately know the other person. Are you ready for the onslaught to come?"

"Do I have a choice?" she asks me.

"Not really. You've signed up for this now. It's too late."

"Yeah," she replies. "I already think I'm crazy for putting my name on the dotted line."

"You're doing this for the money, aren't you?" I ask her. "That's what you need, right?"

"Yep."

"And you're *only* doing it for the money?"

Maddie blinks. "What do you mean?"

"Do you even like me?"

"*Like* you?" Maddie scoffs. "What are you, five years old? I don't even know you, Axel."

"What do you think of me already?"

She pauses, coming up with a good enough answer. "I think you're a show pony."

That actually makes me laugh. Maddie is not amused. "You think I'm shallow, is that it?" I ask her.

"You've done nothing but deserve that title," Maddie replies. "You're smooth with words and with your looks, but I doubt there's much introspection going on inside your head."

Wow. She's good.

"Oh, that's harsh. Maybe you shouldn't judge a book by its cover, Maddie, no matter how smart you may be."

"Let's sit down then, and you tell me about yourself if you're so keen to."

We head back into Lucas' living room and onto the couch.

I sit opposite her again, but then I have a different idea.

"This is fucking uncomfortable," I murmur before sliding over to sit next to Maddie. "Being opposite you makes me feel like we're in some kind of police interrogation room."

"Oh, yeah? Or are you just finding any old excuse to sit next to me?"

I look her in the eyes, trying my hardest to make her feel uncomfortable. It's like a little game we're playing, but Maddie stares right on back.

She's got a real resistant spark in her. Most girls would already have crumbled under the rockstar gaze by now, but not Maddie here. She can hold her own, despite her geeky, shy appearance.

She's an innocent angel who's stumbled into my cave of sin.

The little game is a draw. I decide to speak first.

"Tell me about yourself, Maddie," I say quietly. I want her to feel like she's the only girl I've ever spoken to in this way. "You said you went through some shit. You certainly must've gone through some stuff to talk back to me with your forked tongue. And it takes balls to live on your own in LA, especially the cheap area where you live."

"Should I be taking all that as an insult?"

"No. It's a compliment," I reply. We're really damn close. I can't help my attention quickly jumping down to her soft lips and back up to her eyes. Her mouth is slightly parted. If she were any other girl, I would already be kissing her right now, but that's not in the terms of our silly little contract. I just know for a fact she wouldn't last one minute alone with my mouth. No girl ever does. "Tell me about where you grew up."

"I would've thought Lucas had his spies figure all that out."

"Oh, he did. I just want to hear it from your mouth."

"Well, I grew up in small town Wisconsin. I had a normal, standard American life. Grew up in the suburbs. Not poor, not rich. My parents got divorced, just like most families, and things were pretty messy. As I'm sure they are for most divorced families."

She's deliberately being humble. She's hiding her true self behind a snarky and withdrawn façade, but I'll break those walls down.

"How was it messy? Elaborate."

"My parents were obviously two people not meant for each other," the girl says. "I've had a lot of years to reflect back on that. I'm still not fully over it, but it's the same backstory to lots of people. As I said, I'm standard. Average."

I lean in even closer to her. Maddie freezes. I see her own eyes glance down to my lips.

The next words I whisper.

"There's nothing average about you, Maddie. I mean it."

Maddie suddenly stands up.

"I've got to go," she says, stuttering over her words.

"But you don't know about my life yet," I reply, but she's already grabbing her backpack and getting ready to leave.

"I've read enough on the internet about you, Axel. I know what you're like..."

"Don't believe anything you read on there. Sit down and let me tell you about myself."

Maddie shakes her head. Her movements are jerky. Awkward.

"I'm just *tired*," she says as an excuse. "It's been a long day. I just want my bed. I'll see you soon."

"You have to see me soon," I reply. "You signed a contract."

"Don't remind me," she says.

And then she walks out.

21

MADDIE

THERE ISN'T much for me to pack up inside the dingy motel room, but I still take my time. Most of my things are still in the storage unit that Lucas' hired, and I don't have the effort to go and collect them just yet. If I'm going on tour with Ravaged, then I might as well only pack the essentials.

At least I'm not living out of this crappy room. Goodbye.

As I stand next to the motel room's bed, my phone vibrates in my pocket. I check it. My bank has a new notification for me.

It seems like Lucas has deposited the first half of my payment, and it's already come through.

My mouth drops as I stare dumbly at my phone. The number on my screen is bigger than I've ever seen in any bank account by a long shot. An entire lifetime of earnings is just sitting there in a space where there was nothing just minutes ago, and this is just the first half of what I'm going to receive.

Holy shit.

So. This is all real. Now it dawns on me.

This is actually freaking happening.

This means I've definitely got to uphold my end of the deal now. I've got to spend the next few months with the most arrogant rockstar on the planet in order to actually earn this massive stinking pile of money that's just been deposited in my bank.

But then Axel's words from yesterday on Lucas' couch echo in my head like they have been doing all day. Those words I did not expect *in the slightest* to come pouring from his mouth.

There's nothing average about you, Maddie. I mean it.

As much as I detest Axel and his exasperating bad boy attitude, I have to admit that those words he said made my heart soar. I didn't know how to process what he whispered to me that I freaked out and almost immediately ran away back to the motel. It was just so unanticipated, especially coming from him. Before the meeting at Lucas' place, I'd prepared myself mentally for all the ways Axel would and could react to me. All the little infuriating things he might throw at me. I cycled through all the scenarios in my head, just to make sure. But, despite my calculations, I hadn't expected that he might - at some point - actually be *nice* to me. That he would compliment me like that.

That he would flirt with me.

And that's why I scrambled out of there like a terrified little mouse. I just could not handle a gorgeous rockstar like him genuinely seducing me.

Sure, maybe he simply wanted to get into my panties. He is a red-blooded man after all, but I swear that glint in his eye as he whispered those words to me was more than just lust.

It was something more.

I shake my head and put away my phone.

Maybe it all means nothing. Maybe I'm just overthinking things like I usually do. It wouldn't be the first time.

Stop overthinking, Maddie.

I turn around and zip up my travel bag. It's a bit hard seeing as I've tried to shove in too much inside. It takes me having to basically sit on it before I can manage to bring the zips all the way around.

Packing done, I sit down on my bed and sigh wearily. The next step is to call a cab to take me back to my old condo, get my car, and then drive to Axel's hotel. That's where I'm going to be living before I go on the tour.

My whole life is about to change. I don't know whether to feel excited or anxious. I'm certainly feeling a strange mixture of both right now. There are butterflies in my stomach, and I feel sick. I don't know what awaits me once I step out of the cab and into my new fake relationship.

I'm still summoning up the courage to leave the motel room when there's a sharp knock on the door. The sound makes me jump.

I frown. I'm not expecting anyone. I've already paid the motel and no one else knows where I am.

"Who is it?"

"Me."

Oh. Someone else actually *does* know where I am, and he's here now.

Axel Stoll.

I open the door to the rockstar. He immediately barges past me and sits down on my bed. His lovely black hair is a mess, and he looks pale. There are dark bags under his piercing green eyes. It looks like he needs some tender loving care.

"Are you okay?" I ask him as he lies down on top of the bed.

"I'm fine."

"How did you get here? Taxi? Did the paparazzi follow you?"

"Not to worry, I came on my own. I like driving my motorbike. I've had plenty of experience speeding away from the paparazzi. They can never keep up with me. I'm practically a professional racing bike rider."

"Oh. Are you sure you're okay?" I ask him. "I can get you a glass of water if you'll like. I wouldn't trust the taps in this motel, but I'm sure you'll live."

He's not even looking at me. He's got his eyes closed. His breathing is shallow. I watch his chest slowly rise and fall.

"There's a reason why I'm here." Axel fishes into his pocket and pulls out a keycard, which he throws towards me lazily. He takes out his phone and places it next to his body on the bed. "That's my spare hotel room key for you to use. Man, I'm so tired. I didn't sleep at all last night, what with the whole tabloid thing and the release of the album. A lot is playing on my mind."

"You must be stressed."

It's impossible for me to judge how to approach talking to the man. He's just swanned in here like a loud tornado of energy. There's so much... *life* to the members of Ravaged. That's why they don't seem real. They glide through this world like they're above it all and that everything should bend to their will.

"Do you mind if I lie here for a second?" he asks, voice trailing off. "On this bed?"

"Well, actually, I was just getting ready to head to your hotel..."

But Axel doesn't move.

He actually falls asleep. I can tell by the way he starts to snore.

Great.

Now what do I do? I've never had an internationally renowned musician fall asleep on top of my motel bed before. Do I wake him up? I'm technically his girlfriend, so I think I could be allowed to.

But why is he suddenly my responsibility?

What the hell has happened in my life the last few days? This is the craziest whiplash I've ever experienced. I've now been gifted a rockstar like he's some adopted puppy and now he's fallen asleep and I don't know what to do.

Is it my job to feed him as well?

Suddenly, Axel's phone rings. It's lying next to him on the bed, just where he left it. The phone vibrates loudly. It's an unknown number.

"Axel?" I call out his name, but he doesn't stir. He's definitely not slept in days.

I'm tempted to answer the phone. We are fake dating, after all.

"Hello?" I immediately regret answering as soon as I pick up.

There's a pause on the other end.

"Who's this?"

It's a woman, probably middle-aged.

"Maddie. I'm Axel's girlfriend."

"Girlfriend? I didn't know he had a girlfriend."

She seems amused by her tone, not angry or shocked at all.

"Well, I'm kinda... new," I try to explain.

"I see."

"Axel is asleep, but I can pass on a message if you'll like."

There's another pause.

"Tell him his mother called him. I'm Astrid, by the way."

Oh. His mother.

Crap.

"It's nice to meet you."

"I can't wait to meet you in person, Maddie. Axel having a girlfriend is a surprising development..."

The phone is yanked from my gasp. Axel has woken up, and he's wordlessly taken the phone from me.

"Hello Mom," he whispers.

"I'm sorry," I say to the rockstar as he holds the phone to his ear. "You just weren't waking up, and I thought..."

He walks straight past me and out of the room. Gone.

Is he annoyed with me?

God, why does his moodiness affect me so much? This is exactly why I've been so wary of relationships. I've always been deeply afraid of turning into my own mother, reliant on her husband to the point of an emotional breakdown. I can't let that cycle continue.

I grimace and sit down on the bed where Axel just was a moment ago.

Even if he is the most beautiful man I have ever seen, I need to be careful with the rockstar. Every day I going to have to remind myself that this is a fake relationship. I can't let him affect my feelings. I can't fall for him. I know it's a real risk.

I can't let his sweet words from yesterday imbed themselves in me.

There's nothing average about you, Maddie. I mean it.
No. No. No.

I best protect my heart before I get hurt.

22

AXEL

My mother's voice rings out loud and clear through my headphones as I ride my motorbike through LA's streets.

"Who was that, Axel? A girl?"

"Yes."

"Why is a girl answering your phone?"

I shake my head. It was not good that Maddie had picked up my phone. Rude of her.

Already our fake relationship is off on the wrong foot.

And now she's spoken to my fucking mom.

"It's nothing."

"I'm your mom, Axel," she says in a caring tone. That infuriated me. I'm not a child anymore. "Mothers can sense these kinds of things. Tell me, do you have a secret relationship you're not telling me about?"

For fuck's sake, Maddie. What did you say to her?

"No."

"Well, she did tell me she's your girlfriend."

"Did she now?"

I must've still been asleep when Maddie revealed *that* piece of juicy gossip. I'll need to have a word with the girl and make her understand not to talk to anyone without consulting me first, especially my family.

I should've put that in the damn contract.

"She said she's your girlfriend. Why would she say that if you weren't a couple? Why haven't you introduced us yet, Axel? Why haven't you told me about her? Oh, I would certainly very much like to meet the girl that's nailed down your heart."

And here they come. What I was dreading all along. The questions...

This has come much sooner than expected. I'm cringing at this conversation so hard that I desperately try to change the subject.

"Have you read the tabloids or watched the news lately, Mom? There have been some... rumors flying around about me."

Not a particularly excellent subject to change to, but at least it isn't about Maddie.

"I have heard about the... tape," Mom replies.

My heart beats fast. "You didn't watch it, did you?" I can't hide the panic in my voice.

"Of course not."

I breathe out a sigh of relief. "Thank God."

"These things happen, Axel," Mom says slowly. She's making me squirm, and she knows it. "Especially when you're *you* and you're so much in the public eye. I've been preparing myself for something awful like this to come out at some point from the first moment I saw your name in the newspaper. It's what happens, and don't say you didn't encourage it. I know your reputation, Axel."

"Okay, I get it, Mom."

"But now you might have a new girlfriend? If you do, you better tell me."

"I would, if I did."

"So who's this girl I talked to, then? She seemed sensible and mature. One of you is lying, and she didn't seem the lying type."

"I've got to go, Mom. Bye."

I hang up before she can get another word in.

As I continue to zoom down LA's roads – my motorbike' brutal acceleration hard on my body - I think about Maddie. We're not already a few hours into our fake relationship and it's already becoming complicated, more so than I thought it ever would. She's already fucking *talking* to my mom. This is why I've sworn off proper relationships since I became a member of Ravaged. This is what happens.

Things get complicated.

And when things get complicated, I just want to drown them in my vices. Man, I wish I could call up any of the girls I have on speed dial and get my cock sucked right now, but I actually want to abide by the terms of my conditions with Maddie. No groupies.

She would never find out in a million years if I indulged my cock, and yet I still don't make a move for my phone.

I tap the edge of the handlebars repeatedly.

How does that girl have a hold over me? Already?

I normally make it a habit to break any rule presented to me, but Maddie is somehow making me loyal. For once.

Yeah, loyal to a fake-ass relationship. What a joke I've turned into.

I lean into a fast corner.

"What the fuck have you got yourself into, Axel."

23

MADDIE

I PULL up in my car outside Axel's hotel. It's a very expensive kind of place. I'm betting that the usual clientele here are sports stars and movie actors, not some office drone like me, but this is where I'm going to be staying now, so I better get used to it. I've driven past this place a few times, always imagining what it would be like to stay here. Never thinking I ever would.

Well, now I'll know for real.

But I do have to occupy the same suite as a volatile playboy; that's one slight issue to consider.

Axel was right, there are a hell of a lot of paparazzi waiting outside the hotel for him. A whole gaggle of them all gathered by the front doors. And they're not being secretive about it either, with their laptops and cameras out ready to catch the rockstar or his bandmates. Axel's also true in comparing them to vultures. I see their beady little eyes always searching for Axel or another celebrity. I pity my fake boyfriend for having to deal with this. This side of fame isn't what he signed up for when he first started music. I guess having the world's press in your face every day would screw up anyone's perspective on reality; it's remarkable that Axel and the other members of Ravaged aren't even more crazy.

I park my car across the street and head towards the front doors of the hotel. I notice a few of the paparazzi photographers turn in my direction, mildly interested, but they quickly look away when they realize I'm a nobody. I'm not the kind of girl that Axel would normally be seen with, so I'm nothing to them.

They'll soon find out everything...

But, as I'm about the enter the hotel lobby, I am approached by one of the waiting photographers. He's short and balding. What remains of his hair is greased back. He smells like he's not showered in a few days. I freeze as he talks to me.

"Are you staying here?" he asks me in a gruff voice, nodding towards the hotel.

I'm getting seriously *bad* vibes from this guy.

"I am."

"Have you seen Axel Stoll, by any chance?"

"Who?" I ask.

"Ravaged. You know. The band?"

"Oh."

"They're staying here."

"No, I haven't seen him. I'm not really a fan of his band," I say, pleased with my little deception.

"Sorry to bother," he replies, waving me inside.

I can tell he's not sorry at all. He doesn't give a fuck.

I'm not done with him yet.

"You say he's here? Are you guys here to take photos of him?"

He lifts up his professional camera to display it. "I'm

freelance. Photographer and journalist. Bringing people the stories they need to hear."

"Taking photos of celebrities leaving hotels?"

"Okay," the man smiles as I burst his bubble. "Bringing people the stories they *want* to hear. People love celebrities, and they especially love Axel Stoll."

"I heard about that sex video thing. Not good for his band."

"No, it most certainly is not."

"And he's staying here, you say?"

The man strokes his untidy stubble. "Well, it's true," the man continues. "Axel Stoll *is* staying here, and he's been coming and going a lot. More than should be expected. Disappearing, you might say, and he's very good at it too. I currently work for an entertainment news channel and, trust me, I've been in this game for a long time. I can sense there's a good story brewing somewhere about Axel, and it's not just to do with a pathetic sex tape."

"Didn't he get set up?" I ask him. "He didn't know he was getting filmed, right? Sounds a bit dodgy to me."

"I was the one who helped do that," he replies in a conspiratorial whisper. "But to be honest, Axel did most of the hard work. I simply hired the girl, and he was the one who invited her into his bed. Good little paycheck for me, that."

Wow, this guy.

"Oh. Well. Good luck."

I step into the lobby before the man has a chance to continue the conversation. I better keep an eye on that guy; I have a feeling he's more clued up than the rest of them and is going to snoop around me before too long.

I check my phone as I enter, searching for the message Axel sent me on how to reach his suite. Okay, so I have to go into a private elevator, using Axel's hotel key card to work the thing up to the top floor of the building.

The elevator doors open...

And, holy crap, is the suite beyond any of my wildest dreams.

Now *this* is being a rockstar.

There is a larger floor space dedicated to this hotel room than there was for the entire condo building I lived in until I was kicked out. The suite is probably bigger than a lot of hotels in LA. I am completely gob-smacked by the size and scale of it all. Fit for a king.

There's a massive chandelier just hanging in the middle of the room. I bet it's worth the GDP of a small nation. Massive flatscreen TV on one wall. A balcony that has just the most amazing view of Los Angeles' skyline. Everything is so clean and spotless and exquisite. I'm in awe, and a little bit terrified, just looking at it all.

I enter Axel's room. Of course, true to his form, there's a whole pile of clothes laying scattered on the ground. He's *such* a boy. Typical rockstar behavior. He clearly doesn't give a shit he's staying in one of the most amazing rooms in the hotel industry.

I give him a helping hand by tidying it up. See, I'm fitting into the girlfriend role like an old glove. And this might also be an easy excuse to have a quick peruse of his things. Not that I don't want to overstep any bounds, but he *has* left everything out in the open like a bombsite. Surely if I spot something that's on him, right?

It's so weird that I'm actually here, in the room of the musician I just saw performing to a crowd of thousands the other night. Alone. I still can't shake the feeling that we both inhabit different worlds that should never collide.

But the *money*. I'm here for the money. This is what I'm doing everything for. The money that can change my life, and that of my mom's. That's all I should focus on, and not this annoying man who's somehow taking full residency of my mind...

I find nothing incriminating in the clothes lying around. All I notice is how expensive everything is that Axel owns. All are from the best labels, and he treats them like trash. There would be thousands of dollars' worth of stuff here. I neatly organize the clothes into stacked columns and put them by his massive bed. At least I can see the floor now.

Wow. This bedroom is simply insane.

"What are you doing?"

I'm shocked by Axel from behind. I spin around to face the man. He's leaning on the doorframe that enters the bedroom, staring at me. His perfect jaw clenched. I try to avoid staring back into his deep green eyes.

"Cleaning up," I reply. "It was pure madness here."

"There was method in my madness. I knew where everything was. Before you ruined it."

"Well, that was more than just madness. It needed a woman's touch."

"And you're the right woman to do that?"

"What do you think?"

Without replying to me, Axel steps into the room and immediately takes his shirt off. I involuntarily gasp as I see those exquisite muscles of his again. Flashbacks to me spilling my tea over him and him removing his shirt then come flooding back and I feel a gentle warmth in my nether regions.

Axel raises an eyebrow at me and I immediately spin back around so I'm no longer staring at his naked torso.

"How about, next time, you warn me *before* you get naked," I say in a tense whisper.

"I'm just changing my shirt, Maddie," he replies. "But I can show you my cock if you'll like."

I laugh at that. The man's cheekiness doesn't scare me in the slightest. "There's probably not much to see."

There it is. My inner bad bitch. Back again.

The rockstar growls, and I subtly turn my head as he fetches a fresh shirt. I sneak a glance at his body again when he can't notice me. That *R* tattoo of his stands out.

"You want to bet on that?"

"This conversation would be a field day for HR," I observe.

"Good thing Ravaged hasn't got an HR department then," he replies. "Good thing that you're technically my girlfriend."

"*Technically*, I never agreed to see your cock," I retort.

"Touché. But you will kiss me. When the time comes."

Oh, God. The thought of that. Those famous lips on mine...

Get your head back in the room, Maddie.

But how can I when those tattoos on him are irresistible? They complement his body like a cherry on a freshly baked pie.

This whole fake relationship thing is really going to mess with my head. I despise him one moment, and the next I'm admiring his body and his talent and then the next...

"Why don't you turn around and have a proper look at me?" he asks to my back. "I know you want to."

"You presume a lot about me, don't you? Unlike those groupies of yours, I'm not falling for any of your pre-scripted lines. I'm here in a professional capacity."

"Sure. What's wrong, Maddie? Little bit frightened you might get used to this lifestyle?"

"Not in the slightest."

"Maybe you should, girl."

He doesn't believe me. He thinks he'll be able to wear me down with his honeyed words.

And I'm kind of afraid he might.

"Come with me now," Axel says when he's fully changed.

I face him. "Where are we going?"

"Come."

"So you're not telling me?"

He snarls. "Come with me, Maddie. Let's get the hell out of this place."

"How are we going to get past all the paparazzi waiting outside the hotel?"

"Oh, trust me. I know a secret route," Axel replies. "Only for rockstars... and their *girlfriends*."

"I'm not going until you tell me where we are going. I'm not going to let you pretend to be all mysterious and boss me around, Axel."

He sighs.

And then...

"I'm taking you to meet my band," he says ominously. My heart drops. "Properly this time."

24

MADDIE

Axel takes me to a nightclub, but not just any nightclub. This is *Name...* the most exclusive spot in all of LA. Of course I've never been inside the place before, I've only ever heard about it through entertainment news when some celebrity falls out of it drunk and high or something. This is not a place that I would normally choose to go to, that's for sure. It's probably hard to believe, but I'm not *exactly* a nightclub kind of girl.

But this is where Axel is taking me. Naturally, the most VIP club I know. I don't believe it until we park outside in his car.

Yeah, he's got a car, not just a motorbike. It's a Ferrari. This man certainly knows how to spend his money.

"I hate driving this," he says. "I'd prefer the motorbike."

"Maybe my outfit and heels wouldn't be the best thing on the back of that," I say, glancing down at what I'm wearing. It's the same red dress I wore for him when we signed the contract. The best dress I own. I saw how he looked at me that meeting. How there was the slightest moment of hesitation in his voice when he saw me in this getup at Lucas' place. That slightest moment of realizing that he truly is like any hot-blooded male when presented before a woman in a sexy outfit. That moment of vulnerability from Axel made me feel strong. The first time I felt on a level-playing field with this internationally famous rockstar.

In his flashy Ferrari outside the club, Axel's eyes turn to me, checking me out as if noticing me for the first time, and he growls. "You scrub up well, Maddie."

I blush. "Thanks."

"Yeah, probably best not to have taken the motorbike."

I see the paparazzi waiting outside the club. This must be a regular haunt for them with all the famous people that go through the doors every night. Must be an easy job just waiting for the next upskirt photo.

"You want to introduce me as your girlfriend to the world tonight?" I ask Axel as I stare across at the waiting photographers from the safety of his tinted car.

"No. Not yet," he replies. "This would be the worse way to do it. The front entrance is for those celebrities who want to appear in the news, and you deserve better than some sweaty-ass guy trying to get a photo of your pussy as you step out of the car. I'll take you around the back to the secret entrance."

"There are so many secret entrances for you, Axel. Everywhere. Here... the hotel..."

"It's what you have to do when you're in my position," he says. "I didn't know when I became a musician that I was also signing up to be a spy. You better get used to it."

"I don't think I ever will."

"Let me show you how."

He spins the car around and we arrive behind the nightclub away from the eager cameras. Big security guards with clipboards check inside the vehicle as we roll up to the parking lot doors. Checking who we are. The burly men do a thorough search, but once they know who Axel is, they wave us through. No paparazzi are getting through this blockade.

"Does the rest of the band know it's a fake relationship?" I ask Axel after he hands his car keys over to the valet. "Has Lucas told them?"

Unbeknownst to Axel, I've been so nervous on the drive over. Sure, I've met the other boys, but that was before… all of this. I wonder how they will take me. Will they look down on me? Will they laugh? Will they tease me into tears?

"They do know, yep. Is that a problem?"

"No, just as long as we're on the same page."

I don't think Axel understands how scary this is for me. It's like meeting his family. All this goes against little old introverted me. I glance at the doors leading into the nightclub with trepidation.

This is a world I should not be in.

Axel reaches down and takes my hand. His warm grip makes me feel lightheaded. I do not expect him to hold my hand at all and so I find my heart fluttering unexpectedly as he guides me inside the back entrance of the nightclub.

"Don't worry," he whispers. "Stay with me. I'll look after you."

Kindness? From Axel?

We head through the kitchens – with the loud shouting of chefs and banging of utensils – through to a private area at the back of the nightclub. The most exclusive area of the most exclusive club. There are even more scary-looking security guards in suits hanging around here with little walkie-talkies like in the movies. Yeah, this all *definitely* feels like a movie.

A few days ago I had to summon up the courage to go out to a concert arena to see the same boys I'm about to spend a night with in a private nightclub. Terrified isn't a strong enough word for what I'm feeling.

The rest of Ravaged are waiting in the VIP section. From the vantage point of the room, we can see the rest of the dark nightclub, but no one can approach without going through a wall of security.

There are Drake, Bishop, and Caspian, all sitting together drinking.

Here they are...

They stop their conversation and turn to me when Axel brings us in. I take in a deep breath and ready myself.

This is becoming all too real.

"Boys, this is Maddie," my new fake boyfriend says. "As you may know."

Axel drops my hand.

I awkwardly wave at the famous rock band with my other hand like a total dork.

"Hiya."

Such an awkward loser.

Caspian is the first to acknowledge me. He simply nods, and I have a feeling that's a big welcoming gesture coming from him and his trademark silent stoicism. Drake merely lightly smiles at my entrance, his dimples showing even in the dark nightclub.

And Bishop gets up. A gentleman.

"Please sit, Maddie," he instructs me warmly. He motions to his old spot at the booth.

"Thanks."

"Anything for someone like you," the guitarist says. "I still can't get over how you spilled tea all over Axel. Fucking hilarious."

"Yeah, that was a real sight to behold," Drake agrees. Caspian softly chuckles in approval.

Behind me, Axel growls like a dog. "Back off," he says to Bishop. The tallest member of Ravaged smirks at Axel. I can feel the tension in the air between the two. I saw them poke each other into violence the last time they were at my work, and I don't want that to happen again in front of me, even if they're simply playing.

"It was a total accident," I say, trying to diffuse these young males from fighting each other, as I know they want to do. "But I did enjoy it. A lot."

"I like this one," Bishop says to Axel. "You can keep her, Axel. Really, come and sit with us, Maddie."

I do as he asks and take a seat next to Caspian. The drummer for Ravaged truly is massive, even more so up close. His shirt is practically bursting from his tight muscles. It's all strength and power under there. He regards me with his dark eyes as I smile up at him. I think I see a slight smile pass over his lips.

"You want a drink?" Drake asks me, comfortably leaning back in his seat opposite me like a lothario from an 1800s painting.

"That's my question to ask," Axel says. "She's my fake girlfriend."

I like the possessiveness in his voice. Like I belong to him.

You're losing your mind, Maddie. Over a freaking rockstar.

"Excuse me if your girl finds me more charming than you, Axel," Drake jests.

My fake boyfriend laughs. "Now, that is a joke, Drake. You want a drink, Maddie?"

"Just a glass of white wine, please," I squeak.

"Get the girl a glass of champagne," Drake says. "We're

celebrating her tonight for helping save Ravaged's ass for agreeing to be with this asshole."

I blush.

"Well, you are paying me a pretty handsome sum, guys."

"Yeah, for putting up with Axel," Bishop replies. "We all know how arrogant that guy can be. You couldn't get me to be his fake girlfriend for a billion dollars."

"You don't have the balls to be my fake girlfriend," Axel says.

"Maddie does," Drake adds.

Axel summons a waiter over and orders for us. Soon enough, a bottle of rich champagne arrives with glasses for all members of the band, including me.

I can't help but laugh when Caspian takes a glass. It looks so tiny in his massive hand. Like a toy. He shrugs at me with an amused chuckle.

"Must take a lot for you to get drunk," I remark.

"Like you wouldn't believe."

Bishop pours for all of us and then bids us to raise the glasses in a toast. "I didn't believe it when Lucas told me what was going on with Axel and Maddie here, and I have to say I didn't believe that Axel would let a girl date him, even if it was fake. But I'm glad it was Maddie. Hopefully she'll find more ways to spill tea down him."

I find myself blushing again as the band all cheers to me. I certainly didn't expect this kind of hospitality from the boys. They're known for everything other than being kind to women.

They all want to talk to me about me, including even Caspian. I fend off questions from them about my life. My background story is average compared to these hard-working boys who made it big. I am embarrassed.

All the while, Axel sits next to me. Silent. His leg rubs

up against mine. Does he feel that, or is it just me overthinking things? Does he want to touch me?

Does he know what his touch does to my body?

Eventually, the boys move on to different topics. They chat about their upcoming album and the songs they've written for it. The conversation is too technical and too musical for my understanding. Axel understands this, and so talks to me privately.

"Tell me about your band mates then," I ask him.

"Okay, well, Drake is the founder," Axel whispers into my ear. "He likes to think he's the boss just because he ran the auditions for the band back in high school, but without us he's nothing. He loves to be in front of a crowd. He's the unstoppable force the rest of the band is trying to keep up with. For all our fighting, I have to admit that Drake's got that relentless and infectious energy for life and music. I'll follow him anywhere. He's all about the music, so much so that he's got one rule he lives by, and that's not to get into any relationship with a girl longer than one night..."

"So, like you?"

Axel shakes his head. "Oh, worse than me. He's just more sneaky about it. He hates the very idea of monogamy."

"Poor girls who fall for that trap," I remark.

"He's the most emotional of the group. The most... *tempestuous*. He's the mysterious and dreamy one all the girls fall for, but they don't get very far. He established rules when we started as a band that anyone who uses hard drugs or gets into a relationship more important than the band will be fired."

Drake perks up. Somehow, he overhears our conversation.

"That's true," he shoots back. Axel rolls his eyes. "The rockstar life is about living free from any responsibilities.

We musicians should remain pure. No girlfriends. No distractions. That's how you make musical history."

"What about me?" I ask him. "I'm distracting Axel."

"Yeah, but you're cool. And *fake*, sorry to be blunt."

"Right. No offense taken. But what about living a life, Drake? What about sharing things with someone? Going through life solely focusing on your music and fucking girls without a second's thought doesn't sound much like a life to me."

"Well, that's where you and I differ."

"Oh yeah?"

"You see, so many people never find their passion in life. I'm lucky enough to have found mine, and so have the rest of the boys here, so why not put your heart and soul into it when you've got it? One-hundred-fucking-percent. We don't have time for relationships that are more important than the music."

"But what about love?" I ask him.

Drake laughs.

"I love the music," he replies. "I love the band. That's enough."

"And what about a fulfilling relationship with a partner?"

Drake's dimples grow. His blue eyes are shining. "You're good, Maddie, I give you that. But you won't change my mind."

"I don't think many people can change your mind, Drake," I muse.

"Especially a girl," Ravaged's frontman replies. "No offense."

"None taken. Again."

Axel laughs and points at Drake. "Your philosophy is only that because you were burned by a girl, weren't you? Before Ravaged?"

For the first time, I see a flash of fear cross Drake's famous bright eyes. His dimples fade. "That's not true..."

"You told me once."

"Not in those terms."

"You want to fight about it? Yeah, I see you want to fight me, Drake."

Drake lunges forward and manages to get Axel into a headlock. I lean back, rolling my eyes. Caspian, yet again, is the one that has to break them apart, just like in the office. His giant hands clamp down on their shoulders.

"You have to always get into a fight, don't you?" I ask Axel when he sits back down, taking a drink from his champagne.

"It's how we show love in this band, Maddie. A girl won't understand."

"You're such a child, Axel."

But despite how disapproving I am of their silly behavior, it turns out I really like Ravaged. There's nothing to be intimidated by when you get to know these boys. In fact, they remind me of any other young guy from my hometown, just with a lot more money and that they're getting to do what they love every day.

And the fact that they're super talented and sexy.

"And what about Bishop?" I ask him, quieter this time. I don't want the guitarist to overhear. "What's his deal?"

"Bishop and I have our history," Axel says, clearly hinting at a past he's not keen to fill me on. "If there's one thing to know about Bishop, it's that he does not like to lose. Ever. He's the most competitive guy I know, at anything. Gambling. Art. Music. Hell, even video games. He'll practice Mario Kart for weeks just to beat your ass. And he's the musical genius of the group. He's just one of those lucky people who's fucking good at whatever he turns his hand to. We may have our history, but he's like a brother to me."

"And Caspian?"

"You want to know about his past? Ask him yourself, you won't get much of a response though. He's loyal to a fault, but don't you dare mess with him. I love the big guy."

"You are all like one big family," I say to Axel.

He nods. "That's what we want. We're brothers before rockstars, always have been. We stick to each other no matter what."

His words make me realize how big of a deal it is for him to have me properly meet his bandmates. He's revealing a private side to him that I bet not a lot of other girls get to witness.

"What is your biggest goal now that you all are the biggest rockstars on the planet?" I ask them all, leaning in towards the table dividing us.

Bishop smiles at that question. "We still want to smash Tainted Lives with our next album. They're shit and they deserve it."

"They can't be that bad," I reply.

"They're awful fucking assholes," Drake says.

"You guys and your band rivalries. Must be so stressful," I say. "There must be something else, is there?"

Drake leans forward too. "Madison Square Garden. It's our dream to perform there ever since we first started out."

"And you haven't already? Surely you must have."

"Not until we're ready," Bishop continues. "All our heroes performed there. Bowie. Rolling Stones. Nirvana. We saw a show there together as teenagers and made it our mission to perform on that stage when we're on top of the world. We're so close now. It's only a matter of time. Maybe after this album, we'll feel like we've earned the right to go there."

Someone enters the private area.

Lucas.

The manager looks rushed. Taking care of Ravaged must be a twenty-four-hour occupation. He seems relieved to find us all here. He gives me a wink when he spots me amongst these giant beautiful men.

The band all wave him over enthusiastically. The love they have for him is pretty damn evident.

"I knew I'd find you here, boys."

"Is there a problem, Lucas?" Drake asks. "Please don't be bringing any more paperwork for us to read."

He smiles. "Nope. Worse than that, there's a visitor for you all."

"We're not having any visitors. That's why we've hired security."

"Even I can't say no to her," Ravaged's manager says.

"Who?" Drake asks.

We all turn around. Someone is walking in behind Lucas. A woman. This must be the answer everyone's looking for.

Axel stands up. He's immediately recognized her.

"*Mom?*"

25

AXEL

I don't believe it.

"What are you doing here, Mom? I literally spoke to you this afternoon on the phone, and you were in Crystal River."

There's an audible intake of breath from my other band members behind me as they sit, transfixed, by my own mother walking into the most exclusive nightclub in LA.

Mom just smiles. She loves a bit of drama, this woman. "I've come from Crystal River to see my boy," she announces.

Fuck's sake.

"Mom…"

I feel like a scolded schoolboy, embarrassed by his mom in front of his friends. I can't imagine what's going through Maddie's head right now. She must be so weirded out. I look at her. Just as she was getting used to my boys, now she has my mother to deal with. In the flesh.

"Well, you seemed so secretive on the phone, what with

the scandal you got yourself into the other day and now the fact that an actual girl answered your phone when I called. A girl you said *wasn't* your girlfriend. I got on the first flight over."

"You didn't have to..."

I try, in vain, to explain. Mom has other plans, though. She stops me in mid-sentence by glancing down at the girl sitting next to me.

"Is this the girl I had the pleasure of talking to earlier?" Mom asks, still looking at Maddie, figuring things out all on her own. "Will you be a gentleman, Axel, and introduce us to each other?"

I grunt. I can never turn my mom away, even if she is being totally annoying by rocking up here unannounced in her typical dramatic way.

"This is Maddie Leaver, my girlfriend. Maddie, this is my mom, Astrid Stoll."

I try to rush through introductions, but Mom spins back to me.

"Hang on, Axel. I want to take my time and get to know the woman who snared your heart."

She then brushes past me to sit where I was just sitting, right next to Maddie. I grunt again, but Mom completely ignores me and starts to speak with Maddie. They shake hands.

Oh, both Mom and Maddie are clearly enjoying this. How much it's riling me up.

"Axel hasn't mentioned me yet, has he?" Mom asks my new fake girlfriend.

"Not a word."

"Typical. Well, let me tell you a little bit about myself." The whole band is continuing to listen to this, enraptured. I roll my eyes and grip my glass of champagne tightly. I was planning on these two women never meeting; I didn't need that kind of complication in this fake relationship. Mom doesn't even know the whole thing's a sham, and I want to keep it that way. I remind myself to mention that to Maddie later. Before the cat's out of the bag.

I just want Mom out of here and back to Crystal River before all hell breaks loose.

"Go on," Maddie encourages Mom. "Tell me about yourself, Astrid."

Yep. She's loving this.

"I'm an elementary school teacher back in Crystal River. In fact, I taught all these boys at some point..."

"Mom..."

"Be polite, Axel. I want to talk to Maddie."

Great. I just know that this is all going to be used as ammo against me in the future. Mom loves sniffing around places where she shouldn't sniff. She would've made a brilliant detective in another life.

"You all were taught by Astrid?" Maddie asks the rest of the band.

"Mrs. Stoll was one hell of a good teacher," Drake says.

"Yep," Bishop agrees.

Caspian just nods.

"See?" Mom asks me, turning around. "Everyone wants me here."

"Everyone except for me," I reply churlishly.

"Is Chloe here?" Bishop asks Mom. I shoot him a warning look.

Now is not the time to talk about my younger sibling.

"That's Axel's sister," Mom explains to Maddie. "He'll never mention her as well, though he should. They were very close as kids. I couldn't stop them dressing up in my clothes and dancing along to power ballads."

"Alright, Mom..."

"I thought you two weren't talking."

This time she's looking at Bishop. He shakes his head.

"We haven't been, no. Not for a long time, Astrid."

"Ah. I'll tell her that you say hi."

Bishop blushes. It's incredible. "I don't think she'll like that," he mumbles.

"I see."

"You look like Axel," Maddie remarks to Mom, turning the conversation away.

"It's the green eyes," she replies. "Runs in the family. Chloe has them too."

Oh, she loves to talk about our shared eyes.

Maddie smiles. "I like how you're such a boss," she says. "I didn't suspect Axel had such a splendid mother."

My mother eats that up like sugar.

"Of course I am," she boasts. "I'm going to butcher a bit of Shakespeare, but *some women have matriarch thrust upon them*. Someone's gotta clean up the mess these boys leave in their wake. Sometimes I have to take control and meet the girlfriends my son tries to hide from me."

Maddie giggles at that, and I roll my eyes again. This is exactly how I imagined this meeting between these two women to go, and it's not going well. For me.

For a girl who's shy, Maddie is really warming up to Mom. A bit too fucking much for my liking.

"You're different from how I pictured you," Maddie remarks.

"What do you mean?" Mom asks.

"You're more... *fun*. I don't mean that as an insult, though."

"You think Axel's the cool one of the family? No way. He takes it all from me. My boy might've grown up to be some playboy rockstar with a quiff and everything, but I remember when he was in his diapers."

"Mom..."

But Mom ignores me.

"You're going to have to tell me more about baby Axel," Maddie says, winking at me. I glower back. "I'll like to collect as many embarrassing stories as I can."

"Oh, I shall."

"That's a nice necklace," Maddie compliments, gesturing at the cross that always hangs around Mom's neck.

"I'm a Christian," Mom explains. She turns back to me. "Where's my drink, Axel? I've already been sitting for five minutes. Where are your manners, my boy?"

I fetch Mom a glass of champagne like a dutiful son. Maddie watches me the entire time, a smirk on her lips. I sneer at her as I hand my mother the glass.

"I like you," Maddie tells my mom before they cheer.

This is just great. Fucking perfect.

"You've got to tell me everything. Has Axel asked you about yourself?"

"Yes, he has."

"Good boy, at least I've raised him well in that respect."

I sigh and sit down next to Drake, who's still intently observing my mother and Maddie's interaction.

"Let's talk about something else," I offer the table. "How was your flight over, Mom?"

Everyone ignores me.

"I grew up in Wisconsin," Maddie tells my mother.

"Good. A strong independent midwestern girl to toughen Axel up, just what he needs."

"I'm not exactly that…"

"Sure, you are. I can see it already. You're exactly what Axel needs to get his head out of his own ass. Pardon my French. I would love to meet your mother. Is she in LA or back home in Wisconsin?"

"Back home."

"Well, hopefully, we meet soon. I would very much like

to get to know you more, Miss Leaver. If Axel allows us to and stops his huffing and puffing."

"I'm not huffing and puffing."

"I'm glad I've come here today," Mom announces. "Axel would never have told me about you, Maddie, so I'm glad I've come out properly instead of having to hear about you from Lucas. It's very interesting for Axel to have an actual girlfriend, you see. You must really have something to catch his eye."

She glances between us two.

For like the fiftieth time in the last ten minutes, I groan.

26

MADDIE

"I'm sorry you met my mother," Axel says to me as we leave the nightclub. He's holding my hand again as we head for the back exit through the kitchen, making me go all gooey inside despite my head's resistance.

"Why would you be sorry?" I ask him. "That was a lot of fun. The best trip I've had to a nightclub."

He shakes his head and gingerly lowers his eyes. "She's embarrassing."

It's cute witnessing him squirm like this, and it *was* genuinely fun meeting Astrid Stoll. She's the life and soul of the party. I can see where Axel got his good looks and his charm from. She certainly is not who I expected at all. I didn't even know *who* to expect from a mother of a playboy rockstar. I really like the way Axel – and even the other boys of Ravaged – were respectful and deferential towards her. She has a matriarchal power over them that was amazing to see, and their love for her was evidential.

What's the saying about how the key to a boy's heart is through his mother?

I mean, I don't know much about boys, but what I do know is that how they treat their mother is a big indicator of who their character really is.

And Axel treats his mother like a saintly angel. Even if he does get visibly embarrassed by her.

It warms my heart as I saunter out of the nightclub kitchens with the rockstar holding my hand.

"I'm glad you like her, though," Axel says quietly. Right now, in this moment, he's no longer the cool playboy. He's now just a boy happy that his new girlfriend likes his mom.

Even if I am a *fake* girlfriend.

"She's easy to get on with," I say. "I enjoyed talking to her."

"Mom loves to tease me, especially in public, but I could tell she really enjoyed talking to you. Both of you having a laugh at my expense..."

"Now, *that* was fun. You need to be lowered down a peg or two, Axel. Stop all this music and fame stuff getting to your head."

"Very funny."

"You act like you don't give a damn about anything," I say somberly, "But I can see that, deep down in there, you have a soft heart. You really do care."

Axel diverts his eyes and shakes his head.

"Alright, alright," he barks, hiding himself in a wall of facetious coolness. "No more sentimental crap. This is purely a business transaction we've got going here, not a therapy session. Let's go back to the hotel, shall we?"

I nearly got him there. I nearly got him to lower his guard to peek into what lies beneath.

"Yes, let's."

* * *

I STAND in the middle of Axel's hotel suite and take in a deep breath before I launch into the words I've been thinking of saying the whole car ride back here.

"It's the first night we're going to spend as a couple..."

Axel turns around, his face a stone wall. I can't judge what he's thinking.

"I don't want this to be anything weird," he says. "I don't want to make you feel pressured in any way to act like my girlfriend."

"Why would I feel pressured?"

He sighs and stands by the door to his bedroom. He nods in the room's direction. "You can have my bed, and I'll have the couch."

"I'll feel weird taking up your bed," I reply. "Especially if you're breaking your back on the couch in the other room."

"You're having it, though. I insist, Maddie."

My voice trembles. "I'm fine if you want to share the bed. We can put a pillow between us so it's not weird or anything."

"You want me in the bed with you?" the rockstar asks.

My heart rate quickens. The air is thick with tension. It's like both of us are circling around the topic, neither one of us going to broach anything.

I did tell him no funny business. That was my rule. Am I really trying to tease him to break it on our first night?

I don't know what's up with me. I thought I would be repelled by this man, but seeing him so vulnerable with his mom... and the sweet way he held my hand completely unprompted in the club... it just makes me *rethink* things.

"You have to do all these shows. If you sleep on the couch, then all you'll do is develop a bad spine or something. For no reason when there's a perfectly good bed here."

"I'll live."

"You're really going on the couch?" I ask him. "Just so you don't get near me at all?"

He opens the door to his bedroom for me and then sits down on the couch. "It's all yours."

I make a move towards the room before I stop. Hesitating.

"When will we make this fake relationship public?" I ask him.

"Lucas tells me he's coming up with a plan."

"You really trust him, don't you?"

Axel's green eyes sparkle in the dimly lit hotel room. "He hasn't let me down once."

"Then I'll trust him too."

Getting ready to sleep on the couch, Axel slings off his shirt. My own eyes wander over the tattoos on his tanned skin yet again.

"What is that *R* tattoo?" I ask him, finally summoning up the courage to inquire about the one that intrigues me most.

Axel moves towards me. I freeze in place as he gets close enough that I can smell his piercing aftershave. I feel so small next to him. He's tall. Sexy.

Out of my reach.

"It's for Ravaged," Axel replies in a soft whisper. My eyes dart back down to the tattoo, too afraid to look him in the eye. "All members of the band have it. Us boys are bound together by ink."

"That's something special," I remark.

He takes in a deep breath. Neither of us says a thing for the longest time.

"I'm going to sleep," he eventually tells me.

And yet he doesn't move.

I honestly don't know what he's thinking. What's going through his head. One word from the gorgeous rockstar and I might find myself, despite my better judgment, recklessly falling into his powerful arms. I can't imagine what I would do if he asked to make me his, even for one night.

In the state I'm in now, I might not even fight against it. He would have my heart wrapped around his little finger.

All he has to do is say the words.

You're mine, Maddie.

And then this whole fake relationship would come crashing down as soon as it began.

Am I really that weak?

You're stronger than that, Maddie. Remember, this is a job. Don't let your silly feelings get in the way.

No. No. No.

I'm not going to let a moment of fiery lust ruin this job. Even if Axel can turn on the charm like a tap. Everything about the man is seemingly designed to trap girls like me. No wonder Ravaged sells so many damn albums when all the musicians are like... *this.*

"I hope you sleep well," I squeak out, barely containing the storm brewing inside my chest.

"Tonight was a good night," Axel whispers as he takes one step toward me.

Stay strong, Maddie. You are a professional.

"Yes," I reply. "It really was. Thank you for taking me out to the club."

"No problem."

"It was fun."

I'm taking gibberish, aren't I?

But Axel doesn't seem to mind. His gaze remains unchanged. He continues to stare me down with that penetration that stabs directly into me.

"Goodnight, Miss Leaver," he finally says. His voice is the softest it's ever been. He's practically muttering into my ear from this distance.

A shudder rolls through my body, but I know I'm going to sleep alone tonight. I'll make sure of that.

I'm not falling for his spells.

I'm going to be strong and resist the unresistable.

This *thing* is going to remain fake. And that's final.

"Goodnight, Mr. Stoll."

27

AXEL

"We'll go again but this time from the top."

We all nod in agreement with Drake as we ready ourselves for restarting the song. It's one of the new ones from Staying At Her Place. We're in the same arena in LA we performed at the other night, but this time it's midday, and the place is completely deserted except for our band and a few techies. We're practicing for the world tour we're about to embark on.

Drake pulls the microphone close to his lips like he's about to kiss it and starts to sing.

You didn't forgive me, no
You did not forgive me
when I treated you so bad
But I swear down to you, girl,
That you're the one light
in the darkness
That keeps me going at night

I don't need no words,
no songs,
no promises
I just need you, oh
I just need you

Drake gestures for us to halt the song. Caspian immediately stops the beat. We wait for what Drake has to say. Our lead singer is all about the music, that's for sure. This is both an art *and* a craft for him, and he won't accept any result unless it's perfect. That's probably why we've got to where we are. We're an unbreakable team. We all need each other. When we come together to perform, we're unstoppable.

But, right now, we're not performing up to scratch. And we all sense it.

"I'm not feeling it," Drake mutters, spinning back around to us to gauge our reactions. "There's not enough... *energy*, and that's from all of us. We need to get this song right. We need to make our audience leave with the breath still out of their lungs. We need to beat Tainted Lives on release day."

He's right. I know it. Bishop and Caspian know it. But we're all so damn tired. We've been rehearsing non-stop for hours now, and it really takes its toll on both our bodies and our minds.

I woke up this morning feeling strange. Knowing that Maddie was in the room next door scrambled my head last night. I didn't know how to act around her this morning when I ordered breakfast to the room. She was sweet and nice about everything, which just confused me more. I've never spent a morning with a girl I haven't – or not even *allowed* to have - fucked before. Last night tested the limits of my willpower. I had to restrain myself from kissing her as we said goodnight. Man, how I desired that so much in the moment. It was the next logical step, and one I would've taken if it weren't for all the fucking... *complications* around us.

I had to stop myself from sneaking into the room after

dark. Slide into the bed. Touch her in places she doesn't let anyone touch.

Fuck.

The thought of that makes me hard.

Oh, I could see her admiring my body as I undressed to sleep on that fucking couch. I'm no idiot. My cock was so goddamn ready for her when she ate up my tattoos with her eyes. I just know I could've whispered sweet nothings in her ear and made her mine, just as I fantasize in my deep dreams.

But I won't jeopardize the deal we made, though.

All of my band mates have commented on the fake relationship plan to me in private. Surprisingly, they're all behind it. They see the merit in me changing my shitty public perception.

I just need to make it the next few months not kissing Maddie Leaver except on official business. And, after last night, I know it's gonna be hard.

My phone rings. Drake turns to me.

I check it. Mom.

"I've got to take this," I say.

"Okay, then." Drake is annoyed, but he also knows it's time for a break.

I walk off the stage and answer.

"Hello, Axel. I've come up with an idea."

"Mom, I can't speak long. I'm practicing."

"Okay. Well, let me explain my thinking this morning. Since I'm only in town for a few days before you go on tour, I'll like to meet up with Maddie."

"Okay. And?"

"And I would like to meet her mom."

I sigh.

"You heard what Maddie said last night, right? Her mom lives in Wisconsin. She can't just fly down here."

"And you're a multi-millionaire rockstar, remember? Surely a private jet is something you can afford."

"I'm not worried about a private jet," I say. "I'm more worried about Maddie's reaction to me flying her mom halfway across the country."

"But imagine if you did, Axel."

Oh, Mom sure is pushy.

I sigh again. Mom stays quiet. She knows I can't say no to her.

"Sure, I'll do it. Anything for you, Mom. I'll get Lucas to look into things."

"Excellent. Thank you, Axel."

After we say our goodbyes, I head back to the stage. Lucas is standing there by the front, talking with Drake. When he spots me, he comes bounding over.

"How's Maddie and you after your first night? I trust it went well. How is she?"

I like how caring he is for her. Lucas can be all business, but there's also a caring heart underneath the suit, and that's why I love the man like a brother.

"She's surprisingly okay about everything. She's better than okay."

"Good," Lucas replies. "I knew she'll be a level-headed match. You didn't fuck her, did you? Please tell me you didn't."

"No, Lucas."

Though things got so dangerously close...

"Even better. Keep your hands off her, you understand?"

"I do."

"We all know your spells."

"And so do a lot of women."

"Very funny, Axel."

Here's my chance.

"Lucas, I need to ask a favor from you, if that's alright. A logistics thing. Got a chance to talk over it now?"

Lucas nods, but I can tell his mind is somewhere else. "Ask me later, but I'm sure I can do it. First, I have something to tell you. A little plan I've concocted that needs to be executed today."

"What is it?"

Lucas smiles playfully.

"It's time for you and Maddie to make your relationship public, and I've got just the idea."

28

MADDIE

I frown as I stare at my reflection in the hotel's bathroom mirror. I call out to Axel, who's in the other room.

"So what should I wear to this charity thing again? I feel like I'm overdressed. Is everyone else going to be wearing heels? I don't want to stand out. Ah, I'm freaking out."

I wait a moment for Axel's answer. "I doubt you'll be overdressed, trust me."

I check my lipstick in the mirror. Despite Axel's flippant remark, I *do* feel overdressed. I never really get the chance to go out putting this much effort on. It's been a lot of fun to get ready all afternoon, I have to admit, but now staring at myself in this elegant dress I worry I've gone too far.

Axel bought me this dress. My mouth dropped when I read it was Versace. I can't guess as to how he got my measurements or anything. Or how he got the dress so quickly. I didn't dare ask.

It's certainly a step up from my red dress.

Okay, so there are *some* benefits to fake dating a multi-millionaire, that's for sure.

"Well, who's going to be there?" I ask around the bathroom door.

"You know," comes Axel's reply. "The glitterati of LA. Sports stars, celebrities, hot-shot politicians..."

"And *me*. Wow."

I'm *actually* going to this event, and it isn't for work or as a fan. I'm going as a *guest*. A big special formal occasion. It's going to be like the Academy Awards or something, and I'm going to be right in the middle of it all next to Axel. He didn't seem too bothered telling me about it earlier, about how this is where we'll announce our relationship to the world in front of the world's celebrities and press. I, on the other hand, felt like I was having a heart attack. A day-long drawn-out heart attack, culminating in this freak-out over what I should wear.

I hear voices talking in the room next door. Axel and... Lucas. Ravaged's manager must've just come in. That means it's probably time to actually stop hiding in this bathroom and leave for this charity function. I take in a deep breath and look back at my reflection. I force my frown into a smile.

Say yes to more opportunities. Stop being such a scared little introvert.

Okay. I can do this. I can do this.

I step out.

Axel shocks me. I didn't know what he was going to be wearing until right now, but his appearance tonight takes my breath away.

Holy shit.

He looks... incredible.

My gaze trails up his tailored Tom Ford suit, made of

the finest wool. He's checking his super-expensive Rolex with the expression of an aloof playboy.

He looks every inch a million dollars of pure cool *sex god*. A billionaire bachelor.

"Hello, Maddie," Lucas says. He's standing right next to my fake boyfriend, but my eyes are not on him. "You look absolutely beautiful. Don't you think, Axel?"

I could say the same about Axel.

The bassist of Ravaged smiles at the sight of me. "Yeah," he says softly and – surprisingly – sincerely. "She looks beautiful."

"You look... great, Axel."

The man chuckles confidently, as if he knows exactly what he looks like and needs no encouragement from me. "Thank you, Maddie."

"I need to speak to you alone, if that's alright?" Lucas asks me. I look to Axel. His eyes narrow.

"A bit suspicious," the rockstar mutters.

"It'll only be for a brief moment."

Axel shrugs. "Go ahead."

I follow Lucas into the bedroom where I've been sleeping. He makes sure the door is closed before he speaks.

"Maddie..."

"Oh, you know that Axel is probably listening on the other side of the door," I remark, interrupting the manager.

"Fuck off, Axel," Lucas says to the door.

There's a groan, and then we hear Axel's footsteps stomp away.

There's a sparkle in Lucas' eye. "You're really getting to know him, aren't you?"

I smile.

"Yep."

Lucas' voice then changes. He goes quiet. Serious. "How is everything going between you two?" he asks me.

"Fine."

"Are you sure? There's nothing you want to tell me? Now is the last time you can do or say anything before the entire world knows your name, Maddie."

"It's going to be that bad, huh?"

"For the next few months, sure. But when this is all over, give it a year and everyone will have forgotten about you."

"I hope so," I reply. "This fame thing is not a game I want to play."

"So, you're okay with everything? This is your last chance."

I nod. There are some points you come across in your life when you know it's a turning point in the road. This is one of them. Yeah, I signed the paperwork and everything, but after tonight…

"Axel has been surprisingly great," I say. "I think I can do this. I've signed up knowing this moment will come sooner or later. I can't walk away now."

"Good girl," Lucas replies.

He turns towards the door, but I reach out and take his arm before he opens up.

"Thank you, Lucas," I whisper. "For double checking."

The faintest of smiles crosses his face.

"What are friends for?"

"You're a good man."

"Let's get Axel," Lucas says.

He opens the door and calls my fake boyfriend's name.

"Everything okay?" Axel asks as he steps into the bedroom, adjusting his cuffs.

"Just making sure you're treating Maddie well."

"And am I?"

Lucas nods towards me.

"No complaints," I reply. "Thus far."

"Good." Axel's green eyes fall upon me again, and I sense his gaze over my body. He wants something he knows he can't have.

Me.

"This is going to be a big night for you both," Lucas says. "You nervous?"

"Nope." Axel's response is swift.

"I'm a *bit* nervous," I say.

"No need to be," Lucas replies. "I've already primed up the reporters and paparazzi to search out for you two. You don't have to do anything, Maddie, but look gorgeous. And you're already winning on that front."

I blush. "Okay. Thanks."

"Are you ready?" Axel asks me.

"As ready as I can be."

But really, I don't know what the hell to expect.

* * *

Cameras. Lots of cameras.

And flashes.

I've been expecting a lot of things in the limousine ride over, but not that the first thing that happens to me when I step out of the vehicle was to be blinded by a wall of big black cameras pointed aggressively in my face.

I freeze up. I can't breathe. There are so many noises and colors and blinding lights. So many people demanding my attention. Calling my name.

I don't know how to react. What to do.

Until Axel appears out of nowhere and takes my hand. He squeezes gently, and I'm instantly grounded again. Just like I was at the nightclub.

"Follow me," he whispers into my ear. "Let me take charge."

I don't need to be asked a second time. All I do is take his lead. I'm a nervous ball of fluttering energy, but Axel is completely relaxed. Powerful. Undeterred by this army of photographers and journalists calling his name.

I know that, for as long as he's holding my hand, Axel's got me.

The next few minutes are a total blur of more cameras and questions. I stay quiet as Axel speaks to the assembled throng of people.

He's so charming with everyone, making each reporter feel like he's only talking to them as a friend. He's so experienced in this game.

We slowly head down the red carpet towards the entrance of the charity function, Axel stopping every couple of yards to talk to someone new.

"Are you two together?" a reporter asks.

"Yes," Axel replies. "Her name is Maddie Leaver, and she is my girlfriend."

I swear there are butterflies in my stomach when he says that.

I'm so inundated with all the craziness around me that I don't realize someone's directly asking me a question until Axel squeezes my hand again.

"What is it like dating one of the most eligible and sought-after rockstars on the planet, Maddie Leaver?"

I don't know what to say to that. My mouth dries up.

Axel squeezes my hand again.

"It's the most magical feeling in the world," I reply.

I hope that made sense and I'm not talking gibberish.

There are more reporters and more reporters and more photos and more questions and more people and more smiles and more reporters until we finally reach the end of the red carpet. It's where I finally feel like I can breathe again, away from the pack.

Axel whispers again in my ear as we step inside the center.

"You were fantastic out there, Maddie. I'm proud of you."

I blush.

I have definitely gone down that turning point in the road now. There's no coming back.

29

MADDIE

THERE ARE so many famous people here at the charity thing. It really is as Axel described. LA's glitterati. I'm not the best at spotting celebrities, but I do recognize a few sitting around me. Everyone is either rich, or famous, or both. A table of billionaire CEOs is adjacent to ours. Tech founders. Sitting at a table just two over is the latest Oscar winner for Best Actor. I am in awe.

The charity function goes on well into the night. There's lots of drink and food and caviar and champagne and performances by music acts. All very hoity-toity.

So many people stop by to purposely talk to Axel. With every celebrity that says hello, Axel makes a specific point to introduce me as his girlfriend. That makes me feel special, but also a bit weirded out considering I'm not *really* his girlfriend. Sometimes I even have the sudden urge to blurt out that I'm not – that all this is a sham - but I hold myself back like a pro.

Axel leans back in his seat like a king, and everyone

treats him as such. A member of Ravaged truly means he's on top of the world, especially when it comes to the entertainment industry in LA. He's so freaking confident in these surroundings. He belongs here like water belongs in the ocean.

His confidence rubs off on me, and I find myself finally settling into the seat. My nervousness starts to dissipate. Slowly.

I'm with a man that almost every girl in here wants. I see the jealousy emanating from the surrounding tables. Girls glancing over. The gossipy whispering. I just know that people are curious about me. They're asking my name. Trying to remember if they've met me before.

I bet once they find out who I really am; they are going to be shocked.

I'm not some supermodel, not some actress. I'm merely an assistant.

And yet I've secured this man sitting opposite me.

And it's all... *fake*.

That makes everything seem so pointless and shallow. I have to keep reminding myself that none of this is real. I'm merely a passing guest in Axel's world.

But it is fun to entertain the idea that I am his real girlfriend, even if it's just for tonight.

Our table gets assigned a waitress. I know I shouldn't care, but she's... *well-endowed* and definitely has the hots for Axel. I see her gawking at him every time she comes to get our order. When Axel asks for more champagne, she makes a point of bending over next to his shoulder so that the edge of her tits brushes his skin as she slowly pours into his glass.

When she leaves, I nod at Axel. "I don't want to be the jealous type," I say. "Especially when we aren't technically dating, but that girl has been looking at you all night."

"Was she? I hadn't noticed."

"I'm sure you notice a lot of things, Axel," I reply. "But keep your eyes on me. Remember, I'm your fake girlfriend."

"Oh, I'm going to get you back for that little comment," my fake boyfriend says cheekily, drifting closer to me.

"What do you mean?"

"Kiss me."

My heart stops.

"What?"

"It's the best way to seal the fact that we're a couple in front of this room of reporters and photographers and celebrities and influencers. Kiss me. Now."

"Lucas never said we should do that tonight. It's not in our contract…"

But Axel clearly doesn't care what his manager or our little contract says. He simply leans forward and kisses me on the lips.

His scent overpowers me. The taste of him… his power…

It's safe to say it's the nicest kiss I've ever had. Initially surprised by his boldness, I melt into it. And him.

When our lips part, he barely moves. "There you go," he whispers so quietly that only I can possibly hear. "Our first kiss."

"That's our relationship definitely sealed," I reply, also no longer caring about the stupid contract.

"Wait and see what the tabloids say tomorrow," Axel says with a victorious smirk. "I want to remind you that you just kissed, in public, a man that millions of girls around the globe want. How do you feel about that?"

I bite my lip. "I feel like I need another glass of champagne."

"How about you call over that waitress I don't give a shit about?"

I happily do so. My glass is refilled by the well-endowed flirt.

And Axel doesn't take his eyes off me the entire time.

I really wonder what he's thinking inside that gorgeous head of his.

"What you staring at?" I ask him.

The rockstar smiles, then turns his head. I think I see a slight shade of blush in his cheeks.

"I'm staring at *you*, Maddie."

30

MADDIE

Axel is about to say goodnight to me, and I really don't want him to leave me.

What's going on, Maddie? Why can't you let him go?

"Goodnight, Maddie."

He's about to shut the door to the bedroom. He's about to sleep on the couch in the other room in the hotel suite. I can't have him do that. I can't kick the man out of his own bed, especially after the way he treated me tonight. He made me feel like the only girl in the entire world at the charity thing. The way he stared into my eyes. The way he introduced me to everyone.

And then he *kissed* me.

Yeah, I know it was a fake kiss. But, damn, it felt real.

And he didn't have to kiss me. He was under no obligation to.

Yeah, yeah, yeah. I know. My emotions are getting the better of me, and it's only been a few days of this fake relationship...

But. Still. He doesn't have to sleep on a freaking couch. I'm sure we're comfortable around each other to not make this strange.

"Wait, Axel."

The man stops closing the door between us. His suit is still immaculate. He looks so handsome.

He lifts his chin. I admire that strong jawline of his.

"What is it?" he asks me quietly.

I'm so jittery whilst he is so calm and measured. "Look, I find it kind of weird that we have to sleep separately when we're in this relationship."

Axel raises an eyebrow. "A *fake* relationship."

"Yeah, but even so, I hate how you have to have a crappy night on the couch. Surely, we're friends enough for you to be able to sleep in the bed, even if it's beside me? If we're going to kiss in public, then surely…"

Axel shakes his head. "I can't do that. As you said, no funny business."

"I don't mind," I reply. "I trust you not to do any funny business. We'll put a pillow between us if you really can't help yourself."

He laughs at that. "Maddie…"

He tries to protest yet again, but I jump in. "Just sleep in the bed, Axel. It's one thing I'm going to ask of you, alright? Just have a good night's sleep. Be well-rested for your performances."

Axel pauses. I can see that he's mulling it over. Can he really not trust himself not to get up to any funny business?

I realize I'm biting my lip as I watch him contemplate. I very quickly stop doing that. I certainly don't want to come across as some desperate, horny girl.

I'm not horny. I'm just letting him use the freaking bed as well, that's all.

"You're very keen for this to happen," Axel remarks, finally speaking.

"I just don't want you tired before your tour, that's all."

"That's all?"

"Yep."

Fuck, the tension is unbearable between us.

I just know he wants to kiss me again. But I'm stronger than that. I might be asking him to come to my bed, but still definitely no funny business. I know where one sneaky kiss might lead to.

The contract still stands.

"Okay," Axel replies. "I'll do it. On one condition."

I snort. "This isn't a negotiation. I just want you to get off that couch."

"One condition, Maddie."

"Right. I'll bite. What *one condition*?"

"That my mother meets yours."

The demand hits me like whiplash. I instinctively scoff and make a weird face.

"What?"

"You want this fake relationship to seem real, right?" he asks me. "Then our moms should meet. Plus, my mom did kind of pressure me into talking to you about this."

"My mom lives in Wisconsin," I reply dismissively. "It'll be a miracle before she *considers* coming to LA, even if for just a visit."

"Call her tomorrow," Axel suggests.

"She wouldn't come."

"At least try," Axel says. "Then I can tell my mom and get her off my back about all this."

I roll my eyes. "Fine. If it makes Astrid happy."

"Thank you, Maddie."

"So, you'll stop acting like an idiot and sleep in the bed?"

"Yeah," Axel replies with a smirk. "I will."

"Good."

I head into the bathroom to change, and Axel takes his suit off in the other room. When I emerge, I see that he's stripped down to just his Calvin Klein's. I try very hard not to gawp at his lovely muscular body. It's difficult, to say the least.

That body's going to be sleeping next to me? Oh, God.

He smiles at me and nods towards the bed. It's a little bit awkward, and that makes it cute. I never thought he might also find this a bit nerve-wracking too. It's sweet.

Not being true to our own word, we don't separate ourselves with a pillow. Axel's warmth envelops me.

Is this what I want? This man next to me?

It's too late now.

"Goodnight, Maddie."

Axel's turned away from me. He's so close I swear I can hear his heartbeat.

"Goodnight, Axel."

I keep myself still. I try to breathe in a regular pattern. I try not to think about the kiss we shared only hours ago. I try not to fantasize about Axel attempting any funny business.

I don't know what I would do if he did.

I remain calm. I count out the money from this job. The money that can change the lives of both my mother and me.

And then I slowly drift to sleep.

31

MADDIE

After breakfast, when Axel leaves to practice with his band, I get the courage to call my mom. I've been dreading the call all morning. I even try to catch up on some publicity work for the band that Lucas has sent through to my email simply so that I have a flimsy excuse not to call her.

After the very public kiss last night, I am barred from leaving the hotel. It's such a weird thought to know that there are men with cameras on the street just below that know my face and name now, and who are willing to do almost anything to get a photo of me. As Axel tells me, one step out there and I'll be ambushed. I don't doubt he's lying. I've seen what those men are like.

And so I finally get around to calling my mother. I take out my phone and scroll through for her name.

I know I shouldn't feel so bad calling the woman who gave birth to me. A catch-up with her should be a good thing. A chance for me to get things off my chest and reassure her of my place in the world.

But I know what Mom is like.

And I know I have to ask her to come to LA, for Astrid's sake.

"Hi, Mom."

She answers the phone in a rushed manner, as if I've interrupted a crucial moment in her day. She does this all the time, so it's not unusual. Plus, she doesn't exactly work, so it's not like she's busy. She only sometimes – *rarely* – volunteers at the church she goes to every weekend.

"Maddie. What a surprise. You never call."

"I did a few weeks ago, remember?"

"Oh. Yes."

She's sharp and harsh. I feel like I'm being admonished like I'm twelve again.

"How are you doing today, Mom?" I ask her.

"Not too good. My back hurts. But I did spend the morning reading my Bible. Please tell me you've been doing the same…"

I take in a deep breath and try to steady myself.

Here it comes.

"I've been very busy, Mom," I reply. "My life has gone pretty crazy at the moment. There are actually some things I need to tell you."

Mom is going to focus on the Bible thing, I'm sure of it.

All of this really has nothing to do with religion or the Bible. Everyone's entitled to their belief. But, for Mom, it's all simply an excuse for her to attack me for something I can't refute without seeming morally bad. And I just know that attack is on its way.

"You can never be too busy to not read your Bible, Maddie."

I quickly try to change subjects.

"Like I said, I've got something to tell you."

"I hope this isn't about the money you owe me," she

replies. I want to correct her that I don't technically owe her anything. It's money I'm giving her of my own will. "Because I'm very reliant on it. You've already forsaken me for going to that cursed town."

I ignore that last comment.

"Don't worry about the money, Mom. It's not about that. The thing I want to tell you is that I'm actually starting to date someone."

I rush it out.

There's a long pause as Mom takes it all in. I can imagine her sitting in her chair in the living room, mulling it all over and stroking her chin. Her eyebrows darting down like arrows as she comes to terms with what I just confessed.

I close my eyes, readying for what's to come.

"Is he a good Christian boy?" she eventually asks.

Of course, that's her first question.

"I haven't exactly asked him about his faith yet, Mom."

"And why haven't you?"

"I don't know, Mom. It's not exactly date material to ask someone about their personal relationship to Jesus."

"I think it's the perfect thing to first ask someone. What if he's not Christian, Maddie? Have you thought of that? What if he's... *Muslim?*"

The fear in her voice. I don't think Axel's religion is the first thing she should be worried about the rockstar.

God. She's going to find out he's a rockstar. That's worse than being a Muslim in her books.

"I doubt he's Muslim, Mom."

"You better not be joking around with me, Maddie. You know my poor heart can't take much. You don't want to be the one giving your own mother a heart attack."

"I'm not joking."

"What does he do for a living?"

"He works... in the music industry."

There's a violent intake of breath.

"Lord help us," she replies. "Of course he does so in a cesspit like LA. You do know that if you're sleeping with him, then it's a sin. Nothing before marriage."

"Not everyone can be as strict adherents to the Bible as you are," I remark. "But, no, we're not sleeping together."

Well, maybe in the same bed. But I'm not mentioning that.

I'd once made the mistake of telling Mom that not every Christian needs to be as fundamentalist as her. That people can lead normal lives and still have faith and be good Christians. Let's just say that Mom did not exactly *agree* with that statement.

"There's only one thing I can do," Mom says definitively. "I need to meet this boy. Get a handle on him. Then I'll know if he's right for you or not."

"Well, that's what this call is about, Mom. I want you to meet him. In fact, his mother wants to meet you."

"His mother?"

"We've actually met already."

"You've met his mom?"

"Yes, was that bad?"

There's a huff on the other end. "Nothing."

She's jealous.

"I know it's a big ask, but it would be nice for you to come out here," I say. "Axel is willing to pay for your flight from Wisconsin."

"Honey, you know my thoughts about Los Angeles."

"I certainly do. You've told me enough times."

"You know I detest that pool of sin, but I also don't need some stranger paying for my own flights. I'm coming. To save you, if for nothing else."

I nearly drop my phone. I did not expect that.

"Wait, so you'll actually be here? You're coming?"

"Yes. When is convenient for this Axel fellow and his mother?"

I stutter. "As soon as possible. He's actually leaving for a job in a few days, so the sooner the better."

There's no way I'm dropping the fact of Axel's actual job on my mother right now. Honestly, I'm guessing her heart wouldn't take that news.

"I will get on a flight tomorrow. Be ready for me."

* * *

AFTER THE PHONE call with my mom, I just sit still in quiet and try to process what the hell is going to happen tomorrow.

Mom is coming here. To LA. To meet Axel.

Okay, so that's *not* how I expected the phone call to go.

I thought I'd get a hard no, and then have to tell Astrid that unfortunately Mom can't do it. That would be the end of that.

Would've been a better outcome. For everyone.

Sure, I could've faked the phone call, but I'm so bad at lying I'm sure someone as emotionally intelligent as Astrid would've seen through my charade. I'm already lying too much in regards to this fake relationship.

There's a knock on the hotel suite door. I hesitate before looking through the security camera. Axel's not meant to be home yet.

It's Lucas. I let him in.

"How are you doing, Maddie?" he asks as he steps inside the suite. I offer him a seat and he takes it.

"Okay."

"Good to hear. And last night? How did it go?"

I nod. "Really good, I hope. Did you see that we... kissed?"

He raises an eyebrow. "You haven't checked the news?"

"I'm trying to avoid stuff like that," I reply.

He takes the remote from the living room table and turns on the TV. He switches over to an entertainment channel.

And there is my face.

On the TV.

On the news.

Well, more like *half* my face. You can't see much due to the fact that Axel is in the middle of the frame kissing me.

Holy shit, the kiss from last night? That's all over the news?

I knew it'd be big, but not front-page news big.

"Get ready for this," Lucas tells me, observing my open-mouthed reaction. "This is just the start."

I check my phone messages. Everyone's been trying to contact me. Everyone I know. Even people I thought had completely forgotten about me. They all want to talk to me. Ask me how in the world have I ended up on their social media and TV making out with one of the most famous men on the planet.

"Have I gone viral?" I ask the band manager. "For kissing a rockstar?"

"Yep, it seems like you have."

"Crap." My response is one word. I can't begin to describe what I'm feeling. There are no words beyond ones that would make my mother blush.

"I've dealt with this exact situation plenty of times," Lucas tells me, turning off the TV. "No matter what, it's always insane. Everyone handles sudden fame in different ways. Axel, for instance, bought that crazy motorbike of his. What I suggest you do immediately is turn off your phone and TV and forget all about it for at least a day. Take a moment and make some time for yourself, Maddie. That's the best thing you can do to process what's happening."

"Okay," I reply. "I think I need to sit down first."

32

MADDIE

MAKE SOME TIME FOR MYSELF. Yep. Sure. I can do that.

I mean, I do need to stop thinking about the minor fact that my face is on global news right now. Some time to myself without checking the internet or the TV seems like the correct thing to do.

My own flipping face kissing Axel.

Okay. I'm also not going to think about *that*.

Lucas has gone, leaving me all alone in the hotel suite. Axel will probably be rehearsing with Ravaged for the rest of the day. Other than some light non-urgent publicity work, there's not much for me to do. So, I run myself a bath in the suite's massive bathroom.

Time for myself.

My phone beeps.

I should check it, shouldn't I?

Could be an emergency or something.

I have a quick peek at the phone's notification, even though I really know I shouldn't.

It's Marie from work.

Um, excuse me, Maddie. Am I seeing what I'm really seeing? You're with Axel freaking Stoll? No way, no way, no way. Please tell me I'm dreaming. How the hell has this happened? What did you do? What's he like? I thought you didn't like him? WTF??? Please reply. Please, please, please.

I can't help but smile reading the message. Poor Marie must be experiencing one hell of a whiplash opening up her social media and seeing that. One minute she's taking me to see a band I don't even know the name of, the next I'm kissing the bassist on national news.

What can I even say back to her?

It's been a rollercoaster, Marie! I'll let you know when things have settled down. We'll grab drinks sometime, yeah?

She messages me back immediately.

Okay, fine. Be super mysterious like you are at work. I can't believe it. It was my dream to hook up with a rockstar backstage, but you're living the dream. You rock, girl! I need to hear the full story when things are better for you. Make sure you don't forget the little people like me when you're rich and famous!

I chuckle. That's a very loud Marie message to send.

There is a pang of guilt, though, in the pit of my stomach. This is all fake, isn't it? The relationship... the press around it... All fake. All of it will be gone in a year at most, and then I'll be back to my normal existence as regular old Maddie Leaver from the boring suburbs of Wisconsin. Your average girl-next-door who could never in a million years date a rockstar.

Okay, stop thinking about everything at once and just calm your mind, Maddie. Chill the fuck out.

The first thing to do is turn off my phone, just as Lucas told me to. I throw my phone onto my bed, far away from the bathroom, and then light myself a few scented candles to take to the bath. I turn on the music, and then I find my vibrator.

Me time. Alright.

I step into the inviting warm embrace of the hot bubbling bath. I practically sink into it with a long, happy sigh.

After a moment spent luxuriating in the water, I reach for the vibrator I've placed so conveniently next to the bath. I need to block out the rest of the world, and this is the best way to do that.

I start to slowly touch myself as my mind goes blank. Everything becomes still, but also incredibly heightened as I give in to my deepest impulses. No one can penetrate the calm bubble around me. I'm totally alone and there's no judgment here.

My body shivers with pleasure as I bring the vibrator to bear exactly where it feels best. I close my eyes and my consciousness starts to drift as my body glows from the inside.

My mind wanders to what I'm desiring most.

The kiss I shared with Axel last night...

The powerful way he held my hand completely

unprompted, as if he were showing the entire world that I am his girl. The undivided attention he gave me all night before he leaned in so aggressively to kiss my parted, willing lips.

When I saw him take off his shirt, his tattoos wet and glistening.

His cheeky half-smile.

His green eyes and the intense manner he stares at me.

Oh, God.

I know it's so wrong, but I want him to want me. It's all kinds of fucked up, but I bring myself to climax just thinking of how he stares at me. The lust and charisma of an international rockstar. He wants to make me mine.

You're mine, Maddie...

I hear the water in the bath slosh as my back arches in ecstasy as my vibrator makes me orgasm.

I imagine him saying my name over and over as everything goes gold.

"Maddie... Maddie... Maddie..."

The voice seems so real...

And that's because it is.

Holy shit.

My eyes fly open and the first thing I see is Axel standing in the open doorway of the bathroom, those green eyes I was just imagining staring right back at me.

"What are you doing?" he asks me.

I want to escape. To cover myself.

But I'm so exposed just lying here in this pile of bubbles. Completely nude. My buzzing vibrator in my hand.

"I'm..."

Axel spins around to give me privacy. He's clearly as shocked as I am. The sight he must be seeing...

How long could he have been standing there in the

doorway? Only for a couple of seconds, judging from the panicked expression on his face.

"What are you doing?" I call back accusingly.

"Why are you... doing that in the bath?"

"Look, Axel," I reply, trying hard to retain as much dignity as I can muster. "I still have needs even if you're keeping me in this hotel suite like a kidnapped medieval princess. I'm not completely asexual. Oh, God. This is horrible. This is a nightmare."

"I didn't see anything, I swear. I just walked in."

"You're a terrible liar, Axel," I say as I rise up from the water.

"The door was open," he explains.

"But what the hell are you doing back here so quickly?" I ask Axel's back. "It's not even midday. I thought you guys were going to be practicing until the late afternoon at least."

"Drake has a bad throat today, so we finished early. We can't risk damaging anything this late to the tour."

"Oh, okay."

Calm down. Calm down. Calm down.

He remains turned to me. I unplug the bath and let the water out.

Oh, crap. The towel.

I remember the closest one is a fresh one brought by the hotel staff this morning, and it's currently lying on the couch. I would have to squeeze past Axel completely naked to get it.

"Can I... help you with anything?" Axel asks me awkwardly. At least he hasn't tried sneaking a sneaky peek around, however tempting that must be for him.

"I like how embarrassed you are," I remark with a giggle. "It makes a change from the whole playboy rockstar demeanor you have going on."

"Hilarious."

"But you can help me with something, as long as you promise not to look. Can you get me the towel on the couch?"

"Okay."

"But close your eyes."

"I will."

"You won't look?"

"I won't look, I promise."

He shuffles off and fetches me the towel, one hand covering his eyes. He comes back into the bathroom with the towel stretched out. Despite his promise, I see a bit of green behind his hand. He can't hide those bright eyes of his.

But I don't say a word. I like him taking a quick glance at me all hot, steamy, and wet. Hopefully, this gives *him* something to think about next time he's in the bath all by himself.

I sneak a quick peek myself, this time at his pants. He's clearly erect under there, thanks to me. The outline of his pants teases that he's actually bigger than I imagined.

Oh, I'm definitely saving that mental image for later.

I wrap the towel around myself.

"I'm decent now. You can open your eyes."

"Good."

We're so close in this steamed bathroom. I try really hard not to think about that.

The man just saw me pleasuring myself in the bath. Is this really happening? Should I be more embarrassed than I am, because, somehow, I'm really not.

"I did not see anything," he repeats.

"Yeah, yeah, sure."

"It's your fault for leaving the door open."

"Oh, so you're blaming me now."

"I come in, I see a beautiful woman in the bath. I can't help myself. I'm a red-blooded male."

"You're calling me beautiful? Without Lucas prompting you?"

"You're still a geek, Maddie. I won't let you forget it."

"Well, forgetting my geekiness for one minute, your wish has come true," I tell him.

Axel narrows those pretty green eyes. "What wish?"

"My mother is coming to town."

33

AXEL

"You WANT me to get on that thing?" Maddie asks me.

"Yep."

We're standing in my hotel's parking lot, in the private parking bay reserved for me, looking at my motorbike.

And Maddie is so obviously *terrified*.

"You want me to meet my mother on the back of that?" she asks.

"I'll be driving it," I say. "You won't have to do anything but sit on the back and hold my waist."

"What kind of motorbike is it?" she asks.

I grin. There's nothing I love more than showing off my most prized possession.

"It's a Kawasaki," I say.

"I don't know what that is or means."

"It means it's good. Real fucking good," I explain. "It's from the seventies, the golden decade of rock music. See here? High bars. Teardrop tank. Slinky side-panels. It's exactly my kind of bike."

"And this?" Maddie asks, pointing at the bright red ducktail. "That's very... *loud*."

I shrug. "Red makes it go faster."

"Oh."

"So... what do you think?"

"What do I think about riding up to Mom on the back of this?"

"Yeah?"

"I think it's insane."

"Good idea, huh? I think it'll make a statement. Make it pretty obvious to her that you're dating a rockstar."

"I don't really want to make things that obvious," she says. "Will I die?"

"Riding it?"

"Yep."

"I'm a pretty safe driver," I reassure her. "Although we will have to go fast."

"Why?"

"Because it's a motorbike, and I don't do things half-hearted. Not me. Never."

Maddie bites her lip. She's very concerned. But she still hasn't completely rejected the idea.

"I did tell myself I'd say yes to more things this year," she whispers. "Although dying by riding a motorbike wasn't exactly what I had in mind..."

"So it's a yes, then?"

Maddie groans. "Screw it. Let's do it. As long as I wear a helmet."

* * *

"Hold on tight," I say as Maddie wraps her arms around my waist.

"Don't worry, I am."

The motorbike roars to life. It's loud, louder than the girl's expecting. Maddie lets out a surprised yelp at its ferocity.

It feels good. Her hands around me. Feels *right*.

Now it's time to show her the power of this machine.

I look ahead, out of the hotel's parking lot, and then we zoom the hell out of there.

34

MADDIE

Mom is waiting for me outside the restaurant. A lone figure not dressed at all for LA's harsh sunshine. As we pull up beside her in Axel's nice motorbike, I take in a deep breath and think about tomorrow.

Tomorrow is when Ravaged's tour starts. Tomorrow, with all the stress and craziness of traveling around the world, will be much easier than dealing with Mom for this lunch.

I dismount the bike.

Mom doesn't expect me to be riding on the back of such a thing. I have to call out to her before she even recognizes me.

"Maddie?"

"Hi, Mom."

People have always commented on how similar Mom and I look. Short with light blue eyes and wavy brown hair. Pale skin that shouldn't belong in the Californian sun. That's us. What Mom's wearing doesn't belong in the Californian sun either. She's dressed rather conservatively for Los Angeles heat, like she's going to church in the Mid-West. She's got a scarf around her neck and a long dress that nearly reaches her ankles. She's got flats on as well. Everything's dark colors and no style. I can imagine her thinking that the focus should not be on herself, but on the Lord.

Meanwhile, I've opted for a classic and perfectly fitted pair of jeans and a blazer with sneakers. Nothing too fancy or too casual. Something I can wear on the back of a bike. My outfit's probably *too* casual for someone like my mom, though.

But I don't have to worry about her judgment. She's already looking past me at the man currently removing his helmet with a rockstar flourish.

Here goes.

"Is this him?" she asks me, whispering.

"Yep. Axel, this is my mother, Mary Leaver. Mom, this is Axel Stoll, my boyfriend."

I notice Mom's eyes immediately dart from the dangerous-looking motorbike to scanning Axel up and down like a wild, vicious animal, focusing on the visible tattoos, looking very alarmed.

My fake boyfriend also notices that. He smirks at me. A man well used to being in trouble.

I'm not smirking back.

This is already shaping up to be a very bad idea. Why did I ever agree to this?

I hope to God that Mom doesn't say anything during this lunch to rile up my fake boyfriend. Two hot-headed diametrically opposed people in the same room? It'll be like fireworks, and not in a fun way.

"Hello, Mary," Axel says. He's putting on all the charm for her. "Lovely to meet you. I would've sworn you and Maddie are sisters."

My mother just hums in reply. She's being very guarded. Her eyes flicker around LA's streets. She was never meant to visit a place like this. I bet, in her own mind, all she can see is sin.

I sigh. "Astrid should already be inside. Let's go and find our table, shall we?"

* * *

AXEL'S MOM is already sitting at a table. She stands up and waves us over from across the restaurant as we enter.

The place Axel decided on for lunch is fancy. No doubt he's trying to impress all of us.

Like Name the nightclub and the hotel he's staying at, I've driven past this place many times before, but I never thought I would ever be willing to drop enough money to eat here. I think I've read an article about this restaurant when it opened. Some up-and-coming wonder chef is the owner. It's a hit with the fancy culinary world.

Yep, pretty far removed from your normal drive-thru McDonalds where you'll usually find me.

"Maddie, so wonderful to see you again." Astrid gives me a big hug. There's a painful stab in my heart when I realize my own mother didn't even give me one outside. I hug her back and then introduce her to Mom. Like her son, Astrid is charming and completely ignores my mother's obvious distaste for her and Axel.

My mom, surrounded by similar women like her back home, has never seen people like Astrid and Axel. People who are loud and gregarious and fun-loving. But Astrid takes it all in her stride and tries her hardest to make everyone comfortable.

"It's very lovely to meet you, Mary. Thank you for flying

out here on such short notice.," she says, gesturing at the table. "Please sit. I haven't ordered anything yet."

I make eye contact with Astrid, attempting to psychically express to her my gratitude for the gentle way she handles Mom.

"Couldn't Chloe make it?" Axel asks. "I thought you might be able to talk her out here as well."

"She says she can't get out of work," Astrid replies.

"She does know she doesn't need to work anymore, right? She does know that I am an international rockstar who can pay for her life ten times over, and am willing to do so?"

"You know what your sister is like," Astrid explains. "She won't take a single cent from you. Never has, never will."

"She's infuriating. Is she still practicing?"

"Every day."

"Still too afraid to do anything live?"

"How about you give her a call and find out?"

"I'll like to meet Chloe one day," I add eagerly. "Would be nice to meet Axel's sister."

My fake boyfriend looks at me with a blank expression, and I worry I've gone too far.

"I bet Axel hasn't told you much about her," Astrid says. And it's true. "She's a musician as well. She uploads her videos to YouTube."

"Interesting."

"You're a musician?" Mom asks, her gaze settling on Axel warily.

"I am. A rockstar."

No, no, no, no. We've gone nuclear.

"My daughter wouldn't date a musician. I thought I warned her off men like that. Men like you."

The cat's out of the bag now.

"Well, I am dating Axel."

Mom's laser-like focus switches to me. "That is very out of character for you, Maddie. It's sad to see that it seems like my teachings went straight through your pretty little empty head. I should've known; it's always been like that with you ever since you were a baby. You like to ignore common sense."

My throat dries up as I keep my emotion in check. Under the table, I clench the sides of my chair. I'm not giving my mother the satisfaction of seeing me cry in front of her. I've experienced a lot of her snide comments before.

I can survive this. Just hold on. This'll all be over soon.

Astrid and Axel, however, are very new to this. They both go quiet at my mother's remarks. And I'm instantly embarrassed; I didn't want them to witness this.

But what did you expect, Maddie, bringing Mom here?

It was only a matter of time.

"I am dating Axel, Mom."

Astrid chirps in, sensing the tension. "Obviously, you don't watch the news, Mary. Axel is quite well-known for his music and his band. He's quite successful."

"I don't watch anything that is non-Christian. Success in something does not mean a single iota in the eyes of the Lord."

Silence falls.

I guess it's up to me to move things along.

"What's good here? I've heard some amazing things about this place. I read an article about the owner..."

"What music do you perform?" Mom asks Axel, ignoring me. "I've read up on those modern Christian rock bands. Is it anything like that?"

"No, unfortunately. We're quite different."

I'm glad that Axel isn't being his usual rude self. He's

trying to navigate this carefully. I really appreciate the effort, especially from him.

"Do you believe in Jesus, Axel?"

This is really what I didn't want the topic of conversation to slide to, but it seems like I'm stuck with this.

Oh, Mom. Please don't.

Like a bull in a China shop, she continues her pressing attack.

"Please tell me you believe in Jesus."

"That's a... difficult question." Axel is visibly squirming.

I just want to curl up and hide away for a thousand years. I bury my face in the menu.

"The seafood linguine seems good," I mutter, trying my hardest to force a change in the conversation. Of course, things don't go my way. Not when my mother is involved.

"It's not a difficult question," Mom remarks before spinning to Astrid. "I see that you're wearing a necklace of the cross. Tell me, how can you raise a boy to become the voice of Satan and encourage the Devil's work on earth when you dare wear the icon of the Lord? His *success*, as you call it, makes him practically a demon."

"Let's order," I interject.

But then Mom comes out with her killer line.

"What kind of a mother are you, Astrid Stoll?"

There's silence. Axel's mom stares at my mom in shock. I'm the only person here who's been ready for something like this, and I immediately try to diffuse the tension.

"Mom..."

But she cuts me off by suddenly standing. "I can't believe I've come all this way to break bread with such sinful people. I can't believe I was invited me out here for *this*."

"Please sit, Mom."

"I can't take this anymore," she continues. "I'm not

sitting at this table a moment longer with these kinds of people. A *musician*, of all people. I want you, Maddie, to end this relationship right now. You hear me?"

"No, Mom."

"What do you mean?" she barks back at me.

"I can make my own choices." Despite my defiance, my voice cracks and is so weak. I'm terrified. My legs shake under the table as I will myself not to burst into tears.

You're stronger than this, Maddie. Be strong.

I might've made a resolution to stand up for myself at the beginning of the year, but all that crumbles away when Mom is involved.

"No, you can't make your own choices, Maddie. Not when your choices are this. I am being your responsible mother here. Break up with this godforsaken man. You've seen how relationships with men go, you've heard all my talk about it. You saw what your father put me through. Trust me, this man is even worse. At least your father was a Christian."

"Please, Mom, sit back down. You're being very loud…"

My mother doesn't move. She glares at me.

She really wants me to break up with Axel right now, in this very public place.

Everyone is staring.

Please no. This is a nightmare made real.

I really should've guessed this was how today would've gone. I should never have allowed this to happen. This is my fault.

I tremble. No words come out as I try to rebuff my own mom. I don't know what to say to her. I'm sensing everyone in this restaurant is gawking at me, waiting for my response to my mother's hateful tirade.

But then Astrid stands up. She's taller than my mom.

She towers over her. Her characteristic warmth is gone from her face.

"Honey, my boy is no demon," she says. Though she may be quiet, her voice is strong and powerful. "I am a Christian, so what I'm saying is from a place of love for a fellow believer, but you would know that Jesus Himself dined with sinners."

"Pah." That's my mother's response, but Astrid continues.

"I know my Bible inside and out, Mary, and I can assure you that nothing Axel and Maddie do is sinful. Anyone can be religious and have faith without the need to abuse their own child, or to get in other people's faces. Or be rude. What would Jesus think of all this? Would He be on your side? Maddie is an adult. She can make her own choices, and you should support her in whatever she does as a mother. *That's* what I know a good mother does, so don't you dare try to insult her or me or my son. Your daughter is one of the most loveliest people I've had the privilege of meeting, and you should thank God every day for that."

Mom takes it all in, but she doesn't reply to Astrid. She turns her fire back onto me.

"How dare you associate yourself with such a witch," she barks. "You've always tried to run to the dark side all your life, and I'm the one always having to pull you away from temptation. You never make things easy, Maddie, don't you? You've always been such a pain. You need to end this relationship right now and promise me you'll never see either of these two heathens ever again."

"Please sit down, Mom." I can't hold my emotions back any longer. Tears stream down my face. I must be a horrible sight.

And then Axel rises. He really towers over my mother,

but he doesn't physically threaten her at all. He merely crosses his arms and speaks in a near-whisper.

"You're Maddie's mother, so I'm going to say this respectfully, Mrs. Leaver. I respect Maddie enough not to indulge my impulses and insult you in the same way you've just been going at, unhinged, for the last ten minutes, but I want you to understand one thing. I *know* Maddie. I know things about Maddie that she doesn't know I know. I know that Maddie spends most of her paycheck every month paying for your bills. I know she's nearly gone homeless for you without a single word of protest. She's not some demon-loving woman, she's an angel, and I know that most of all. Somehow you're too blind to see that, even as her mother. Maddie is my angel. Maybe look to your own house before you judge someone else's."

The table falls silent yet again. Mom straightens her back. She doesn't say a single word – she doesn't even look at me – before she's storming for the exit.

Which leaves just Axel, Astrid, and I at the table.

Silence again.

"I've got to go to the bathroom," I whisper, before I rush off.

35

MADDIE

My crying finally stops. I dry my eyes and wash my hands before I reapply my makeup in the mirror.

I'm in the restaurant bathroom, glad that neither Astrid nor Axel have decided to follow me in here to check if I'm okay. I just need a minute – or five – to make sure I've recovered from whatever the hell that was that just happened with my mother. That entire episode just then was more than one of her usual rants. That was pure venom spitting from her, spraying everyone in sight.

And I hate how Axel and Astrid had to see it.

They must feel so much pity for me, and that's what I hate the most about what just occurred. I'm so damn embarrassed that they saw my own mom treating me like that. Saying those words. Insulting me and *them*.

Mom's aggressive words *should* sting, but I actually don't feel any hurt from her. Mom's insults today have ridden over me like a slight gust of wind, which has never happened before.

I'm actually happy.

Axel stood up for me. In front of Mom.

Axel called me an angel. Sure, it wasn't *me* that stood up to her – I didn't fulfill my New Year's resolution – but Axel spoke for the both of us.

Ready to face my fake boyfriend and his mom, I check myself one last time in the mirror. I can't get rid of all traces of my tears, but at least now I appear stoic.

Strong.

I'm not going to let Mom get me down.

I stroll out of the bathroom with my head held high, and then I nearly run into a man I recognize immediately.

"Winston?"

My boss and I avoid collapsing into each other as he leaves the male bathroom. He instinctively grabs my shoulder to stop us both before it's too late, and then he looks me up and down. He's clearly as surprised as I am.

"Maddie?"

"What are you doing here?" I ask. It's pretty stupid to ask, seeing as we're in a restaurant, but I just blurt it out awkwardly anyway.

"I'm having a business lunch... how's Axel? How's all that going? I saw it on the news."

I blush. I'm constantly forgetting how weird and unusual it must be for people that know me to suddenly get confronted by a viral photo of me kissing one of the most famous men on the planet.

"Yeah, it's been a whirlwind couple of days."

"I bet," Winston replies. He looks uneasy talking any further about his employee's love life. "I saw the reports you've posted into work. Fantastic stuff, Maddie."

"Thanks."

"And now you and Axel are together?"

He doesn't know it's fake. Lucas has really tightly kept

that under wraps.

"It's a long story," I reply sheepishly. "Actually, he's here somewhere. I'm having lunch with Axel and his mom."

"I'll come and say hi."

"Oh, you don't have to do that."

Winston shrugs. "I'm in the good books with the nieces, talking about how I've met Ravaged. Maybe I can get a photo with him and then I'll be the coolest uncle in the world."

I laugh. "That's fair enough."

My boss follows me back to the table. If he's noticed the dried tears on my face, then he doesn't mention them. I'm thankful.

Astrid and Axel both look up as I approach, concern etched on their faces. It's kinda cute how much Axel seems to care. He's let me see a little bit past his cool exterior. He gets up to invite me back to the table. Now, that's sweet.

But Astrid's worry changes immediately into shock when she sees Winston following behind me.

"Winston?" she blurts out.

"Astrid?" my boss exclaims

Wait, they know each other?

"What..."

Astrid is at a loss for words. Both Axel and I spin our heads between the two.

"How long has it been?" Winston asks Axel's mom. "Years?"

"Decades," she corrects him sternly.

Are they old friends?

They don't go in for a hug as old friends should. Instead, they maintain a formal distance of a few yards apart in the middle of the restaurant. It's like some kind of Western standoff. This isn't two acquaintances seeing each other after years apart.

This is something more.

"How do you know Maddie?" Winston asks her.

"She's currently dating my son."

Oh, Astrid is cold.

"Your son is Axel Stoll? I didn't know you had a child."

"I got married."

"Oh, I see."

"I changed my last name."

"Right."

"Yep."

This is awkward.

"Well, Maddie is actually one of my employees."

Astrid remains fixated on Winston. "Is she?" she asks.

"Yes."

"Good for you. She's a nice girl."

I want to sit down. This is so stiff. Astrid's face makes her seem like she's about to bite Winston's head off. His presence has completely erased her lovely smile.

"It would be nice to talk to you, Astrid. About how things... ended."

Axel's mom crosses her arms. "Now is not the time or the place."

"I see."

"Goodbye, Winston."

Astrid's word is final. She wants him gone, and even my boss can see that.

"Okay, goodbye, Astrid. I hope we see each other again." Astrid's lips go tight. "It was nice seeing you, Maddie."

"You too, Winston."

He risks one last look at Astrid before he turns and heads to the other side of the restaurant where I presume his table is.

"Let's sit back down," Astrid suggests. I feel like those

words are a subtle hint that she doesn't want either Axel or me to talk about what just happened.

But what *did* just happen? She and Winston knew each other a long time ago? Were they just friends, or was there more to it than that? With that little interaction, it seems like it's the latter. And things didn't seem to end well at all. I've got so many questions.

Winston was apologetic, and Astrid was stern. Something must've really got to her decades ago. Something to do with him. His behavior, perhaps? Did they actually date?

Axel, being a gentleman, pulls out my chair for me to sit.

"Thanks," I breathlessly whisper to the man. He surprises me every moment. I had really dismissed him as just some arrogant, aloof playboy, but then – with every action he takes towards me – he reveals more of the real man underneath.

It's only when we're all comfortable at the table that the apologies fly.

It's Astrid's turn first.

"I'm so sorry for how we behaved, Maddie."

Then Axel.

"I didn't mean to insult your mom like that. I didn't mean for things to get so heated."

I wave them both away with a flick of my wrist. I can't stand apologies, especially from these two. Especially when they did absolutely nothing wrong.

"I know, I know. There's no need to say sorry at all; that was just my mother. You're both in the right. I should've expected something like that to happen. I shouldn't have thought things would somehow be different just because you were here."

"Is she always like that?" Axel asks.

I just nod.

Astrid reaches out and takes my hand.

"I am *so* sorry, though, Maddie. You shouldn't have to deal with that."

I take her hand with my other and gently squeeze. "It's okay. You did nothing wrong. In fact, just the opposite. Both of you."

"Are you okay?" Astrid asks.

"Yeah. I just find it... *hard* to talk back to Mom. I shouldn't, but with her I simply can't be myself. I transform into being a little girl whenever I'm around her; too scared to do a thing. She's got a hold over me, and it's like I can't escape her shadow... Sorry, I'm rambling on. I hate talking about Mom to other people. I'm sorry to put you through all that."

"There's nothing to be sorry for," Astrid replies softly. "Maddie, you don't need to rely on anyone except yourself. You are enough."

Something is caught in my throat. "Thank you, Astrid."

She smiles, and it fills me with warmth. Under the table, Axel tenderly places his hand on my leg. It isn't sexual in any way, just him expressing a feeling in the best way possible.

We sit in comfortable silence, together, for a moment.

And then I ask the question that I know is on both Axel's and my minds.

"How the hell do you know my boss, Astrid?"

"Yeah?" Even Axel has perked up.

The woman coyly blushes.

"He's an old flame of mine."

Just as I suspected.

"So you're going to keep quiet about this?" I ask.

"It's a story for another day," Astrid replies. "Shall we still have lunch?"

36

AXEL

At the end of our meal, Maddie excuses herself.

"I know this sounds silly, but I need to go to the bathroom again," she says cutely.

I just smile and nod. "Go."

She needs to compose herself after what the hell just happened with her mother. Holy shit, I did not expect that at all. To be honest, I'm still in shock at what that woman said. What she was like. No wonder Maddie's always so cautious and her defenses are so high when she's grown up with a mother like that.

Once she leaves, I glance at my own mom sitting across from me.

"I think I did something wrong," I say.

I've been thinking that ever since Maddie's mom stormed out. Because of words that I've said. I shouldn't have gotten involved with all that. I shouldn't have stood up to the woman.

That was not part of my fake boyfriend contract with

Maddie.

But I had to say something; there was an overwhelming urge in that moment to stand up for the girl I've really gotten to know over the last few days and tell her mother the truth. I hated how Mary spoke to her. How can a mother say things like that to her daughter?

Maddie has been through some shit, that's for sure.

"You did nothing wrong," Mom assures me. "You did something *right*."

"How could you know? She ran to the bathroom in tears afterwards. Was that me? My fault?"

I don't know why I'm caring so much. I never would normally.

But I care about my fake girlfriend.

"I saw Maddie's face," Mom explains. "I know these things. For a man who's made millions of girls around the world fall in love with you, Axel, you're pretty ignorant of how the female mind works, aren't you?"

I just blink at my mother.

"I just hope she isn't insulted or hurt," I reply dumbly.

Mom takes a long pause to study my face intently. It's uncomfortable. I try to look everywhere but at her.

"You really love Maddie, don't you?" Mom asks.

Right. That's enough for me.

I can't deal with these kinds of questions from Mom.

I flag down a passing server.

"I'll have a beer, please."

"You don't want to talk about it?" Mom asks me.

Nope.

"What the hell was that with the publicity guy?" I ask her in response. "The guy who's Maddie's boss? Winston *what's-his-name*?"

"It's something I'm not ready to divulge yet."

"Does Chloe know about this guy?"

"No," Mom replies. "Winston is from a distant time when I was a different woman, long before you and your sister came into my life. You do know I lived a life before you two entered it, don't you?"

"I know now."

Maddie's returning from the bathroom. It's a long walk from the other side of the restaurant to our table.

I take a sneak peek at her face. No tears this time. The thought that I might've said something that upset her forms an unfamiliar ache in my heart.

She hasn't even made it back to the table when Mom leans over to whisper to me.

"She looks tough. She's been through a lot. Axel, make sure you take good care of this girl. I like her too much to let anything bad happen to her."

"Yep."

"You promise? Maddie doesn't know the rockstar life. She really doesn't know what she's getting into here. Don't you dare fuck her around, okay?"

"I won't."

"I know you, Axel. You told me that you've always wanted to live that musician's life. You wanted to get out of Crystal River. You said you wanted to experience the world as a rockstar. You even got a nickname in the press for your antics. You've always protested against relationships, so don't you dare screw up this one. That girl is a good soul…"

Mom falls silent as Maddie reaches the table.

"Hello, guys. Sorry about that," my fake girlfriend says. "What are you talking about?"

Oh, she is smart. She knows something's up between Mom and me.

"Nothing," I reply. I stand up. Mom watches me carefully. "Let's go back home. The tour starts tomorrow. First stop's Canada."

37

MADDIE

"Now you see what my mother is like?" I ask Axel as he unlocks to door to his hotel suite. "Now you see why I was so worried about her meeting you and Astrid?"

The man chuckles as he collapses onto the couch, exhausted. We've been out all afternoon at the concert arena. Drake called Axel straight after we left the restaurant, summoning him to rehearse with the band all afternoon. I decided to come along. I sat up in the seats overlooking the stage, enjoying being a witness to this talented little band play to an empty arena. With only me in the audience, it felt like they were playing just for me.

A few days ago I didn't know a word of their songs, now entire lyrics are floating annoyingly around my head.

You are everything, girl
Everything to me

"Lunch today was... interesting," Axel says diplomatically, half-closing his eyes as he rests on the couch. Man, he really looks tired.

"Can you see now why I might be a bit insecure and unable to trust relationships?" I continue.

Axel just chuckles again. He leans his head back against a pillow. "You have absolutely nothing to be insecure about," he replies in his deep, resonate voice.

I don't know about that.

I take a seat opposite him with an enormous yawn. Seems like I'm tired too, and I'm not the one who's been non-stop playing a bass guitar for the last few hours.

I study Axel's sharp features as he closes his eyes. His strong jawline. His tousled hair. Those dimples. He's incredibly gorgeous. And cute. But he's also a rockstar and an infamous playboy. There have been hundreds of girls who've fallen in love, up close, with this man's perfect face. There's not a chance in a million years a man like this would fall for an ordinary girl like me. That's what I've got to remember about this whole little thing we've got going on. This is all fake. A simple contract. It will all end, and soon.

"Come on, let's get to bed," I announce, standing up and gesturing Axel to follow me to the bedroom. "I need my beauty sleep before the flight tomorrow."

The rockstar drowsily gets up from the couch and follows me to bed. He strips down to just his underpants and slides in while I get ready in the bathroom. He's still awake when I return.

We lie in bed for a long time in silence. I can sense, right next to me, that he's still awake. I wonder what he's thinking. Does he know I'm not asleep yet? Is he waiting for me to say something?

For the last few days, I've had the constant overwhelming urge to pinch myself. I surprise myself all the time thinking about this crazy-ass situation I've somehow fallen into. I'm now a rockstar's girlfriend. My face is out there on the news and social media right now. There are thousands of girls trying to figure out who I am. Probably thousands of journalists as well, come to think of it. I'm some nobody who's been photographed kissing one of the sexiest men on the planet. What a ride it's been, and it's only going to get crazier.

And that same man is lying next to me.

Yep, I really want to pinch myself.

"Are you awake?"

I hear Axel's whisper in the dark.

"Yes."

With my answer, Axel slowly turns over so that he's facing me. I can't see him in the pitch blackness of the room, but I can feel his warmth. His hot breath on my neck.

I feel his arm move towards me under the covers until he reaches my thigh. He rests his hand there. My heart rate quickens. I let out an involuntary gasp.

And then the rest of his body moves towards me until he's so close.

And then he's kissing me.

Oh, God.

I don't want to give in to him. I don't want to be another one of his girls. His one-night flings.

And so, against my own body's desire, I pull back.

"I can't do this," I breathlessly stutter. "I can't."

"Okay," Axel replies. I still can't see him properly, but I know his eyes are burning into me. "I'm sorry. This is the longest time I've gone without touching someone."

"What, a few days?"

"Yep. I couldn't control myself."

I like that. I like how even the mere presence of me in his bed unlocks his desires. His burning need for me. This rockstar who's willing to break a contract just to have *me*.

"Let's just forget about it," I whisper back.

Forgetting about it is the very last thing I want to do. In another life, I would've fallen into that kiss. Fallen into whatever Axel's next move was going to be. But I can't trust him. Mom's words echo in my head from when I was a girl.

You can't trust men.

Especially the playboy kind, for sure. I know how this all goes. He's after one thing and when this tour and this deal is over then he'll discard me like he's done to countless women.

He can't control himself? Yeah, that's what he probably says to all the girls.

We don't say another word to each other. I turn over and fall asleep with my mother's voice from my childhood still ringing loud and clear, warning me off men.

Men just like Axel.

38

AXEL

All my boys arrive at the airport at the same time. Our chauffeured-driven limousines pull up outside the VIP entrance to the airport within minutes of each other as if we choreographed this, but we haven't. Great minds think alike and all that.

"Perfectly timed," I announce with a grin as I step out of the vehicle. Drake and Caspian both grin back like cheeky schoolboys. Even Caspian does a satisfied nod as he slides out of his limo, large backpack in his hands like he's a tourist on vacation.

But this isn't a vacation. This tour means *work*.

Drake summons us all over with a flick of his wrist where he embraces us all in a hug.

"Here's to the start of the best tour yet," he says as we huddle around each other. We truly are brothers when we can greet each other like this. "Let's smash the competition and have a fucking *good* time."

I turn back to my limo to see Maddie with a smile on

her face.

"Watching us?" I ask her.

"Can't not to," she replies. "You guys are cute together."

At least she's still on speaking terms with me after last night. After I stupidly nearly ruined everything we've got going simply because I wanted to kiss her.

Hey, I took my chance and went for it.

And she rejected me.

"We're rockstars, not dolls. We ain't cute," I say.

I've gone casual today. Just my hoodie on. I want to be comfortable on this damn flight to Canada.

"The rockstar doth protest too much, methinks," Maddie replies.

"Shut up." I pull her bag out from the trunk. No way am I letting some other guy carry her stuff. "Come, have you ever flown on a private plane before?"

Maddie shakes her head. "Nope."

"Well, now's your chance. See that?"

"What?"

I point towards the airfield where a sleek jet is waiting to go.

"That's ours."

* * *

THERE's another jet parked next to ours. A group of people stand outside it, probably waiting to embark, I guess. I don't give them a second's notice as we head towards our plane. Well, that's until Bishop opens his lips and swears.

"Holy fuck, that's *them*."

I squint at the group.

And then I'm swearing as well.

"Yeah, it's fucking them. I can recognize those cheap skinny jeans and stupid smug faces anywhere."

Maddie next to me furrows her brow. "Who are they?"

Drake answers for me. The two words I hate most in the English language.

"Tainted Lives."

Maddie's mouth drops.

"Your rival band? Those guys? They're here as well?"

"The one and the same," I reply. "The assholes themselves in all their shit glory."

"*Of course* their plane is next to ours," Bishop seethes.

"They can't do anything without doing it next to us," Drake adds.

We pass by the group to board our own plane.

Oz Cantor, the famous frontman of Tainted Lives spots us at the same time as we spot him. He nudges his bandmates. They all face us. As we pass, Oz opens his arms wide aggressively.

"Well, well, well," he cackles. "If it isn't our lowly little competition, Ravaged."

He pronounces our band's name like it's poison he's spitting from his mouth.

He's just like he's like in photos. Bright red curly hair. Pale, freckly skin. Dark green sneering eyes.

To me, he's fucking *ugly* as fuck.

"Oz," Drake greets, trying to move past him without a fight developing. That plan doesn't work with a guy like Oz. He's determined not to let us slip from his grasp.

"You guys better get that plane started. You have an album to promote, don't you? You need all the help you can get, seeing as you are vastly behind us in record sales. Isn't that right?"

"Look," Drake replies. "We don't want any trouble, Oz."

We'll be on our way, and you be on yours," I add. "We don't have to say anything to each other."

Oz laughs directly back in my face. We must be no

further than ten yards apart from each other on the tarmac of the airport. I can practically see the disgust in his eyes from this distance.

His fellow bandmates chuckle along with their leader, their bags lying next to them. It's like the rest of Tainted Lives have no personality at all other than to act as simple *yes men* to the frontman.

"We *don't* have to say something to each other, but I want to," Oz gloats. "Both our new albums are coming out on the same day, and we're going to beat you guys to pulp. You know what? Me and the guys have been making some bets on how many more copies we're going to sell than you on release day. I gotta let you in on a little secret… the numbers are pretty big."

It's Bishop's turn to speak. "Just back away, Oz. We simply want to fly out in peace."

Oz laughs mockingly again. "You guys think you're so tough and cool. You guys are, in fact, nothing but *posers*."

"One day, I swear, Tainted Lives will be a support act for our tour," I reply. "Nothing else but a little backup at the beginning of our show when everyone's still getting their drinks and finding their seats in a sold-out stadium under our names. I promise one day you'll wish you're even one-tenth of our band."

"As if," Oz retorts. I see my words have had an effect on him, though, despite his bravado. "We're going to be bigger than you. No one is going to remember you guys at all in a year's time. Ravaged will end up in the trashcan of music history. I won't stop until you're Tainted Lives' supporting act."

I smirk and take Maddie's hand. "Well, it's been real nice catching up with you, Oz, but we've got a flight to catch."

"Is that your girl?"

The question makes me stop. It's not a simple question. It's a goddamn *threat*.

"What?"

"Is that your girl?" Oz repeats. "I saw her on my Instagram. I recognize her. At first, I saw all those negative comments and thought she was quite pretty but seeing her in person makes me admit that she's a bit too plain for a guy like you, Axel."

What the actual...

The next moment is pure instinct and adrenaline.

I take a step forward and fake a punch towards the frontman. I clench back my arm. All pretend. He stumbles back with arms raised, cowering away.

"No one talks to my girl like that," I seethe, holding myself back from the fucker. "I guess you're all words and no bite, though. Tiny little Oz with his tiny little cock, unable to get his dick sucked, right?"

"Fuck you."

Oz's reply is very unimaginative.

I slowly turn back around to Maddie. "Let's get on the plane," I say to her. "Ignore him."

She looks at me with both sadness and fear. It's the words that Oz has just said to her. Those barbed words of pain and humiliation. Sure, I was able to frighten him, but I wish I could do so much more to avenge my girl.

All I want to do is take her in a tight embrace and tell her she has nothing to worry about.

She isn't plain at all.

As I look at her, it happens.

I don't see the spray of water until it's too late.

It comes from behind me. A directed torrent of water that completely drenches Maddie and makes her yelp.

What the fuck?

I spin around.

It's Oz. He's got a hose in his hands. One that they keep on the runway to wash down planes with.

And he's spraying Maddie with water.

"Look," Oz gleefully announces. "I'm giving her a clean for you, Axel. Maybe she won't be so plain anymore."

I lunge towards the man, but Bishop grabs me before I can get the opportunity to place my hands around the bastard's neck. I watch as Caspian, towering over Oz, gently removes the hose from the man's hands without any resistance and switches it off. There is some deep fucking fear in Oz's eyes as he stares up at Ravaged's massive drummer. Caspian doesn't say a word.

"He's not worth our time, Axel," Bishop whispers into my ear, calming me down. "I know you're angry, but this is not the place for retaliation. Make sure your girl is okay."

He's right. Maddie is more important.

Sensing a shift in my manner, Bishop lets me go.

"You're lucky Bishop was here to stop me," I warn the lead singer of Tainted Lives. "Next time you won't be so lucky."

Maddie has already run into the private jet. I follow closely behind. She needs me.

I reach out to stop her once we're inside.

"You okay?" I ask.

"I am."

She's shivering. She's pretending to be brave for me, but I see right past it.

"Maddie..."

She cuts me off.

"I don't like to see you angry," she tells me. "That's what I care about most. I honestly don't give a shit about Tainted Lives and their stupid water prank or anything, only about you."

She doesn't know how sweet she's being. How much

her words mean to me.

"You must be cold," I reply. I fetch her a towel from the plane's bathroom. I wrap her in it and hold her close against my warmth until she stops shaking. Maddie doesn't protest.

"Thank you," she murmurs.

I let her sit before I take off my hoodie. "Wear this," I say to her as I hand it over.

"Thank you," she repeats.

"My hoodie looks better on you," I remark when she fits it over her head. She blushes.

The rest of Ravaged board the plane. They all apologize for Oz's behavior.

Maddie just smiles along.

"I see what you guys mean," she says, just as the plane takes off. "Tainted Lives *are* pretty shit."

That makes us all laugh.

* * *

MADDIE NAPS once the plane reaches altitude. She must be pretty tired, and so am I.

I watch her sleep. She leans back in her seat with my hoodie on. Her soft cheeks glisten with the water. Her hair is still wet.

She looks so goddamn cute.

Maybe this is what life is all about. Finding someone. Maybe that would bring me more joy than trying to live that rockstar lifestyle I crave. That's what Mom would have me think, anyway.

Maybe I need a girl like Maddie to feel complete.

But she rejected me last night when I made my advances. And, somehow, that hurts me more than I ever thought a rejection would.

This girl, man. This girl...

39

MADDIE

Lucas takes Axel and me straight into a separate limousine, separating us from the other members of Ravaged when the private plane lands in Vancouver.

"I've got to talk to you two," he tells us when he gestures towards the limousine on the runway. We both follow him.

"A few days ago I'd never been in a limo," I say when I take a seat inside the vehicle. "Today I've been in two."

"Welcome to my world," Axel nudges me.

"Are you going to keep saying that?"

"Only if you keep expressing how amazed you are by everything."

"Well, I am."

"Stop getting so sulky," Axel teases. "It's too adorable."

"Ugh. Don't call me adorable."

Lucas shuts the door and orders the driver to take us to the downtown hotel we're going to be staying at.

"What do you want to talk to us about, Lucas?" Axel

asks as we pull away from the airport. "Sounds pretty ominous making us get in here with you like this. Alone."

Lucas spins around from the front seat. He's not here to joke around. I can tell from his eyes he's purely business.

"Listen, we need to make a splash," he says.

"A splash?" I ask.

"We need to get you both out there in the spotlight, especially today. It will be perfect for the first day on the tour to put you two center. Get your faces out on everything. Bombard social media and the tabloids."

"Sounds pretty intense, man," Axel whistles.

"Look, I've run the numbers – I've sure you've seen them as well, Maddie – and you are already proving yourselves a hit with the fans," Lucas continues, ignoring the rockstar. "People love this new mysterious girl that Axel seems enamored with. Everyone loves you two. It's a real kind of *prince and the commoner* type thing. People just love that you're just a normal girl, Maddie, who's been swept off her feet into this life. It's like a fairytale come true. Cinderella and all that jazz. Ravaged's social media is going crazy, and it's time we feed it again."

"Oh, God," I whisper. "It's all starting to feel so real."

"That's not all. There are even hashtags about you two. *Axelsgirl*."

My fake boyfriend scoffs. "*Axelsgirl*?"

"I'm not the biggest fan of social media," I say. Sure, I have an Instagram and Facebook account, but they're mainly to keep up with family and friends from back home rather than scroll through all day.

"Trust me," Axel tells me. "Don't go on it."

"Yeah, things are blowing up madly," Lucas adds. "Most things seem to be positive about you, though. People love Maddie Leaver, even though they don't know who the hell you are. See, Axel, didn't I tell you she's a good choice?"

Axel turns to look at me. "She was a good choice."

There are butterflies in my stomach as the man stares me in the eyes. All I think about is the kiss last night. How much I wanted the man. But how I turned him away.

And then how much he was willing to fight for me at the airport this morning despite my rejection of him last night. How vicious he acted in the face of my humiliation by Tainted Lives. How far he was prepared to go to protect my honor.

"I think this fake relationship is going to work out wonders," Lucas says. "I'm a genius. Don't thank me all at once."

"Okay, Lucas. Don't let all this get to your ego," Axel replies. "It's big enough already; soon you'll be asking for a pay rise."

"My personal favorite is the nickname fans have come up for you both," Lucas continues.

"What?" I ask, blinking. "A nickname?"

It's all absurd, this.

"You know, like Rpatz or Kimye," he explains. "Your one is Maxel."

"I love it," Axel says.

"I'm not too sure," I reply. "Maxel? Sounds like a superhero. Or a type of dog."

"So, what's this *splash* you want to tell us about?" Axel asks as we reach downtown Vancouver. The tall skyscrapers rise up around us. I look outside. I've been to Canada once or twice, but never to this city. This must be what it's like as a rockstar. So much travel. So many cities. I wonder if Axel even gets a chance to explore all these places or if it's just a blur of arenas and hotels.

"We need to beat Tainted Lives," Lucas says.

"I'm all on board with that," I reply. "After what they've just done."

Lucas raises an eyebrow. He was late to the plane this morning and didn't witness that confrontation.

"Maddie had a run-in with the assholes at the airport today," Axel helpfully clarifies. "They were their usual selves. And by that, I mean they were assholes."

"I see."

"So, what's this plan you've made?" I ask the band's manager. He's being deliberately secretive, as if he wants to keep both Axel and me in suspense. He certainly likes a pinch of drama, Lucas.

"After the performance tonight, I want you two to go on a nice romantic date somewhere," Lucas says. "I'll find you a spot. I'll make sure the paparazzi are there to snap photos of you two. What do you think?"

I shrug. "I signed a contract."

"Good. You guys have got to act all loved up, alright? Are you two in?"

Axel and I both turn to each other at the same time. There's a slight smirk on his face. It's the Axel I know.

"Yeah," my fake boyfriend says, speaking for both of us. "We're in."

40

MADDIE

True to Lucas' word, the paparazzi are waiting for us outside Vancouver's most elite restaurant. Waiting for the perfect shot of the most talked-about couple on planet earth.

Me and Axel Stoll.

As I step out of the limo – the third I've been in just *today* – I immediately spot the leader of the pack of photographers lining up for us. I never got his name the last – and first – time I met him outside Axel's hotel, but I know who he is alright. He's greasy, just as I remember. The same man who confessed to me that he was the one who set up Axel's sex tape. The one who spoke to me the day before I got famous. The one who scratched his messy stubble and gloated that he *had* Axel.

Well, now he clearly knows who I am. I can practically see the cartoon dollar signs in his eyes as he glares at me from the pavement.

"I remember you," he growls at me. I try to ignore him, but he pushes up against me. His stench is overwhelming. I want to cough. "You thought you were having fun at my expense, huh? A little joke before you got famous?"

Shit.

But Axel is already here beside me.

"Come on," Axel replies to the man. "Let us pass."

The paparazzo is undeterred. "You snuck past me once, Miss Maddie Leaver, but that was before I learned who you are. This time you ain't so lucky. I want an upskirt photo of you. I *really* want one. Can't you give one to me? How about you go back to your car and let me take one of you, huh? You wouldn't believe the demand there is for pictures of your pussy."

Axel flies in for the rescue.

"Fuck. Off."

My fake boyfriend takes my hand and pulls me inside the restaurant as flashes from the waiting paparazzi's cameras light up around us.

"I need a minute," I say, breathless, once we make it safely inside the exclusive establishment.

"You okay?" Axel asks me, concern on his face.

"I'm fine, just need a second to get over the little fact that somehow I've gotten incredibly famous overnight," I reply.

"It was wrong for him to say that kind of shit," Axel seethes. "I should go out there and show him a piece of me for disrespecting you like that."

I squeeze his hand.

"Trust me," I reply. "I've handled greasy men who've said bad comments to me in the past. Besides, I've met that guy before."

"You've met him before?"

"Yep."

"Wow, I'm sorry. That's Harold, he's a real dick. He's the worst of the worse."

"I've noticed."

"The rest of Ravaged hate him as well, and we've gotten to know him intimately over the years. He's prolific, to say the least. There isn't a dirty method he won't try to get uncompromising and exclusive photos of celebrities. He's infamous with famous people. A real character."

"I'm not surprised," I remark. "He fits the part perfectly."

The maître-D arrives and accompanies us to the back corner of the fancy restaurant where there's a candlelit table waiting just for us.

"I looked up this place online," I say to Axel as we sit. "And I discovered it's one of the most exclusive joints in all of Vancouver. It's apparently booked out for months, so how the hell did Lucas get a table for us here last minute?"

"Oh, Lucas has his way," Axel explains. "He's a master of the dark arts. I don't want to know what that man can do. It's pretty damn scary."

"How did your show go?" I ask. Ravaged have just performed at Vancouver's biggest arena tonight.

"Great," Axel says. "It's good to be performing again."

"What do you prefer?" I ask, genuinely curious. "Being in the studio or on the road?"

"On the road, for sure. Bishop and Caspian prefer the studio where we are purely creative. Coming up with new songs and all that. But Drake and I love the performances. We're the extroverts of the group."

"You really love being part of Ravaged, don't you?"

"Every single moment," Axel replies with fire in his eyes. Passion. "It's what I was born to do. And these are my brothers. I will die for them, and they'll do the same for me. Music and my boys. What else could I ask for?"

Axel orders for us. First of all, the wine. The most expensive bottle on the list.

"I hope you're paying," I say. Axel just smirks his irresistible smirk.

I dare not drink the stuff, thinking how many dollars each sip must be. I'm guessing the bottle is the same price as a condo back in Wisconsin. But Axel gulps it down, and I must follow.

And I start to get tipsy. No wonder it's so expensive when it must have a pretty high alcohol percentage.

"Right," I announce, slurring my words. "I'm going to get rough here."

Axel chuckles. "Oh, no. What does this mean?"

"I'm going to as you some personal questions that little Miss sober me wouldn't dare ask."

Axel laughs again. "Personal? I like the sound of that. Not many girls survive asking me personal questions."

"Well, ain't I lucky I'm not like most girls, then."

"Touché."

"Let's go through some basic ones," I say. "We really have to know each other for this whole fake relationship thing to work, right?"

Axel is just staring at me. Penetratingly.

"What?" I ask him.

He doesn't answer. He continues to stare.

"What?"

"You just look so good right now," he whispers.

I instinctively turn my head, not wanting him to notice the sudden blush that's spread over my cheeks.

"Um… let's go to these questions then," I stutter.

Axel continues to stare.

"Sure," he replies, evidently loving how much he's made color rush to my face.

"Okay. Favorite color?"

"Green."

"Like your eyes, got it."

"Next question, Maddie."

"Favorite kind of food?"

"Italian. These are easy."

"Give me a second. I'm coming to the hard ones," I reply. "Your biggest fear?"

Axel leans back in his seat. "Oh, that's a good one."

"You gotta give me an answer."

He takes a moment to think about it. He actually *seriously* thinks about it before answering in that dry witty way of his.

"Being normal."

"What does that mean?"

"I hated the small town life and everyone's small minds about things back there. Their attitudes about who you can be and who you can't. I always wanted to see the world instead of being normal. Having a normal life. That's the scariest thing in the whole freaking world for me."

"Oh."

Axel takes a sip of his wine. He furrows his brow. He's about to tell me something, something I reckon he's building up the courage to tell me.

He leans in close.

"I had a best friend when I grew up in Crystal River who was amazing at the guitar as well. Better than anyone I knew. He had the talent and the promise to be next fucking level, you understand? Gabe. We were inseparable as kids. Real close. We did nothing without the other, relying on each other as best friends. I mean, everyone thought we were twins, and we basically were. We would do anything for each other. We learned guitar together. We sang together. We were inseparable. And then, one day out of the blue, he was diagnosed with a rare form of childhood cancer that ate his little body up. I couldn't do a damn thing about it. Gabe died before he even reached ten years old, and it broke me. My best friend was robbed of his life way too young, and I've never forgotten that. Gabe wanted to explore the world and live life as a rockstar just like the ones he saw on TV. *That's* why I want to experience the world and soak up everything it can offer me. *That's* why I'm in the position I'm in now. I don't want to let that boy I was once best friends with down, even if he only now exists in my memory. I want to have the life Gabe never could have."

There are tears forming at the corners of Axel's perfect eyes. A cloud of grief hangs over him. His sadness makes me want to cry as well.

"People who come into our lives are more than just a memory," I whisper back in reply, my voice cracking under the melancholy I'm feeling from the stoic man. "Even if they're gone, they've changed our soul. They always do."

Axel nods. He's holding back those tears with everything he's got. He still wants to be perceived as the strong man. The cool rockstar. He should know he doesn't need to do that in front of me; I've seen enough of him to know the real man underneath that hard, playboy exterior. "I think that's the case too," he murmurs.

"You know you can talk to me," I tell him. "I may be your fake girlfriend and all, but I'm here. I can listen."

"Yeah, I know. Thanks, Maddie."

And then he straightens his back. The moment of emotion on his face is gone as fast as it came. He's back to being the charming cocky I-don't-give-a-damn-about-anything Axel the rest of the world knows.

For a moment there, I pierced through the façade. I've probably gone further than any girl's gone before, and he allowed me – for that brief moment – to see beyond the mask.

"Is that why you sleep around?" I ask. It's the alcohol that's allowing me to be so blunt. "Is that why you're addicted to the novelty of a new girl in every new hotel bed you sleep in? You want to *experience* the world?"

Axel leans back and chuckles again. He waves away my question like it's silly. "Maybe that's part of it. You're a real armchair psychologist, Maddie."

"You can still explore the world with a partner by your side," I tell him. "The right partner who may not want to settle in the suburbs and lead a normal life. The right partner who will follow you where you go."

"You're probably right, Maddie," he says dismissively. "You always seem to be. Now, where the fuck's our food?"

* * *

THE ENTIRE COHORT of paparazzi is still waiting for us as we step outside the restaurant.

I instinctively shy away from the probing cameras that are thrust towards my face.

Axel relishes the attention. He stands beside me, confident and basking in the fame.

He faces me then.

"How's this for a kiss?" he asks rhetorically.

Before I have a chance to react, he lifts me into his arms, making my legs wrap around his muscular waist, and deeply kisses me in front of everyone.

Wow. Freaking wow.

I better hold on tight, because I think I'm going to swoon.

I can hear the clicks of the paparazzi cameras behind me taking photos to document this crazy act, but I don't care.

This is the best kiss in the world.

41

MADDIE

We are silent the entire journey back to the hotel from the restaurant. I can practically hear my heart beating fast as the limo whizzes us through Vancouver's streets.

That kiss... My God, that kiss...

I'm dizzy. Elated with what just happened.

Wild.

The rockstar raised me up with just his arms. He drew me close against his body. He kissed me like I mean the world to him.

It was the most breathless I've ever been. Period.

I was really – *literally* – swept off my feet.

I sneak a glance over at Axel as we ride along. He's completely still. Staring dead ahead with those cold green eyes of his.

Can he hear my heart beating in my chest? He's not doing anything. How can he not be going crazy over what just happened?

Was that kiss even real or was it all a play for the

cameras? A little bait for the tabloids and nothing more? Axel had taken me completely by surprise with that grand gesture. I mean, come on, no way could someone fake something like that, even if what we're doing is one big lie. It can't have just meant *nothing*. There is no actor on earth who could kiss like that and not have it mean a thing.

I just don't know. Axel is one hell of a man.

What is going on in that brooding head of his?

My gaze lingers on his lips. Those full lips that took my own back there outside the restaurant with the confidence and skill that only comes from a man who knows *exactly* what he's doing.

Everything's a rush for me. We arrive back at the hotel, going underground through the secret entrance reserved for celebrities like Axel. We ride the elevator up to Axel's suite and then we enter the massive luxury room. All of that without saying a word to each other. I keep my eyes on the rockstar all the time, hoping to discover an answer to all my burning questions in him. In a look or something. But the man is impassive.

Emotionless.

Distant.

We get ourselves ready for bed, still without a word being exchanged.

I watch him remove his suit. He does so carefully. Gently. I watch those hands of his. Those talented hands that can play both a guitar and my feelings. Those hands that were wrapped around my waist as he pulled me in for that kiss...

He'd been so vulnerable to me at the restaurant. So open. Talking about Gabe like that... I just know that he doesn't speak about his childhood friend often or to everybody. I feel like I've been let into a corner of his humanity; his past that you can't find on a Wikipedia page.

There's a reason why he's so ambitious and determined to make it as a rockstar, and it's something none of his millions of fans could ever guess. A tragedy in his childhood that he's buried deep within, and which spurs him to pick up that bass guitar every day.

And he let *me* in on that secret.

He must trust me. He must view me as more than just some prop to enhance his reputation in the press.

I'm not like most other girls...

"Goodnight."

He speaks, barely looking in my direction as he says so.

It's the only word he's said to me since taking me in his arms outside the restaurant. A word that puts a dagger in my heart and a halt to my fantasies.

Is that it then? All over?

He must be telling me that the kiss meant nothing. That now it's time we go to sleep and simply and completely forget about the most magical moment in my life.

"Goodnight," I reply.

We slide into bed.

He turns the light off.

And then we're plunged into darkness.

There's more silence. This time it's deafening.

I lie still.

But then there's movement. Axel is moving. In the bed. Towards me.

I offer no resistance. I don't even move. I don't want to.

What's he doing?

I feel his hand on my cheek, tenderly guiding my face towards his side.

This?

And then he's kissing me. Slowly at first, and then with passion.

I feel his tongue, and I don't want him to stop. I've got

no energy left to refuse the man. No more reasons why I shouldn't do what we're doing.

The truth is... despite everything telling me this is wrong and against our fake relationship contract...

Screw the contract; I *want* this.

As if sensing the shift in my mind, Axel pulls back from the kiss and speaks the words I've longed to hear from him.

"I want you, Maddie. I *really* want you."

I don't reply. Instead, I reach for his face and pull him back towards my lips. There are no words left to say.

I want him. I want him. I want him.

Under the covers, his hand gently slips down my half-naked body until he's at the rim of my panties. I shudder as I imagine what he's going to do next.

I don't need to imagine much.

"Go ahead," I whisper to the man. "Touch me. You can do whatever you want."

He smiles then at my pleading, but I don't get much of a chance to swoon before he's kissing me yet again. Passionate and forceful.

Oh, God. This is too much to handle...

My panties prove no obstacle for the rockstar as his hand slides in.

"*Yes*," he breathes. "You are so addictive, Maddie."

"Please, Axel," I whine impatiently, his mouth still on mine. "Please..."

I've completely surrendered to what's about to happen. Even if I wanted to, I can offer no resistance. The rockstar's got me. Hook, line, and sinker.

Deep under the bedsheets, his middle finger guides over my folds and I instinctively toss my head back, shutting my eyes and holding onto the man - and the bed - for dear life.

"You want me to continue?" he asks with a cocky, confident calmness that stirs the tumultuous emotions inside me even more. I can barely mutter my approval, but I need him to keep going so bad it makes me dizzy.

And Axel can sense that.

His fingertip drifts into my wetness, parting me as easily as I need him inside me. I swallow in quivering anticipation as Axel's finger uncovers my clit and begins circling it masterfully. I moan and my mind goes blank.

"I've been wanting – *needing* – to do this for a hell of a long time," he murmurs into my ear. The air from his lips is scorching hot on my skin.

"How long?" I ask, stumbling over the words.

"Ever since I saw you naked in the bath touching yourself. Maddie, you wouldn't be able to comprehend how much that's made me want you. How much that's made me desire to touch you like the way you were touching yourself when I walked in. All the times I've fantasized about that moment... seeing you like that..."

Two fingers slip into me. His free hand grabs my hair and pulls my face back to his. His tongue works into my mouth as his fingers dig deep inside me.

I can barely breathe. I can't even gasp in pleasure. With my hair, he possesses my mouth against his own as his tongue mirrors the magic his fingers are committing in my pussy. My whole body rocks in unison with whatever he does. Axel is in complete control.

He *owns* my body.

We're so close.

"Don't stop," I groan. "Please don't stop. Tell me what you would've done..."

His thumb rubs my clit in small circles. The taste and smell of his overwhelms me. My legs go stiff. He's building me up and up and up...

"I wish I had walked in and sat by that bath and took the vibrator out of your hands," he growls under his breath in his deep manly voice. "I wish I had put my hand under the hot soapy water. I wish I had found your pussy like I've found it now. I wish I had made you scream my name in pleasure."

I'm on the edge of the cliff.

"I promised myself I would be careful around you," he continues in barely a whisper. "I promised myself I wouldn't do this. But... seeing you... so close to me. I can't think straight, girl."

And then I fall. My back arches as I gasp against his lips. Axel moans in victory as I call out his name.

"*Axel...*"

His fingers don't stop. He brings me back to the brink yet again like a fresh set of waves crashing on the shore.

"Don't you dare stop," I rasp between gulps of air. "Don't you dare."

But he does stop.

No, no, no.

"What..."

I open my eyes. Axel has let go of me and has stretched over to collect a strip of condoms. I don't know where the hell he's produced them from, but he hastily rips one open and rolls it over his member.

Oh, God. That shaft. So much... weight. Wow.

I gawk longingly at the space between his legs as my inner thighs wet with my need. I'm still so stunned by what his fingers have done to me. All I ponder about in my swinging mind is this irresistible man and gifting him the pleasure he yearns from my body.

And then he says it.

"You're mine, Maddie."

All my dreams come true...

He grunts as he climbs on top of my form and enters me in one swift, graceful movement. I moan as his arousal fills me entirely. His hands give my breasts attention, wrapping around my arched back to undo my bra. His eyes brim with lust as he takes in my freed tits. His thumb, still wet from my pussy, pinches my left nipple, making my eyes roll back into my head. I don't know what to focus on as he simultaneously plays with my breasts and rhythmically thrusts deep into my sex.

His necklace going wild around his neck, Axel bites at it and keeps it restrained between his teeth. It's so hot.

"This is what I've been wishing to do to you most of all," he snarls. "You are *mine*, Maddie."

"I'm yours..."

He makes the most intense sounds as he fucks me. Raw and primal noises of thrill as he claims me with every pump inside me. Making me his. He's brutal. Strong. Determined. I can't do anything besides give in to his pleasure and allow him to use me for his own desires.

And that turns me on so much I feel like I've gone crazy.

"I can never take my eyes off you," he growls. "It's not because I'm horny all the time, it's just that you're so fucking sexy."

"Oh, Axel..."

"Do you know how much I want you? How much I fucking *need* you?"

"I think about you a little more than I should," I whisper back.

Axel snarls. "There is no one like you, Maddie Leaver."

My hands grip the side of the bed as Axel roars one last time before finishing inside me, compelling me down into the soft mattress with a moan escaping from my own lips.

Spent, Axel finds his place next to me. He grunts again, softly this time, as he comes to rest with his arm enveloped around my breasts as if he doesn't want to let go. His eyes shut in blissful contentment.

I let out a long and satisfied sigh, and his heat mingles with mine. His sexy dark wavy hair, sweaty with exhaustion, wets the bed between us. I lean over and kiss his perfect cheek. Axel, eyes still closed, murmurs something indecipherable. I take it as a *thanks*.

I roll my head back onto the soft pillow and close my own eyes.

You know, I could lie like this all day until tomorrow evening and not move a muscle...

The night takes me, and I fall into the deepest sleep.

42

MADDIE

We've had sex. We've had sex. We've had *freaking* sex.

This morning has been a whirlwind. So much so that I've not had time to properly process what crazy decision I had made last night in that hotel bed.

I mean, Axel and I… we freaking broke our contract.

No funny business? Yeah. Right.

That flew out the door the minute that sexy rockstar dared to pull my face in for a kiss. And the weird thing is that I don't even feel like I've done something wrong.

It had felt *right*. It still feels right.

Have I gone over the edge?

Like I've said, I still haven't had time to even think through it all. We have to be at the airport incredibly early to board the private jet for the next stop of the tour. We were both too bleary-eyed this morning to even talk to each other when our alarm went off, let alone sit down and deeply discuss what the hell we've just done.

And what we do from here…

"Holy shit, there's a lot of people," I remark in the back of the limo as we pull up to the airport. I quickly grasp that this must be the first thing I've actually said to Axel all morning.

He leans past me to look out my window. He's so close. I could pucker my lips and kiss his neck if I wanted to.

Where do we stand with each other? Was last night a fatal mistake? Are we no longer fake boyfriend and fake girlfriend?

"Those are fans," Axel replies. He betrays nothing in his voice.

I wish that man could lower his cool guard down for a minute.

I follow his sight out the window at the waiting crowd. He's right, they are fans. They line up at the fence that forms the perimeter of the airport with signs for each of the members of Ravaged. There's a lot of cheering as our limo approaches. The driver is wary of accidentally running over some excited fangirl, so he creeps up to the gate leading onto the runway.

I try to duck from the attention that the fans are giving us. And I'm also so worried about making eye contact with Axel and betraying my burgeoning feelings for him. I look down at my phone and scroll aimlessly through social media instead. My Instagram has gone insane the last few days – ever since my "relationship" with Axel went public – that I have no choice but to see everyone's opinion of me and to see all the people try to send messages my way.

But the photo from last night – the one where Axel has me lifted in his arms as he kisses me – has gone up to another whole level entirely. It's fair to say that the photo is a hit. Looking through my social media, I can see that people's responses to it have been out of this world. There's fan fiction about the moment. I'm getting messages from everyone I know. Marie from work has even sent me more messages proclaiming her complete disbelief in the whole thing. She's practically drooling over it.

I don't know how to even *think* about it all. I wish it all could just disappear, but that's the job I've signed up for. This is my fifteen minutes of fame.

"I need to sign some things for the fans," Axel explains to me before he asks the driver to pull up in front of the adoring crowd. "It shouldn't take too long."

"Okay."

His words hit me in a way I do not anticipate. I feel kinda sad that I might have to board the plane by myself. It somehow feels like Axel is abandoning me. After last night, I just want to hold on to the man and never let go.

"I want you to come along," Axel continues, and it's like sunshine piercing through the crowds.

He doesn't want me to leave his side. This must mean good things.

We get out of the limo, and the fan screaming immediately intensifies. They're calling Axel's name over and over. It's like he's some cult leader or something.

But then I hear something else.

They're also calling my name.

Holy shit. No freaking way.

Of course, I'm famous as well. I've not really thought about things that way. That people see me as famous as Axel now. We come as a combined package. What was that nickname Lucas said we have now?

Wow, this is really something.

I want to tell them that they shouldn't be calling my name. That just a few days ago I was broke and in tears. That I've been a nobody all my life and actually prefer it that way.

Just like the charity function, Axel silently reaches for

my hand and holds me tight. Helping me. He brings us over to the crowd and starts signing posters of his face like it's the most normal thing to do.

"I love you."

"You're the best, Axel."

The fans all repeat how much they adore the man I've come to know. He takes it all with an easy smile and thanks. Meanwhile, I am overwhelmed. Of course I am. I'm a normal human being in this crazy situation.

A girl, seemingly my age, tries to say something directly to me. Seems like a question, but I can't make it out, so I lean close. She repeats.

"What's it like having Axel's cock in your mouth?"

I don't say a thing back in response. I'm in shock.

Axel notices something is wrong and looks at me.

"That's enough for today," he announces to the crowd. "I love my Canadian fans and I love Vancouver."

Still holding my hand protectively, he pulls me towards the gate to the airport. Security opens it for him, and we pass through.

I'm still shaking from the question.

I did not expect that at all.

"Are you okay?" Axel asks me on the tarmac.

"Yeah, I am."

"What did they say to you?"

I shrug. "Nothing."

"I should go back and confront them."

"It wasn't what they said," I lie. "I'm just... *tired.*"

Axel eyes me suspiciously.

"Are you sure you're okay?" he asks.

"Yeah. Just... last night..."

"Look, if you're having second thoughts, I understand," he says.

I wave him off. "We don't have to talk about it."

"You can leave now, if you want," he says. "Any time. Just talk to Lucas and he'll terminate the contract."

"Do you want me to leave?" I ask him.

Axel sighs.

What is he thinking?

He glances at the far-distant crowd of fans by the airport gate and then back at me. "No. I really don't."

"I don't either," I say. "Last night was... I can't put it into words."

"Neither can I," he replies.

"It was magical," I say.

There. I've said it. I've put it all on the line.

Axel smirks at that. Victory.

"Yeah, it wasn't so bad," he says.

I groan. "Typical Axel, shrugging it off like a cool rockstar."

"That's because I am, baby," he sneers jokily. But then his face turns serious, and he nods towards Ravaged's private jet. "I wouldn't mind you coming along, though. You've grown on me these last few days, Maddie."

"Yeah? I'm not too geeky for you?"

"Maybe a little, but I can look past it. What do you say, wanna come with me?"

I nod.

"I would very much like that."

"Good," Axel replies.

"Good," I reply.

We both look over at the private jet in unison.

"Shall we go and see the world?" he asks.

He takes my hand again.

"Yes, please."

We head up the steps together.

Lucas and the rest of the band are waiting for us on the plane.

"Last night's photo was the perfect touch," Lucas says as his way of greeting.

"Good morning to you too, Lucas," Axel replies.

"Well done, you two." Lucas does look elated. "That photo drastically helped bump pre-orders for the album; you can see it in the data."

"Oh nice," I reply, nodding. At least I'm doing a good job faking that I'm in love with this man currently holding my hand.

The other members of Ravaged thank me in turn.

"You're a natural," Drake tells me.

"People love you," Bishop adds. "And you seem to actually like Axel, though we don't know why."

"Shut up," Axel replies.

"Don't worry about sales or numbers," Caspian grunts at me. "Your wellbeing, Maddie, is more important than anything."

"Thanks, Caspian."

Axel's phone rings and he drops my hand to answer it.

"It's Astrid," he says. He listens to his mother for a moment before turning back around and handing the phone to me with a quizzical expression on his face. "She's asking for you."

Me?

I apprehensively take the phone from him and lift it to my ear.

"Hello?"

"Hi, Maddie. Can you do me a favor and stand away from my son for a moment?"

I mouth sorry to Axel and head towards the plane's bathroom. I speak to Astrid again the moment I lock the door.

"Is something serious happening?" I ask her.

"No," she replies. "I'm just checking to see if you're fine.

I've seen the news, and the photo, and I just want to check that you're handling everything okay. Are you, Maddie?"

"Yes, I am. Thank you."

I don't know about that.

"Is Axel being on good form? Is he looking after you?"

"He sure is."

"Ah, good. You know that if you ever need to talk to me about anything, I'm always there for you, right?"

"Yeah, thank you. You're amazing. You don't have to be like this, checking in on me and all that."

I really do want her to know how thankful I am. She's been too kind towards me. More than she needs to be.

"Maddie, you are family now," Astrid continues. "Of course I'll check on you. As of the minute you started dating my son, you're a member of Ravaged."

Yeah. I guess I am.

43

MADDIE

Ravaged's tour continues. All over the world. Everything is a blur of places and venues and hotels. One stop. Two stop. We travel all over North America, stopping at so many places that they become indistinguishable from hotel to arena to airport. Another city. Another country.

Another hotel room to fuck in.

Yeah, there is a *lot* of fucking on this little tour.

Let's just say that Axel makes time for me. Way more than what should be required in this deal…

Well, whatever the hell this deal has turned into.

It's so very different from what I'd imagined it would be when we started out on all of this. When I signed the contract, I thought I would be counting down the days until I was freed from the snare of this impulsive, arrogant asshole rockstar, but things have not turned out like that.

No, not at all.

Now we really are doing all the naughty things social

media is rumoring we're doing behind closed doors. We've taken this whole "fake" thing a bit too far.

And, hell, I'm *loving* it.

Let's just say we're always leaving each hotel room a mess due to our unbridled lust.

My God, Axel. That gorgeous rockstar with the green eyes that make me lose my breath every time they train on me. What can I say about the man other than the fact he's the best fuck I've ever had? He's unstoppable. I'm unable to say no to his power. He's always hungry for me, even straight after a show when he's shattered. I can see that hunger in his piercing eyes. He *always* wants me. He's *always* raring to go. Hard. It's an effort to keep up, for sure, but I relish every moment.

He knows how to touch me in places that make me squirm. Make me yelp out his name. Make my whole body shiver until I'm reaching the delightful cusp of orgasm.

My God, the orgasms. The constant fucking orgasms.

Every time I cry out, Axel loves it. I can tell it's his favorite moment when I climax. It's what turns him on even more.

Oh, I think he likes me. It's a sneaking suspicion.

In the time when Axel is not fucking my brains out, I'm usually just doing publicity work for Ravaged, as agreed in my deal. Sorting through reports and the like. It's interesting seeing how Axel's and mine fake relationship is impacting the public's perception of the band. It's good. Real good. I gotta hand it to Lucas; he's come up with a great idea and it's working wonders. People love that Axel found a girl. Especially someone like me...

A commoner.

I guess that's how everyone views me. I don't mind. I'm pretty normal in every way; the polar opposite of Axel. I think that helps in my favor with Ravaged's fans. Pre-orders for the upcoming album have shot up considerably.

I check in with Winston every couple of days, making sure I'm doing the right work. The fact is, I don't *really* have to work. I guess it's all a formality. But I want to. I don't want to be dead weight.

And I'm always ready for Axel to come home.

Oh, boy, am I ready.

After every show, he storms through the hotel door with a wild look. He takes me and pins me on the bed, stripping me down with both his hands and his eyes. I let him do so willingly. It's so hot to witness this powerful man take me as his girl. The sheer energy he has. The bountiful lust he has for me. All of that turns me on.

I don't dare question this relationship. It feels real. No one can fake the look in Axel's eyes as he fucks me.

One night, late at night as we're drinking champagne Axel's ordered to the room after another crazy sex session, I ask him a question.

"Will you teach me the bass guitar? Just a few notes?"

I'm sitting on the edge of the bed, wearing one of Axel's shirts. It's massive on me but tight on his muscles.

The man smirks and silently takes out his guitar from the case. He connects it to the amp. He moves in so that he's sitting behind me, his legs wrapped around mine. He places the bass guitar in my hands and whispers into my ear.

"Let me show you a thing or two, Maddie."

He teaches me a few rudimentary chords and scales, all the while pushing his semi-naked body against mine. I can feel his eager erection pressing into my lower back, and it turns me on. I just fall into the sound of his smooth, deep voice as he calmly instructs me on how to play his instrument. The man is so passionate about his music. So authoritative. His total command over the guitar makes me so goddamn horny.

    I play the chords back to Axel.
He laughs.
I laugh.
And then I'm kissing him.
I don't stop kissing him all night.

44

AXEL

I SEE Maddie in the crowd at the show and my cock immediately goes hard. It's not good when something like this happens as you're on stage in front of thousands of fans, but I just can't help myself. Seeing her there... the woman I'm going to fuck tonight. Man, it just makes me feel a lust deep within.

She's swaying to our music. She's so radiant there. One of the stage lights catches her and the sight of her illuminated in green forms a lump in my throat. She's so close to me on the front row that I bet she's drenched in my sweat.

I only have to reach out and I'll touch her.

I love that she's watching me perform at my best. I know how my talent makes her wild.

Oh, I can't wait to make her mine tonight...

My fingers strum up and down the bass guitar to the song. I turn away from the crowd – and especially Maddie there dancing away – to focus on Ravaged's frontman. Drake gestures at us to repeat the final verse of the song, making the crowd cheer and scream out the lyrics back to us.

I love this. I love being on stage, performing, with my bandmates.

And yet I can't take my mind off Maddie.

She's been the best thing that's happened to me for a long time, and I'm not even talking about just the sex. She somehow makes me a *better* person. That's sickening to think about, but it's true. It's like I want to be a better man around her. She pushes me that way.

I've clearly got something wrong with me.

I can't take my eyes off her.

Like the rest of the crowd, she's screaming along with the famous lyrics of this song. Words that we all created in Ravaged.

It's so fucking hot.

* * *

THERE ARE ALWAYS VIP fans waiting for us after the show. Rich people who've paid top dollar to meet the famous rock band straight off the stage like we're just trophies to be taken photos with. They've been put, waiting, in a special area backstage on the way back to our dressing room.

I *should* stop and say hello. I should sign their record sleeves. I *should* have my photo taken with the millionaires who've paid extortionate amounts just to greet me.

But instead, I stroll straight up to my woman who's waiting for me past these VIPs, and I whisper in her ear before she has a chance to react.

"I want to see your ass waiting to be fucked in my bed when I enter the door. So you better hurry back to the hotel, sweetheart."

Maddie gasps softly. Then she bites her lip.

I reach down and kiss her passionately. I don't care who sees us. I don't care that the entire room probably has their focus on the two of us.

I only care about this girl.

Our lips part, and then she's skipping away out of the room. I watch her ass as she leaves, practically drooling after her.

I think it's fair to say the next few hours of signing autographs and taking photos with the waiting VIPs are the most painful of my life.

45

AXEL

Another city. Another show. Another night with Maddie.

How many more nights will we get the chance to spend together? Just the rest of the nights of the tour, that's all, and there's not many of those left.

I don't want to think about it.

"Come on, we're in Chicago," I say to Maddie as we lie in bed together. She wants to stay here, but I've got other plans. "I'm taking you out for this city's famous pizza."

Maddie snuggles against my arm. It's so strange that I even allow her to do this. The minute any other girl would try this trick I'd have them thrown out of my hotel room.

But not Maddie.

I welcome her cuddles.

I sound like such a child. I've gone fucking soft.

"Okay, let's do it."

I glance down at the top of her cute head and smile. "Great."

"Should I call for the driver?" she asks me, rising up to meet my gaze.

"No," I reply bluntly. "No driver tonight. I just want a normal night with you. Like two normal people going for a normal date to get normal Chicago pizza. No more private planes and private limos and screaming fans. Not for one night. Let me be a normal fake boyfriend."

She nods. She gets it, thank fuck.

"Okay."

We manage to prize ourselves away from bed and get changed. Maddie watches me strip.

"I want to ask you," she says. "Your tattoo on the underside of your collarbone. *Don't let anybody get in your way.* What is that?"

"It's a quote from the band Oasis," I tell her. "You like it?"

"Yeah, I like it."

To hide from any lurking paparazzi outside, I purposely wear a beanie and large glasses.

"What are those?" Maddie asks me, her mouth hanging open at the sight of my comically round glasses.

"My incognito disguise."

"You actually own those glasses? You take them around with you?"

"Yeah," I reply. "In case I want to head out without a crowd following me around."

"And they actually work?"

I shrug. "They have before."

Maddie snorts derisively. "You look like a child molester."

"Gee, thanks."

We leave the hotel like any other guest and walk downtown Chicago's streets like any other ordinary person. It's nighttime, but there are still a lot of people on the roads.

The city is beautiful now. The skyscrapers all light up around us as we wander. It feels so weird being out and about like this, without an armed guard or with a horde of fans chasing me down.

It's almost like... *normality*.

"I'm like a princess who's been locked in a tower all her life sneaking into the nearby town," I remark to Maddie. She giggles.

"Welcome to being a regular person," she says. "The view's pretty good down here. Sometimes."

I constantly check behind me for any paparazzi. I'm not naïve enough to think that they may not be following me. I know their dirty tricks, especially Harold's. The dude's a real professional creep who'll follow me anywhere.

But no one's following us tonight.

Maybe I can live out this normal fantasy for one night...

We reach a cool-looking pizza place.

"Wanna go inside?" Maddie asks me, nodding towards the restaurant.

I take in a deep breath, readying myself for what's about to unfold. I won't admit it to my fake girlfriend, but I'm secretly terrified of situations like these. If someone in there recognizes me, then I will have to make Maddie and I run back to the hotel before we're swamped. It can actually be quite dangerous, especially with no security around to bring order to any crowds.

"I am fucking hungry," I say.

But, despite my fears, nothing happens. There's no crush of autograph seekers. No crowd control. Maddie simply orders a few slices for us to take away, and we leave.

Simple as that.

Normal fucking people.

We walk and talk through the streets.

"The tour has gone by so fast," Maddie says. I hear a touch of melancholy in her voice. She's sad too, it seems.

She has really grown to like me, hasn't she? A few weeks ago and she was ready to kill me in that office, now she can't get enough of me.

I'm not the only one to be changed by this fake relationship...

I don't know where we both stand. We've not really talked about what we've been doing. This whole next level of the relationship. It feels like something that once we talk about it, then it'll make it all *real*. Right now, it's like we're living in a dream.

A dream where I'm not a famous rockstar and she's a girl hired to do a publicity stunt.

A dream where we live in a world where maybe we *could* be boyfriend-girlfriend.

But we both know this is going to end. Soon.

"Yeah, it has," I reply, trying to keep neutral. No need to divulge any emotion.

"Like a tornado."

"Exactly."

"I've seen so much," she says quietly. "So much of the world. It'll be weird going home. It'll be weird trying to tell Mom about all this."

"Have you two spoken?" I ask.

Maddie shakes her head sorrowfully. "Nope."

"Has she said *anything* at all to you since that lunch?"

"No," Maddie replies. "We obviously have a rather... delicate relationship, my mother and me. The divorce between her and Dad was not good."

"Did it have a big impact on you? Even though you were only a kid?"

"I remember bits of it very clearly," she says. "I remember Mom telling me that all men are bad and that is why you should never trust a man, nor his attempts to woo you. They just want to get into your bed, *remember that*. She liked to also tell me that we all live in sin and deserve the pain in our lives. Yeah, the relationship has always been kinda delicate between her and me."

"It seems like your mom's attitudes have changed little since then," I remark.

"No. Mom is stuck in the nineties. The divorce drove her to fundamentalism, and that's where I lost her. To have religion or not is a personal thing, and I don't want to judge her for that, but it's when it becomes a barrier between us that things get difficult. But, hey, she's the only mother I've got, so I can't really cut her off. I just want her to be happy. I just want us to have a good relationship. It's hard, though, as you've seen."

I let her words sink in. "You're a good daughter, Maddie." I'm totally sincere.

I see a small tear glisten in her eyes. She quickly diverts her face away from mine.

"Thanks."

We round the corner and enter a park that has an amazing view of Lake Michigan. We simply stop and admire the water. The city behind us sparkles in the night. We're alone here.

It feels like a moment to say something.

"Thank you, Maddie, for coming along on this tour. Everything is better because of you being here."

Maddie takes in a sharp breath. "Thank you too, Axel."

"Good."

"I've had the time of my life doing this."

I laugh, breaking the tension. "We didn't get along at first, didn't we?"

"That's certainly true," Maddie replies. "But you've grown on me."

"Oh, have I?"

"The whole emo playboy rockstar seems to have a soft side underneath."

I snort. "Never."

"But thank you," Maddie whispers. "You've made this whole thing something else."

"So have you, Maddie," I reply. "So have you."

"So," she asks. "What next?"

I can barely contain my animalistic urge. "How about you and I head back to the hotel and I see that lovely ass of yours?"

46

AXEL

"What do you want me to do to you?"

My head is creeping up Maddie's leg. I decide to pin her wrist down to the bed with my other hand. That makes the girl smirk. She bites her lower lip as my fingers glide along her skin; she's unable to resist the expression of lust that passes across her pretty little face.

"I want you to fuck me," she says matter-of-factly. "Right fucking *now*."

And then, prizing herself free out of my grip, she spins around, revealing her enticing ass towards me.

Now that makes me hard.

"You really want me?" I ask her, my cock jolting awake. I'm definitely not begging. Simply asking with every fiber of my being.

"If you think you can have me," she teases. "If you think you possess what it takes to fuck a girl like me."

Fuck. She's good.

"And what kind of girl are you, Maddie? A good girl? A little geek in awe of the famous rockstar?"

She glowers at me from behind that perfect ass of hers.

"I'm a girl who wants to get down and dirty, Axel Stoll. If you think you've got it in you."

Damn.

"You want me inside you? This is so very different from the shy Maddie I've come to know. She wouldn't dare be a bad girl."

She wriggles her ass.

No...

"Shut up and take me," she commands. "I'll be a bad girl for you only if you fuck me like a man."

"You don't have to tell me twice," I reply with a growl. I immediately reach for the rim of her jeans, pulling them down to reveal that pink bare ass I've been fixated on in the darkest moments of my dreams. Maddie groans as I manhandle her.

I give her ass a little sharp spank.

Maddie yelps in surprise and pleasure, hardening my cock even more.

"*That's* for talking back to me," I explain in a deep voice, grabbing her wet sex with the palm of my hand. I'm determined to show this teasing naughty girl who's boss. "And for being such a bad girl."

"Mmm." Maddie's moan of approval is music to my ears. All the encouragement I need to grab her hair and pull her head back towards my mouth. My lips kiss the exposed part of her neck, leaving a wet mark of ownership as my free hand forces her back down, pushing her head into the soft mattress. This unleashes another ear-shattering moan from the girl.

Man, I love it when she does that.

I can't contain myself any longer. My lust for the girl is too overpowering.

"I'm going to fuck you," I sneer menacingly into her ear. "I'm going to do what I want with you, Maddie. I'm going to fuck you from behind. I want to feel your ass against my cock as I ram inside you over and over until you can't take anymore. Until you are begging with my name in your throat."

"Oh, *Axel...*"

I yank her hair back, making her yelp in pleasure yet again.

"Don't you dare say another word, Maddie Leaver," I order. "You understand me?"

She nods.

"I'm going to take control," I say. "And you do nothing but enjoy it. Surrender yourself to me."

She nods again.

"Now," I say, turning her head around to face my erect cock. "I want you to help me put on my condom. With your sweet, sexy mouth."

With a smile of delight, she obliges my command. She takes the condom packet I hand her and rips it open. Between her teeth, she grasps the condom. Her mouth covers my cock as she uses her lips to slide the latex covering over my thick, pulsating member. I watch her submissive act the entire time with fire in my belly.

This is so fucking hot.

Done with my command, Maddie flicks her light brown hair back out of her face and looks up at me with expectant eyes.

I turn her around with my brute strength and drive her forward back into the mattress, my right hand controlling her back and my left hand squeezing her gorgeous ass. I angle my cock for her wet sex between her legs and then I come inside her with a moan from both her and me. Maddie whimpers into the bedding as I tilt my head back and allow myself the pleasure of feeling her inside warmth.

I don't slow down. I don't give her a chance to collect her senses before I'm giving her long and heavy strokes. Her bare ass bounces against my pelvis as I fill her soft, wet pussy with my manhood. My sweaty hair sticks to my forehead as I thrust into her, my mouth open uncontrollably.

"You feel so good, Maddie," I grunt. "Your body was made for me. You're *completely* mine."

Intensity satiates me.

Maddie gasps as her pussy accommodates me. I lean over her in an effort to thrust in even deeper. Maddie can't clench back her screams. Going against my explicit instruction of remaining silent, she commences to repeatedly moan my name over and over out that sweet mouth of hers.

"Axel... Axel... Axel..."

Hearing her sugary voice gasp for me forces me to the point of climax. I can't stop myself now.

Who's really in control here? Her or me?

My hand squeezes her ass tighter, eliciting another yelp from the girl, as I'm brought racing to the edge.

"Oh fuck, Maddie."

"I want you to finish for me," she whispers. "I want you to cum."

I cry out her name one more time before I unleash myself inside her. Maddie utters my name again as I finish.

"Axel..."

My body is covered in sweat as I pull out of her. Maddie turns around, admiring my naked torso. I like it when she looks at me like that. That desire in her eyes.

"Not too bad," she says.

I growl. "Is that your verdict? Not too bad?"

"Yep."

I flick my wet hair away from my eyes and lower myself to her level. "I'll show you *not too bad*, Maddie."

Before she can reply, I shoot forward for a long, hard kiss. She melts into my mouth. She tastes of exhaustion and lust.

Feeling her lips on mine, my cock is already hardening. Ready for round two.

I'm really going to show her not too bad.

A taste of your lips calls to me
A thing I can never forget
I wish
Oh, how I wish
I can call you mine

47

MADDIE

I DON'T SLEEP all night, and neither does Axel. It's Staying At Her Place's release day. D-Day. Or *A-Day* as I like to call it. Axel doesn't like that I do.

But whatever the day's title is, it's officially here. The new album unleashed onto the public.

And we've yet to see the rating results, and it's *killing* us with anticipation.

It's also the last day of the tour. We're in Boston, hunkered down in our hotel as we wait for how Staying At Her Place is received.

Sure, the band cares about reviews and the social media reaction, but what they're really looking at are sales. Do their fans *like* it? Do they like it enough to make sure it beats Tainted Lives' new album?

That's the question that remains unanswered.

I sneakily listen to a few tracks from the rival band's album on my earphones. For obvious reasons, I don't tell Axel what I'm doing. I know he wouldn't like it. Tainted

Lives are good. No wonder they're competing with Ravaged. But I still think Axel's band is better. I am a *bit* biased, though.

Axel, meanwhile, spends the night trying to sleep by listening to classic rock songs that inspired him as a kid.

It's actually kind of sweet.

The morning arrives, and as soon as Axel and I make our coffee, the rest of the band comes storming into our suite.

"You guys all look tired," I remark.

Drake shrugs. "Couldn't sleep."

"Me neither," adds Bishop.

Caspian nods along.

"I thought you were all cool rockstars who didn't give a shit," I say.

"If there's anything to give a shit about," Drake replies. "It's our new album. You know how much sweat and fucking tears have gone into this?"

"I imagine quite a lot," I reply.

"That's putting it mildly."

"Has anyone heard from Lucas yet?" Bishop asks. "He'll be the one who finds out any information first."

"No news at all," Axel confirms, shaking his head.

"Damn."

"We'll just have to wait until there's any news," Drake says.

"Agreed," Caspian replies.

"I'm going back to my room," Bishop announces. "Tell Lucas to call me."

"I'll walk with you," Caspian says.

Drake follows them out the door. "This is it, guys. The moment we've waited for."

I wave goodbye to the boys and sit down on the couch

with a sigh. *I'm* stressing out and I'm not even a member of the band.

"I can't imagine what's going through your head now," I say to Axel. "I'd be going crazy if I were you, but you seem so calm."

Axel saunters over to me. "Breakfast? I'm going to order some for myself."

"Yes, please."

He smiles and picks up the phone for reception. "I'm always hungry when I'm nervous."

"Okay, you order something, and I'll have a shower. I need to do *something* to take my mind off all this, even if it's just to wash my hair."

I take my time in the bathroom. I keep expecting Axel to burst through the door with news from Lucas, but it never comes. I just close my eyes and run the warm water over my face and try to drown out all the stress on my mind.

I hope today goes well. For Axel's sake.

I emerge from the bathroom to see a sight arrayed before me.

"You've ordered everything on the breakfast menu?" I ask Axel, open-mouthed.

The suite's main table is covered with all the dishes that the hotel has to offer in the morning. Axel stands there at the side of the table proudly.

"I did tell you I get hungry when nervous," he says. "I couldn't decide what to get, so I got everything."

"How much did this all cost?"

"I don't know, and I don't care. I have enough money for a hundred lifetimes."

"You're crazy, Axel. You know that?"

"Sorry, but I've already started eating," he says. "I couldn't wait any longer. You take long-ass showers."

"That's because I'm a girl and actually clean myself, unlike you."

I take a seat at the table and help myself to bacon and scrambled eggs.

Axel grins at me from across the table. He thinks he's so cool by doing all this. He's so excited that he's like a boy on his birthday. Well, at least it keeps him from stressing out over the album's release.

There's a loud ring. It's Axel's phone. He takes it out of his pocket and puts it on loudspeaker for me to hear.

"Hi, Lucas," he says. "It's Maddie and me here."

"Hey guys."

"You've got news?"

"I have."

"Well, tell us. Quit being so dramatic."

"It's good."

"Yeah?"

"*Real* good, Axel. The final numbers are yet to come in, but it's safe to say that Ravaged has smashed Tainted Lives out of the water."

"Lucas, don't fuck me about..."

"I'm not fucking you about, Axel. This is looking to be one of the best opening days ever in music history."

"Fuck off."

"I'll tell the rest of the boys."

Lucas hangs up, and Axel immediately leaps up from his chair. He does a little geeky dance around the room with the biggest smile on his face.

I rush over to him and kiss him.

"We need to put on some fucking music," he says, already reaching for his phone.

From the speakers, the room erupts in the first song from Staying At Her Place. A fast-beat track. Axel spins away from me into the center of the room, dancing along to the music ecstatically. I laugh from the sidelines as he brings out a parade of the most awkward dance moves just to show off to me. The shuffle. Raising the roof. The cowboy. All the classics you'd find at a cheesy wedding. Axel's feeling free; unembarrassed to be so joyful around me.

And it's beautiful.

"I can't believe it," he whispers to me as the music fades, his beautiful green eyes full of tears. "We did it."

"Yes, you did it."

"You were right there beside me," he tells me. "All the way."

I nod towards the suite's record player.

"Put on the album," I say. "Properly. Not through your phone, but on vinyl."

"Of course."

Axel takes the new album out of its sleeve and places it on the record player. Ravaged's music once again fills the room.

I bid Axel to come to me with a curl of my finger.

"I'm going to give you a reward," I coo.

I slowly – and seductively – lower myself down onto my knees. I undo Axel's pants until I see his bulge. Axel groans in expectation.

I torment him for a minute with my tongue, but then Axel grabs my hair and sexily thrusts my head towards his crotch, practically begging me to stop fucking around.

My mouth becomes full of him. He groans again. His hips sway into me as I suck him off while his music plays around us.

48

AXEL

Maddie's tongue teases the tip of my penis. Her mouth wets my cock as she takes me in. She drags her tongue under me, closing her lips around the head. I'm pulsating inside her mouth.

I lean back, unable to control even my own body.

"I can't resist you, Maddie."

She likes that. Her deep moan at my comment is proof enough.

My hand grabs her hair, encouraging her to work harder and stronger. I really can't resist her.

"I'm going to finish," I grunt. She's making me reach this so fast. I've never felt anything like this before. Her mouth is so goddamn perfect.

Maddie's tongue swirls around my tip, continuing to torture me. I'm struggling to clench myself back with every ounce of strength within me.

Ravaged's music continues to play in the background. The new record-breaking album.

"I'm not going to last much longer," I whisper.

She blinks up at me. It's so sexy.

She's loving this domination she has over me. My hips jerk and vibrate. My life force is threatening to blow.

All I'm thinking about is Maddie and her goddamn beautiful mouth and the awful amazing things her tongue can do to me.

My album is on top of the charts and I'm getting the best fucking blowjob of my life.

I'm on the fucking top of the world.

I peek down at Maddie. Her soft lips around my shaft. Her hand around my hard cock.

Fuck, the things she does to me.

This girl sure knows how to make me feel like a king.

49

MADDIE

Without a doubt, the boys of Ravaged appreciate how to throw a party. We party all day, celebrating Staying At Her Place's massive chart-topping success. Drinks flow. The music's loud. We dance our souls away.

By the time we catch the band's private jet back to Los Angeles, it's the morning after A-Day. The Boston show last night was a chaos of drunken antics on stage. The audience didn't seem to mind the rockstars turning up excited and drunk out of their minds. In fact, they *loved* it. There was a real party atmosphere in the stadium as Axel and his band mates tore through their famous songs with wild abandon.

I myself was pretty drunk off champagne by that point as well; so much so that I ended up screaming every word of their songs. I've really come to learn all of Ravaged's lyrics off by heart now, and it shows when I see them live. My voice is nearly gone from all the shrieking.

When we're boarding the plane, I get a phone call from Winston. When his name flashes up on my screen, I feel a bit sick. That might have to do with all the alcohol I consumed yesterday. I'm really feeling it today.

But I still answer. I'm professional, even when I'm totally hungover.

"Hi, Winston."

"Hello, Maddie."

"Is there a problem?" I ask.

I may still be a little bit drunk.

"No problem," Winston replies. "I'm just calling to admit that I was wrong."

"Wrong about what?"

"Your performance. Your job. Maddie, I've seen Ravaged's album sales figures. They're incredible. You've really done a great job. You know that you'll always have a job with me if you ever want to properly get back into the marketing game."

"Thank you, Winston."

"You've really done good, Maddie."

Maybe it's because I'm still tipsy that I ask Winston the next question. I certainly wouldn't have done it sober. "Winston, you and Astrid Stoll, what's the deal with that? I haven't forgotten about that restaurant..."

There's a long sigh down the line and I immediately regret ever asking my boss the question.

Such a loose-lipped idiot, Maddie.

But instead of getting mad, Winston just quietly speaks up.

"Keep this between us, Maddie, but Astrid Stoll is the girl who got away."

* * *

Lucas sits down next to Axel and me as we're about to descend into LA. Axel is fast asleep while I'm trying my best not to throw up. This hangover is not going well.

"How's everything going?" Lucas asks me softly, trying not to wake the rockstar.

"Good. I had a bit too much yesterday, though. I had a bit too much fun and now I'm feeling it."

"So did I," Lucas replies. "How has the fake relationship gone these last few weeks?"

Do I tell the manager that we've broken our contract about a million times in bed over the last few weeks? Do I tell him this no longer feels like a fake relationship, although Axel and I haven't even properly spoken about it yet?

Do I tell him that I have doubts about everything but still can't stop myself from falling for rockstar temptation?

There is technically nothing fake about this relationship, and yet I still don't really know what Axel thinks about me.

Oh boy, it's such a mess.

"Yeah, all good."

That's my reply.

"You know that it's going to end after today, right?"

It's what I've been dreading. Lucas doesn't need to remind me. After today, there are no more excuses for Axel to see me. No more shared hotel rooms. No more time spent together.

After today, that's it.

The finality of this fake relationship is worse than my hangover, or any hangover can be. The thought that this is the end of the greatest few weeks of my life really makes me want to vomit.

"Yeah. All over."

"You should get your share of the money in the next few days once it's cleared through the banks."

"Thanks, Lucas."

"I'm glad we had you, Maddie," he says quietly. "This wouldn't have been the success it was if it wasn't for you."

I just nod.

I really want to be sick. This is the worst day of my life. Tomorrow I will be just a memory for Axel.

This was never real.

This was always fake.

Lucas gently wakes up Axel by rubbing his shoulder. The rockstar groans in discomfort.

"We're about to land," Lucas tells him.

"Wonderful. I could sleep for a week."

"I know it's not the best time to go over things, but I thought I'll give you guys a heads up over what's going to happen," Lucas tells us both. "We'll pretend the relationship lasts a few more months and then simmer it out. But you two won't have to see each other in the meantime. You won't have to do a thing, Maddie."

"Sure."

"Then what we can do is have Ravaged release a break-up album. We won't use your name at all, Maddie."

"That sounds great," Axel replies. His tone is completely neutral. I can't guess what he really thinks.

Is that all I am? A commodity to sell more albums?

"So, everything is all over?" I ask Lucas, hoping to get Axel's attention. I want him to realize, like me, how final this all is. "Just like that?"

"Yes," Lucas replies. "But first, I've got a great idea for one last thing before the tour ends properly. Something that'll boost those sales records even more. It's a genius idea, coming from a genius."

"What is it?" Axel asks.

Lucas grins. "How about I get you two on a talk show together? Tonight?"

50

MADDIE

In LA, Astrid is waiting for us at the airport. The boys of Ravaged rush off the plane and embrace her in one big hug. I stand at the steps leading from the jet and smile on. There's a lot of love between them all.

"Well done," Astrid congratulates the band.

She gives me a little wave and that makes me comfortable enough to join them.

"How was the tour?" she asks me. "Did the boys treat you right?"

"You know we do, Mrs. Stoll," Drake replies.

Astrid raises an eyebrow towards me, waiting for my answer.

"They were better than good, Astrid."

"Good to hear."

She still doesn't know about the little fact I'm not really her son's girlfriend. She's still been kept in the dark about that by Lucas and Axel. It doesn't feel right, especially now that it's definite the contract is coming to an end.

She has the right to know before all this comes public. I don't want her to think Axel's played me around or broken my heart.

Although he will after tonight. And it's all my damn fault for letting my heart get involved in this simple business transaction.

"Maddie has really helped," Axel says to his mother. "I don't want to think about what we would've done without her, or where the album would be."

"Or your reputation," Astrid adds.

I blush. "Shut up, Axel."

I playfully punch his arm. He doesn't even flinch.

"Well, it's the truth," he replies.

"Yeah," Bishop says as he wraps an arm around my shoulder. "I first thought it was going to be a terrible mistake having this girl along for the ride, but she's actually made Axel bearable for once."

"Don't make me fight you in front of my mother, Bishop."

"You wouldn't even last ten seconds against me, Axel, and you know it."

"Good to see all your recent success hasn't stopped you two acting like little boys," Astrid remarks.

Caspian growls. He doesn't want any trouble. "Paparazzi can see us," he warns. "We're out in the open here."

"Your album has been a massive success," Astrid continues. "Even I've been listening to it. I mean, you can't *not* to when it's the only thing the radio plays."

"So no Tainted Lives?" Bishop asks.

Astrid winks. "Who's that again?"

The boys laugh, and all of them except Axel head back to the plane to collect their things.

"So it was a good tour, then?" Astrid asks us both, her

eyes dancing between us. "You two are okay?"

"Yeah," I reply, trying hard to swallow the lump in my throat.

Axel just nods at his mom.

It's so infuriating that I can't see what that man's thinking. It could be my overreactive imagination, but I swear he's been completely unmoved by the fact I'm going.

Does he want me out of his life? Has he tired of me?

What does he even think of me?

Who knew fake dating a rockstar would be so stressful?

"Is it alright if I just talk to Astrid?" I quietly ask Axel. "Just one-on-one?"

"Fine." He might seem fine, but the look he throws me is full of suspicion.

Truth be told, I've been meaning to talk to Astrid. I didn't think I would get the chance to, but I feel like she needs to know something about what has been going on. She's been way too kind to me, and I've felt like a total fraud around her.

This is all totally spur of the moment, but my gut tells me she should know. Lucas and Axel are wrong in keeping this a secret from her.

Axel wanders back to join his bandmates, and so I wait until he's definitely out of earshot before I turn back to Astrid.

"There's something I want you to know."

Astrid regards me with concern. I hate having to do this to her – to tell her I've been lying to her – but I know I won't be able to live with myself if I don't.

"You know you can talk to me about anything, Maddie. It's just what I told you on that call when you first started the tour."

Her words hit me more than I thought they would. Everything comes back to me. These last few weeks that have been the best and also the worst of my life. Weeks where I've truly felt something more than I ever thought I would and also weeks where I've felt like I've lost myself. I've been building up all of this within myself and I've spoken to no one about it. Not my mother, not Lucas. And certainly not Axel. It's like my heart has been wrapped up tight in wire and I can't breathe.

So as Astrid looks at me with genuine care, the tears start to well.

"No one understands what this has been like," I say, mumbling and stumbling over my words. "I've had to keep it all to myself and now I don't think I can go on. God, I sound so self-pitying."

"No, you don't," Astrid replies. "Just tell me what's going on, Maddie."

I try to speak again, but the tears make it all incomprehensible. Astrid sees this happening and rubs her hand on my shoulder. Her caring touch gives me the strength to just get it out.

"The relationship I've had with your son is fake." That sentence carries with it weeks of buttoned-up stress. I just say it coldly. I need to tell her this, and there's no point ducking and diving around the point. I don't care about the contract and not being allowed to tell anyone. "It was all for album sales. None of it was real. I thought it... might've been at some point, but I was being delusional. It was all a business deal to sell some albums and make Axel look respectable in front of the press and fans. I've been lying to you, Astrid, and that's the worst thing of all. I'm so, so sorry."

"I know."

"What?" I ask her.

"Oh, I knew all that, Maddie."

"That the relationship has been fake?"

"Yes."

"Did Lucas and Axel tell you?"

Astrid shakes her head. "I didn't need anyone to tell me, Maddie. I'm a mom, and I know my own son. I knew what the situation was the minute I met you."

"Oh."

"But I also knew something had to be done about Axel. I knew his nickname. I knew his reputation. I know what my son needs. He needs a girl. I knew it would take time and a strong woman to break through into his heart, and it turns out that you are just the strong woman needed. Just as I suspected the first time I met you in that ridiculous nightclub."

Now it's my turn to shake my head. "I don't know if that's the case, Astrid. I don't know if I'm the girl Axel needs or wants."

There's a long pause as Astrid thinks about my comment. She doesn't seem surprised at all by my confession. She's not angry at me.

She's complimenting me.

Her eyes flicker towards the private plane behind me. Towards Axel. None of the band can hear our little interaction.

Finally, she speaks.

"Time will tell, Maddie. Time will tell."

51

MADDIE

I DON'T GET to see Axel all day once we're driven away from the airport in separate cars. Boom. He's gone just like that. Lucas tells me that he's off doing a whole round of press interviews for the new album whilst I'm taken to my new condo. Lucas had the storage unit guys send all my stuff here already. Everything's neatly unpacked by the time I arrive at the place.

I walk in and stand in the middle of the spacious living room and let out a sigh. At least I can afford this place now, thanks to all the money I've earned being a rockstar's fake girlfriend.

But everything feels so empty. There's no Axel here. I've literally been dropped off without even a goodbye.

Time to start the rest of your life, Maddie Leaver.

I start to unpack my bags from the tour, but I give up pretty quickly. I have no energy for this just yet.

I just need time.

Time to get over what were the unexpectedly best weeks of my life. Time to move on past Axel Stoll. Time to be a normal human being again, no longer on the front pages of newspapers and social media feeds.

Instead of unpacking, I simply take a shower. One of my *long-ass* ones, as Axel would say.

Oh, Axel.

How can I already be missing that man?

That man I once despised, but who showed me his vulnerable side. The man who would go to any lengths to protect me. Make me feel special. Who cared for me.

I miss him so much.

I cry in the shower thinking of how it's all coming to an end.

After tonight, it certainly will. I just have to get through this damn talk show. Another fake situation where I have to act like nothing is wrong sitting next to Axel when actually my insides spin around in agony. Tonight will be the last time I see the man in person. From now on, I'll only be seeing him in advertising, and on social media. I will hear his voice, but he won't be talking to me. He'll be on the radio; a rockstar talking to his fans.

I will become nothing but a footnote on Axel Stoll's Wikipedia page.

I have only myself to blame. I was the one who allowed my heart to be put on the line. Axel seems to be coping perfectly fine without me. He's not the one who allowed feelings to develop.

I'm the one getting hurt here.

And it's all my damn fault.

After my long-ass shower, I just sit on the couch until there's a knock on the door.

"Hello?"

A man is standing there outside my condo.

"I'm here to collect you to the TV studio, Miss Leaver."

I follow him to the limo parked outside just for me.

Not long now before all this rockstar glitz and glamor is gone from my life.

* * *

I DO GET to see Axel again. This time it's when I'm in the makeup chair at the TV studio. I was bundled through the back entrance away from any fans by a horde of security guards and forced into this random room where someone applies strong makeup to my face. Apparently, you need a lot for TV.

Axel comes in late. He's clearly had a rough and long day doing interviews. There's an entire crew surrounding him when he comes in. They guide him to the chair next to me and he sits with a sigh.

"Had a good day?" I ask him, trying my damn hardest to act nonchalant and not that this is the moment I've been waiting for since I stepped off the plane.

"Yes."

It's his only reply. Nothing flows between us. He doesn't even look at me, instead regarding his handsome reflection in the makeup mirror. It's like he's a different man. The tour has ended and I'm now just another girl to him. Another past fling, as I've always feared.

We don't say another word to each other as makeup is applied to us by an entire team of artists. Then, suddenly, I'm whisked to another part backstage.

"This is where you can watch the beginning of the show," a production runner tells me in a hushed voice. I want to ask them where Axel is, but I bite my tongue. I'll surely see him again in the moment, out there on stage with all the lights and cameras trained on me.

I have no choice but to just stand here and watch the talk show. Back in Wisconsin, I used to watch some of this. I liked it back then, but being here and up close to all the action makes the whole thing seem hollow in a way. Fake entertainment. I used to watch all this before I met Axel and the entire world flipped on its head.

The host is all merry and dramatic. It's as false as the damn relationship.

He suddenly says my name. I've been daydreaming – completely forgetting that I'm about to head out on this stage – that I have to shake my head to compose myself.

Behind me, Axel appears.

"Out we go," he whispers into my ear. I wish he doesn't stop talking.

But then we're out in view of all the cameras. The stage lights are blinding, just as the paparazzi camera flashes once had been. I find myself going through the motions of what I've seen guests do on talk shows before...

Wave to the crowd.

Hug the host.

Smile.

Sit down.

Pretend like your whole life isn't crumbling apart inside.

Axel takes his place next to me. Unlike all the other times on the tour during our contract, he's not holding my hand to guide me through this wild experience.

I strain my eyes and try to look into the audience. They're all a blur. I do make out one figure sitting in the front row, though.

Astrid.

What's she doing here?

She's nodding at me. Encouraging me to be strong with that caring expression of hers I've come to love.

At least I have one friend in this crazy world.

There are some questions from the host aimed at Axel. Things about the album. Congratulating him and the band on the success. The rockstar grins his charismatic smile and answers smoothly. It's like none of this even remotely touches him.

Meanwhile, I, on the other hand, feel like I'm a walking stick of nervous sweat.

"And how is the relationship going between you two?"

Suddenly the question is directed at me.

I don't know what to say. I didn't even think of an answer.

Do I lie?

But before I can open my mouth and make a total fool of myself, Axel takes my hand and speaks for the both of us. His touch, although wanted, doesn't feel right.

Fake.

"Oh, things are great. We can't get enough of each other."

I want to stand up and tell everyone that this is all fabricated. All bullshit. I'm just some girl who was broke and desperate enough to be manipulated by some sexy rockstar to do his bidding. Make him look good. None of this is real.

But I don't.

I just sit there and smile like a dutiful partner.

I laugh in all the right places.

Axel and the rest of the band appear to perform a song from Staying At Her Place. They must've arrived during the interview; I didn't see them earlier.

Then the lights go down and I'm guided off the stage into the wings. The host quickly thanks me, and I'm scurried away into the darkness.

Lucas appears by my side.

"Good job, Maddie. I've asked the bank to transfer the rest of those funds into your account immediately."

"You're rich now."

It's Axel. He's swooped in by my shoulder like a bat.

"Thanks."

"You never have to worry about a thing for the rest of your life," he says.

"Is this the end?" I ask him, knowing the answer already.

"I guess so," he replies.

"I guess you'll go back to your exciting life, then. Without a partner. Without a care in the world. Good old Active Axel."

"Yes."

So. That's the end of our deal and he can't even give me a proper goodbye? I know I'm being selfish, but I'm getting so irate by his sheer ineptitude for showing any kind of emotion towards me. Not even a *sliver* of affection for the girl he's spent weeks fucking.

"Are you going to say anything to me, Axel?"

He shrugs. Lucas watches on. "What's there to add?"

"You could say goodbye. You could say that I meant – *mean* – something to you. Do I mean something to you?"

The man just shrugs again. "I don't know what you're getting at, Maddie. We did a business transaction. Now it's over. Done."

"Just like that?"

"Just like that."

My hands curl into fists. I want to cry *and* lash out at the man in unison.

But instead, I raise my chin in his direction and direct all my anger at that smug, arrogant, gorgeous face of his.

"You're a real asshole, you know that?"

The words come flying out of my mouth. I can't take them back now, nor do I want to.

I simply spin around on the spot and march out of there.//
I hear him call my name behind me. Once. Twice.//
But I don't care.//
I'm out of that world. That fake bullshit rockstar world.//
Forever.

52

AXEL

MADDIE IS GONE.

That's it?

Yep. It's over. All done.

And I am the *asshole*?

Give me a fucking break.

I'm surrounded by people here backstage at the talk show. Producers and crew and production runners all swarming around me like busy bees.

And yet I feel totally alone in this crowd of people.

Before I even have a moment to process the girl that I've just spent weeks getting to know intimately walking away from me for the last time, my mother appears by my side in that silent, graceful way of hers.

"You know I love you, Axel, but you're an idiot if you let that woman go."

I sigh. Mom is the last person I want to talk to right now. Especially about Maddie. I can already sense there's an argument or, even worse, a *lecture* brewing in the air.

"She left of her own free accord," I reply bluntly.

That's not enough for Mom.

"Did she?"

I bristle at my mom's passive aggressiveness. She knows how to make me squirm.

"She's got my money," I retort. "She isn't sticking around. This is her own choice."

"You think she wants to leave?" Mom asks with a raised eyebrow. "Come on, Axel, you're smarter than that. I raised you to be more aware than this. Do you not know her? Do you not know her feelings for you?"

"Mom..."

God, I sound like such a whining schoolboy when it comes to her little lectures.

"You do not need me to tell you that Maddie Leaver would have traveled with you to the ends of the earth, Axel. She gave up everything for you. A normal life. Her own mother."

"So you know everything was fake, then?"

She smiles. "Was it, though? *Really*? Was it ever fake?"

"We signed a business deal."

"What you two had – *have* – is a whole lot more than a piece of paper."

I wave away her stupid rhetorical questions. "I don't want to talk about this."

"You say you want to soak up what the world has to offer you? Well, Axel, Maddie is, by far, the best thing that's been offered. I know my own son better than he knows himself, it seems. I know what you truly think about Maddie. Cut out the rest of that rockstar bullshit and you will find that you are just two kids in love."

I grunt. "Leave me alone, Mom."

She shakes her head. I can sense her disappointment in me. And that stings.

"Goodnight, Axel."

"Goodnight, Mom."

And just like Maddie, she walks away. I watch her go.

But *fuck me*, I know she's right. Every word she said to me.

She's always fucking right.

53

MADDIE

I cry in the taxi all the way back to my new fancy condo. God, I must be such a lovely sight for the poor taxi driver. I mean, I do try to hide my sobbing, but who am I kidding? I must look like such a mess.

I should never have trusted Axel Stoll with my heart.

I should have listened to my mother and her words of wisdom about men and relationships. Axel simply has proven my crazy Mom right. All men really are out for one thing and that one thing only.

This is all my own making. My own fault.

The taxi pulls up to my place. I wipe my eyes before I pay the taxi driver, handing him a big tip for having to deal with my sorry ass, then step outside into the night air of LA.

Thank God my new neighbors can't see me crying in the darkness.

I glance around just in case anyone's peeking through their windows. I'm so paranoid.

And I'm so alone.

My God, I feel alone.

Yeah, I have all the money from Lucas and Ravaged for a job well done, but that means nothing when you have a broken heart. No amount of money can fix a wound like that.

The way he didn't seem to care. The way he just... let me go. Forever. Without a word in protest.

Simply to seem cool.

Yeah. I should've known the deal when I started to lose my feelings to a rockstar. Totally my fault. I played with fire and got burned.

I lean against the wall of my condo building. I spot some motorbike parked across the street. It must've been there when the taxi pulled up.

Oh.

That motorbike. And the rider...

It can't be...

Axel Stoll takes off his helmet, revealing that impossible face of his.

"Stay away," I tell him. I don't want him seeing me like this. In tears and breaking down.

He shouldn't be here. How is he even here?

"I'm happy to wait," he says.

"Wait for what?"

"For you."

"Just go away, Axel."

He stands next to his motorbike across the street from me. The distance between us is far.

"I've got a million places to be tonight with this whole album release. Parties. Interviews. But trust me when I say, Maddie, there is nowhere else I'd rather be than with you. Here."

"Bullshit," I retort sharply. "You *literally* just told me the relationship is over. Don't give me this crap."

He sighs. "That was wrong of me to say."

"Yeah, so wrong. Now it's time for you to go, as you promised."

"It's hard to process what's going through my head and my heart right now."

I cross my arms and stare him down. I've already put up with his bullshit for far too long to trust his words easily again. "Really?"

"I know you can't trust me, but just give me a chance."

"I've given you a chance, but a chance for *what*, exactly?"

"A chance for us," he says. "For us to be together."

My breathing stops. He wants to continue the relationship? He's not discarding me?

Is that really what he's saying here?

I still don't know. I still can't trust him.

As if sensing my hesitancy, Axel makes a move towards me. He crosses the street and strolls straight up to me. I don't move and I don't say a thing as the rockstar walks confidently towards me until he leans over and whispers his smooth voice into my ear.

"I love you, Maddie Leaver."

My mouth opens and closes. I feel the ground shift below my feet. I no longer know what is up or what is down.

He loves me?

All this time?

"The relationship was never fake," he says quietly, like it's a secret he's telling me. "It never was, even from the very start."

"No," I whisper back. "It wasn't for me. It was never fake."

"Let's stop fucking about then," Axel replies. "And let's give this a try. I love you, Maddie. I'm sorry if it's taken me too long to even say that, but it's true. I love you. I loved you from when you spilled that tea over me. I loved you when you screamed out my band's lyrics in the crowd. I loved that you waited up for me in my hotel room. I love your intelligence, your kindness, and the fact you really do seem to fucking care for me. I should've told you all these things a long time ago, but that was me being an idiot. I'm sorry. I love you, and I will keep repeating that until you can trust me again."

I take in a long breath.

"Get down on your knees," I say.

"What?"

"You heard me," I retort. "Get down on your knees and say that."

Axel growls. A sound from the back of his throat. Getting down on his knees is everything this proud, cocky man is against.

And I want to see it happen.

I want him to do it for me.

"I don't beg," he snarls. "I don't grovel. I don't get on my knees for anyone."

I raise an eyebrow.

"Well, you can do it for me."

Another growl from the rockstar.

And Axel lowers himself in front of me.

He's on his knees.

"I love you, Maddie," he whispers. "It's insane, but I fucking love you."

Wow.

"Okay, you can stand up now."

He does so and takes a step towards me.

"I love you," he repeats. "I love you. I love you. I love you."

I shake my head. The tears return. It's good to see the man grovel for me. His green eyes are so close to mine that

I can see deep inside them, and I know he's telling the truth.

"I'm the idiot," I reply. "I'm the idiot for falling for a rockstar. The sexiest rockstar on the planet."

"Oh, I like that."

His smile. His fucking charming smile.

"I love you, Axel."

And there are the words that have been caught in my throat for weeks. Those words that have been begging to be released into the world.

Saying them makes everything true. All my feelings for him. Everything I've falsely tried to hold back.

This is what love is. I never got any of this from Mom. Loving Axel makes me feel like I'm flying with no effort.

"Maddie, I've been waiting for you to say that. I've been waiting for you for years."

"Stop being so sentimental, Axel. It doesn't fit you," I say. He laughs.

"So you'll have me?"

"Maybe."

"Maybe? I just got down on my fucking *knees* for you."

"I'll have you... as long as it isn't fake."

"You think this is fake, Maddie?" he asks before he kisses me.

"No," I say as I peel away from his beautiful lips. "That didn't seem fake. Not at all."

"You're mine, Maddie."

I nod.

"I'm yours, Axel."

"Nothing's fake between us," he says. "I want to take you by the hand and declare to the world that you have my heart."

"Maybe write a song for me first."

"Oh, I'm planning to."

He kisses me again.

"I just have one question," I say.

"What?"

"How did you get here so fast?" I ask.

"You have a problem with my speed?"

"No, it's just kind of mysterious; how did you get here before me?"

"I'm fast on a motorbike, remember? I wasn't joking when I said I am practically a professional racing driver."

That makes me laugh.

"You want to see my new place?" I ask him.

The rockstar I love smiles that irresistible smile of his.

"There's nowhere I'd rather be."

54

MADDIE

Okay, truth be told I don't really show Axel my new place.

We barely even get through the door before we're kissing like the world is about to end. His tongue is in my mouth before I even get the chance to flick on the lights so that we're in darkness by the doorway to my new condo with Axel's arms around my body pushing me towards the wall.

Yeah, some tour this is turning out to be...

My hips angle towards his own. My breasts heave up against his thick muscular chest. My back is completely against the wall now.

This time, things feel different. This isn't just sex. This isn't just another conquest for Axel to gloat over. I'm not simply another fuck to tally off his list.

This is *love*.

As we kiss, he gently lifts my arms above my head, pinning me to the condo wall. He grinds into me, bodies coming together as one.

I feel so hot.

We stare deep into each other's eyes as we make out. His greenness dazzles me. My cheeks burn as his tongue grazes mine.

He just got down on his knees for me. He just told me he loves me. None of this is fake.

Axel takes my wrists with one hand as his other hand slowly unbuttons my blouse. He's stripping me down. There's only one direction this is all heading towards, and that thought makes me gasp with giddy anticipation.

"Maddie..."

It's a strangled snarl of my name, delivered in that ice-cold Axel tone. My clit hums in appreciation. I'm becoming so wet.

He's winning me with so much care and so much of his trademark confidence. Here is a man who knows precisely what he wants. And he's going to get it, no matter what.

I am what he wants.

I can't remain detached. I give myself fully to this experience. This is all so real. So bristling full of emotion...

He jerks down his pants, and then his briefs, exposing his long, hard cock. I blow a sigh of need at the spectacle of his manhood displayed so impressively.

"You're hard for me?" I ask, my voice not even a whisper. His grasp around my wrist tightens.

"I'm always hard for you, Maddie."

"Don't I know that."

Axel unzips my jeans and pulls them down to my knees, exposing my panties. He doesn't allow them to stay there for too long. Soon he's bringing them down too. My wetness creeps down my thighs. I tremble as the tip of his veiny cock brushes against my opening.

His lips find mine again. "Your pretty mouth..."

"What do you want to do to me, Axel?"

He likes that. A lot. He sucks in a breath in excitement.

"What *can* I do to you?"

I lean towards his ear. "Anything you want."

He takes his erection in his hand and guides it towards my wet pussy.

With an involuntary gasp emerging from deep within me, Axel enters my body. He's so long and smooth and perfect for my inviting pussy. It's like my whole constitution wraps around his member eagerly. Tears fill my eyes as he buries himself in my soaking sex.

His sheer masculinity surrounds me.

"Maddie..."

One more time he utters my name, and that's when I know I've got a hold of him he can't shake.

That raw, untamed nature of his brought to heel by *me*.

That power turns me on.

"You're the only girl for me," he says. "The only one I need."

"Then show me," I command with a smirk.

Taking his time, Axel soothingly thrusts. Filling me. Playing with me. All I want is his power and he's giving me his heart.

"I'm going to do this nice and slow," he says. "I want to *feel* all of you. I want to *understand* you. I want to *savor* every part of you, Maddie."

"You have me completely."

"You're mine," he says once again. Those words take me back to the first time we had sex. Back in his hotel. Back when we were still faking what we had between us. Time has changed. This is so fucking real.

"I'm yours," I affirm breathlessly.

With my words, Axel groans and tunnels in deep with one powerful thrust. He practically drives me up the wall with his strength. My eyes go wide, and my mouth opens in a surprised gasp. Axel shuts me up with a long kiss on my exposed neck. His teeth nibble at my skin. I let out a contentment sigh.

"I love you, Maddie Leaver."

Those words hit me more than anything.

"Say that again," I say. "Repeat it like you did outside."

Axel grins and lifts his head to my ear.

"I love you," he whispers over and over. "I love you. I love you."

Hearing that sentence sends a chill of delight down my spine.

Axel lets go of my wrists, and his free hand drops to my pussy. Both his hands are there now. I grab his shoulders for support as his fingers glide towards my clit.

My whole body twists when he circles my engorged sex. He finds my clit and tenderly teases it to boiling point.

"That feels so good," I moan. "Don't stop."

"Beg for it, Maddie."

"Please don't stop, Axel."

"That's better, my girl. My good girl."

His hips move faster now. I can tell he's close to finishing. He's holding himself back.

But I can't give too much thought to that. The tips of his fingers are doing too much with my sex. My own hands grip even tighter around his muscular shoulders. Axel doesn't seem to mind in the slightest that my nails are probably starting to scratch him in unrestrained pleasure.

"I fucking love you, Maddie."

Oh God, those words...

"Keep saying that," I say. "You're going to make me climax saying just that."

That spurs on the man.

"I love you, Maddie. I love you. I love you."

I can't take it anymore. My core rocks with his thrusting

cock and his fingers dancing on my clit as I'm brought to a sudden and powerful orgasm against the wall of my new condo.

Love is one hell of an aphrodisiac.

This is certainly not fake.

55

MADDIE

The next morning, I decide to finally call my mother. It has been a long time since we've last spoken.

Well, we've actually not spoken since that disastrous lunch.

There are things I need to get off my chest. Things I need to go over with her about. I'm searching for closure.

And now it's time.

I tell Axel what I'm planning to do, and that I'm going on a walk to do so. He asks me if he should come. No, I need to be on my own for this.

I need to do this alone.

I walk around the block before I bring up the courage to dial her number. Surprisingly, Mom picks up.

"Maddie?"

"Hi, Mom."

I hear her take in a deep breath.

Time to ready myself...

"How are you?"

"I'm okay, Mom."

"I saw you and that *boy* on the news."

"Did you?"

"And I got the newspaper because I was walking past the store and saw your face on the front page. Again, you were with that musician."

"Oh. Well, that's nice."

I would very much like to tell my mother that his name is actually Axel, but I hold my tongue back. There's no need to fall into that trap. That is not what this phone call is about.

"What are you calling me about, Maddie? You better not be wasting time."

Here goes.

"I'm just calling to let you know that you were wrong."

There's a pause.

"Wrong?" she asks me. "When was I wrong? Wrong about what, Maddie?"

My hand is shaking. I've never spoken to Mom like this. Her sharp tone of voice... I feel like I'm just a little girl again getting into trouble. About to be sent to my room to read my Bible from cover to cover.

Stand up for yourself, Maddie.

"You were wrong when I was a child and you told me over and over again that all men can't be trusted, but I'm calling to let you know I've got some evidence to back up the exact opposite."

I can practically hear her eyes rolling on the other end.

"Oh, come on, Maddie. Don't tell me you've actually gone soft over this sinner. What possible evidence do you have?"

"I love Axel Stoll," I reply. I feel the confidence return to my chest. I stand up tall and I stop walking. I'm facing her down, over the phone. "And, Mom, I know for a damn fact that Axel Stoll loves me. *That's* my evidence."

And then without waiting for an answer from her – because I don't need one – I hang up and walk back to my *real* boyfriend with the biggest smile on my face.

If I risk it all
Would you be there?
If I put my heart on the line
Would you take it?

Some say we're too different
Some may doubt our love
But I don't think they're right, no
To me, we are enough

How can I live
when you're in this world?
My blood burns
Burns so hot
Because, for you, I will risk it all

EPILOGUE

THREE MONTHS LATER

AXEL

I PULL up outside my place on my motorbike and allow myself a moment to sit on the back of my beast and think.

My mind wanders back over the last few months. The *best* three months of my life.

Maddie Leaver.

God, that girl. She's completely snared my heart. She's everything to me. My world. My love. I had felt like such an idiot that I didn't tell her sooner my true feelings for her, but I'm glad I did. I'm glad I drove to her place and confronted her. Practically *begged* her to forgive me.

I've told her a million times since then that that one moment is the only time she'll ever witness this rockstar boy beg. I'm not the pleading type.

But, hey, I got my woman. That was worth anything, even getting on my knees for.

She told me how she called her mom. How she told her that she loves me. How she finally got some much-overdue closure. I told her that I'm proud of her. I told her that I'll always be right behind her as her biggest fan, just as she is mine.

What a few months it's been. I bought a new place in LA the week after the album's release. This pad is massive. A pool. Stunning views over the city. So many rooms. Enough space for a family. In fact, I immediately asked Maddie – the moment she came over to inspect the place – if she would move in with me. She was surprised but said yes straight away. She had no need to be surprised. I bought the place for us.

And we've both made it our home.

"It's still pretty far from the suburbs and a normal life," Maddie told me.

I had to agree.

This is certainly not the life I feared when I thought of a relationship. I want to kick myself for being so wrong all those years. Like Mom said, it took a woman like Maddie Leaver to come flying into my life with all her strength and intelligence to change me.

And she has changed me. For the better. Every single fucking day.

Don't get me wrong, I'm still the fucking coolest rockstar on the planet. Just because I've got a girl doesn't mean I stopped being an international sex symbol. But now I don't care at all about the girls in the audience who flash their tits at me or shoot me dirty looks backstage. I go straight home to the one woman I give a shit about.

The one woman I just know I'm gonna love until the end of my days.

Whenever I look at her, I realize that this is what I've

always wanted. Not the crazy rockstar life. Not suburbia. But my *own* life. With my *own* partner.

I even got another tattoo to add to my collection, this one for Maddie. This one is as important to me as the R that stands for Ravaged over my heart.

It's a date. Written on the underside of my right wrist, where I can always see it when I play my bass guitar.

The date I met the love of my life.

Maddie is still working publicity for Ravaged. The rest of the boys didn't care that our relationship had started off fake; they're just happy she's still in our weird big family.

I glance at myself in the motorbike's side mirror and chuckle.

You're one hell of a lucky bastard, Axel, to land a girl like this.

Well, now it's time to see her.

I dismount from the bike and head up to the front door.

The first thing I sense when I get inside is the overwhelmingly delicious smell of freshly baked cookies. My mouth instantly waters as I rush to the kitchen to be greeted by a sight of a whole mountain of choc chip ones. I snatch one and try it.

Maddie slowly walks in as I crunch away at her creation. She stands by the doorway and watches me silently.

"These are fucking amazing," I announce to her, pointing at my very full mouth. "You should definitely start a business making them."

She remains silent. Which is weird.

I try changing the topic.

"You wouldn't believe what Drake did at rehearsal today..."

She still doesn't reply.

Something is wrong.

Instead, she lifts up her arm to show me something. I can't see what it is in her hand.

"*Axel...*"

Her voice is tiny. Like she's in shock. Like she's still processing something unbelievable.

And then it hits me. I realize what the strange little object she's holding up to me actually is.

And my entire universe changes in one instant.

She's holding a pregnancy test.

And it's positive.

Want to read what happens next?

Go to rebeccacastle.com to find the links for Ravaged By Lust (Ravaged Rockstars II)

ABOUT THE AUTHOR

Rebecca has had the storytelling bug since… forever!

What Rebecca likes most is writing steamy hot filthy romances with sweet happy endings sprinkled with some delicious bad boys.

Born and raised in an Aussie coastal town, she loves travelling around the world - meeting new people and discovering their stories.

Aside from adventuring she also enjoys a good rainy day in with a good book or at a hot beach catching the sun.

She's a world-class napping professional. You'll most likely find her asleep snuggled up on a sofa somewhere cozy.

For other titles and information please visit
rebeccacastle.com

facebook.com/rebeccacastleauthor
instagram.com/rebeccacastle.author

Printed in Dunstable, United Kingdom